Business Not As Usual

Business Not As Usual

SHARON C. COOPER

JOVE
NEW YORK

A JOVE BOOK
Published by Berkley
An imprint of Penguin Random House LLC
penguinrandomhouse.com

Library of Congress Cataloging-in-Publication Data

Names: Cooper, Sharon C., author.
Title: Business not as usual / Sharon C. Cooper.
Description: First edition. | New York: Jove, 2022.
Identifiers: LCCN 2021045315 (print) | LCCN 2021045316 (ebook) |
ISBN 9780593335253 (trade paperback) | ISBN 9780593335260 (ebook)
Subjects: LCGFT: Romance fiction.
Classification: LCC PS3603.O582985 B87 2022 (print) |
LCC PS3603.O582985 (ebook) | DDC 813/.6—dc23/eng/20211006
LC record available at https://lccn.loc.gov/2021045315
LC ebook record available at https://lccn.loc.gov/2021045316

First Edition: April 2022

Printed in the United States of America
1st Printing

Book design by George Towne

To my amazing husband—my real-life hero—Al

Chapter One

ONE, TWO, THREE . . .

Dreamy Daniels closed her eyes and counted to keep from exploding as Gordon Mathison, her helicopter boss, paced the narrow space behind her desk. She should be used to his peeking over her shoulder while she worked and questioning everything she did, but not today. Today she wanted to hog-tie him to his desk chair, in his office, and stuff a pair of his boring black socks into his mouth.

But she wouldn't.

Why? Because he couldn't help himself. Gordon was an anxious genius with horrible people skills who drove her and anyone else in his orbit absolutely batty most days.

Dreamy opened her eyes and gripped the edge of her file-laden desk, then blew out a long, cleansing breath, willing herself to think before she spoke. Once she was sure her professional demeanor was securely in place and there was no chance of saying what she really wanted to—like Get the hell away from my desk—she leaned back in her seat. Slowly swiveling her gray tweed chair around to face her boss, she waited until he realized she was watching him.

Gordon stopped pacing, and eagerness bounced off him in waves. "You're done?" he asked, excitement lacing his words as his green eyes gleamed like those of a child who'd just received his desired Christmas present.

"Of course I'm not done!" she growled through clenched teeth. Frustration seeped out with every word. So much for maintaining professionalism. "Gordon, you gave me the assignment five minutes ago. I can't just fold my arms, blink my eyes, and nod my head like a genie and expect the report to magically appear, especially with you hovering behind me. Don't you have some fancy tech idea to work on?"

At around five nine with a slim build and olive skin, he appeared younger than his thirty years. His thick, dark hair stood up and out every which way, looking as if he had run his fingers through it one too many times. Add that to the dark rings under his eyes, and it was safe to say he hadn't been sleeping well. Dreamy could understand why he might've been on edge. He had a lot riding on his upcoming meeting.

He huffed out a breath and ran his left hand through his hair and shoved his other hand into the front pocket of his navy-blue dress pants. Normally, his attire consisted of jeans and a button-down shirt with the sleeves rolled up to reveal his forearms. But today he wore his navy-blue suit, the only suit he owned, along with a white dress shirt. Since arriving in the office an hour ago, he had shed the jacket, and the boring blue-and-white-striped tie was askew. Obviously, he'd been tugging on it.

"Yeah, yeah, I have plenty to work on, but I need this information. Karter Redford will be here later this afternoon," Gordon said of the venture capitalist he planned to hit up for money for a new product idea he had created. "Are you going to be able to get that report to me in time?"

"Don't I always?"

"Yes, but this one is really important."

"Aren't they all?"

"Well, yeah, but . . ."

For the last few months, Dreamy had gotten to know Gordon better than most. His need to be involved in every detail, his lack of delegating skills, and his inability to trust his staff to do their jobs was enough for Mother Teresa to consider him a lost cause.

Dreamy rubbed her temples. The man might be a tech genius, but in the real world, he worked her last nerve. "Gordon, I'll email the information to you once I'm done."

"You do that. I'll just go back to my office." He turned on his heel and Dreamy swiveled her chair back around and watched as he marched down the short hallway toward his office.

She leaned forward and banged her head on top of the desk a few times. Not enough to cause damage, but enough to work out the irritation drumming through her body. She'd had just about enough of Gordon's micromanaging, but she needed her job. He was lucky her one-week gig down at the Purple Pony Strip Club hadn't worked out. If only she could've walked in those five-inch heels without stumbling every few feet. It also probably would've helped if she could've stayed upright on that slippery pole. Who knew the damn thing spun?

"Hey, chica! Clearly you have forgotten that your walls are made of glass. What are you trying to do, knock some sense into your head?"

Dreamy lifted her head as Mariana strolled into the office suite grinning.

"Ha. Ha. Ha. I see you've got jokes. I was just letting off a little steam."

Stylishly dressed in a red wrap dress that accentuated her curves,

Mariana dropped down in the chair next to the desk. Her tawny brown skin with minimal makeup glowed under the fluorescent lights, but the grin she'd had moments ago slid from her pretty face.

"What's wrong? I'm used to your bright smile greeting me whenever I stop by. What's got you banging your head on the desk? Wait, let me guess. Mr. Man is being his usual pain-in-the-butt self."

Dreamy nodded, determined not to let Gordon get to her any more than he already had. The only reason she had survived working for him over the last eight months was because she maintained a positive attitude. She refused to let him run her out of the office the way she'd heard he'd done with his last three assistants. Three assistants in six months? Not a good record.

Dreamy told her friend about the short conversation. "I should be used to him standing over me, waiting for whatever project he's thrown my way. But some days, like today, it bugs the heck out of me. I've talked to him about the hovering, but it's like talking to a steel beam. At least the beam is doing some of the heavy lifting. Mr. M just makes everything heavier. He's stressing me the hell out."

"Mr. M?"

"*M* is for *Micromanager*," Dreamy explained.

"You mean Micromaniac?"

Dreamy laughed at the title that fit Gordon to a tee.

"But seriously, I feel for you. I'm just glad he's not my boss. Otherwise, I probably would've strangled him by now. Okay, enough about Mr. Micromaniac. Are you feeling lucky? I heard Powerball is at one hundred twenty million dollars."

Dreamy rubbed her palms together. "Yes. I know I've said that before, but for real this time. This is going to be my big break."

Most people who knew she was banking on winning the lottery thought she was delusional, but not Mariana. She knew Dreamy played the lottery faithfully, and not once did she tell her she was crazy or that she was just wasting her money. Her exact words were *anything is possible if you believe.*

"Okay, just remember your girl when you hit it big." Mariana didn't play the lottery for religious reasons, but she'd already made it clear that she wouldn't turn down a gift from someone who did win.

"You know I got you."

Dreamy had already identified people she planned to give gifts to once she won, and Mariana topped the list. They met years ago at a homeless shelter where they had volunteered to feed the hungry on Thanksgiving Day. They'd been friends ever since. She knew Mariana was one of the kindest, most giving people when she spied her scooping extra mashed potatoes onto every plate.

If it hadn't been for her, Dreamy wouldn't have landed the job with Gordon. After Dreamy had been laid off for months and was settling for any type of work, like the strip club gig, Mariana had told her about the secretarial position. It had come right on time, because Dreamy had been down to her last hundred dollars.

Now it was time for her to start thinking bigger, because her ultimate goal was to be a badass boss lady.

Thanks to her small-business class and the assignment to create a business plan, she had already begun pulling ideas together. The nonprofit she wanted to start one day would cater to women looking to become entrepreneurs.

Granted, the idea was lofty, especially since she had limited business experience and no money. But she never let a few obstacles keep her from going after what she wanted.

Dreamy propped her elbow onto the desk and rested her chin in her hand as she stared out the glass wall in front of her desk. It gave her a panoramic view into the main hallway of the top floor.

"I need to get my act together. I don't plan on working here forever, but right now, all of my goals seem so out of reach," she murmured.

Mariana waved her off. "It's only a matter of time. Soon you'll have your bachelor's degree and, after that, I have no doubt greater things will follow."

Dreamy hoped so. Recently, her self-esteem had taken a big hit. Her boyfriend . . . well, her ex-boyfriend, Brandon, dumped her the day after he made partner at his law firm. Their relationship hadn't been perfect, but she thought with time, it could develop into the type of relationship she dreamed of having. Instead, it exploded in a heap of a mess in front of his co-workers, who were there at the party celebrating his promotion.

Not cultured.

Not sophisticated.

Not educated enough, the jerk had told her. She might not be polished or classy, but what she lacked in sophistication, she made up for in resilience. No matter how often things didn't go her way, she never quit. Which was why at twenty-eight, she was still trying to finish college.

Between the obscene amount they charged for tuition, and having to care for her ailing grandfather, she'd ended up dropping out of school after her first year. Dreamy had returned to college a few years ago, and now she only had one more semester before she graduated with a public administration degree. Then she'd look for a job that paid more than her secretary's salary, and from there, she'd dive deeper into starting her nonprofit. That's assuming she didn't win the lottery first.

"I just have to keep believing in myself," she said.

Mariana frowned. "I don't know what's going on with you right now, but whatever's got you in your feelings, get over it, because you're amazing. Your confidence alone is going to take you places."

Dreamy gave a slight smile. On the outside, she put on a front to make people think she had it all together. She wanted them to believe that her self-confidence was fully intact. Yet, since breaking up with Brandon, there were days when his negative words rattled around in her mind like a crappy 1980s song playing on loop. She knew everyone experienced moments of self-doubt, but it had been almost two months since their breakup. She shouldn't even be thinking about his bougie ass.

I am beautiful. I am confident. I am lovable. I am a lottery winner.

That was her new mantra. She had added the part about the lottery winner a couple of weeks ago. Now all she had to do was keep reciting the chant until every single word stuck.

"Now, if you want to climb the corporate ladder or own your own business," Mariana said, "start making small changes and build on that. Maybe start with tweaking your wardrobe. I get that you're eccentric. Which is one of many things I love about you, but I don't think skinny pants with humongous flowers covering them and an equally bold striped shirt really say, *I'm a boss, and I mean business.*"

Dreamy glanced down at her attire. "What? This is boho-chic."

"Okay, but fluorescent yellow, green, blue, and that splash of hot pink in those pants don't exactly scream corporate America."

Dreamy studied her outfit. Yeah, the flowers and stripes were bold, and maybe there was some rule about putting the two patterns together, but both pieces had the same colors.

"I love you and the colors are cute against your dark skin, but they're a bit much for this boring office. You look like a walking, talking flower garden. The shoes are cute, though."

Dreamy laughed at the "flower garden" comment, then turned her left foot to the side to admire her Mary Jane heels that were killing her feet. She had two weaknesses in life: shoes and wigs. She had very little restraint when it came to buying either . . . but especially shoes.

"They are cute, aren't they? They came in the mail yesterday, and I couldn't wait to wear them. I just wish they weren't so noisy when I walk. I paid a pretty penny for them. Yet I can hear the squeaking all the way down the hall. I'm going to need to lube them up with some WD-40."

"Was that you earlier? I wondered if a cat was being stepped on."

"Girl, yes. But I'm sure once I break them in, they'll be fine."

Mariana shook her head and grinned. "You're too much. You gotta stop buying shoes from Discount Joe's. He uses fake leather. That's why you sound like you're killing someone's pet with every step you take."

"You might be right, but I told you I stopped shopping there when I got this job. These little beauties weren't cheap. As for my outfit, when I win this money, maybe I'll get a stylist to hook me up. But first, I'm getting a nurse to come to the house a few times a week to help Gramps."

"Good plan, and how is he? You haven't mentioned him lately."

"Girrrl, that man is going to be the death of me and Jordyn," Dreamy said of her cousin. The three of them lived together in a sketchy part of Hollywood in a house that was an earthquake away from crumbling around them. Dreamy frequently prayed nothing higher than 3.2 on the Richter scale ever hit the city. "There are days when I think Gramps won't be here with us much longer, and other days when I think he's faking his illnesses. I got home last night and a woman was coming out of his bedroom adjusting her gray wig. He had the nerve to say that she was his nurse making a house call."

Mariana's mouth dropped open. "Get out! Are you serious?" She burst out laughing.

Dreamy couldn't help but join in. The old woman had smoothed down her house dress, planted on a smile, and walked out of the house as if nothing had happened.

"Well, he might be old, but he ain't dead," Mariana said between giggles. "I just love that man."

Everyone, including Dreamy, loved Slick Lester, as most people called him. He was a handful at times, but he was Dreamy's whole world. She had lived with him and her grandmother since she was twelve, the day her mother had dumped her on their doorstep. Her grandmother passed away a few years ago. Shortly after that, Gramps suffered a mild stroke.

Now, years later, their grandfather had bounced back almost to one hundred percent, but other ailments started creeping in as he aged. High blood pressure along with back and hip issues plagued him, but he didn't let any of it stop him from loving life. He marched to his own beat, doing whatever the hell he wanted, and was unapologetic about how he chose to live his life.

Mariana wiped tears from her eyes and stood. "Okay, thanks for the laugh. Let me get back to work before *my* boss starts looking for me. Good luck in getting that report done."

"Thanks. It shouldn't take too long."

After Mariana left the office, Dreamy started working on Gordon's report, and her mind went back to thoughts of Brandon. While they dated, she thought she had hit the jackpot of love. They'd gotten along great. He was nice, handsome, and financially stable. Spending time together had been challenging with her attending night school and him working long hours, but they managed. Everything was great. Until he dumped her.

It's just as easy to fall in love with a rich man as it is a poor one, her mother, Tarrah, had once said.

What a load of crap. Her mother hadn't known what she was talking about. Hell, Dreamy shouldn't have been listening to anything the woman had to say anyway. What type of mother abandoned her daughter to follow a man to New York?

Dreamy shook her head, remembering how she'd been left on

her grandparents' doorstep. Literally. Her grandma and grandpa had taken her in, provided for her, and showered her with unwavering love. She never knew her father but would be forever grateful for her grandparents' sacrifices. There's nothing she wouldn't do for her gramps, but her mother better never ask for anything. Ever.

Tarrah knew that. The rare occasions when they did talk, their conversations were stiff. Her mother either was condescending or offered unsolicited advice, especially when it came to men. Which was one subject Dreamy had no intention of discussing with anyone anytime soon.

Nope. She was done with men . . . at least for awhile. Right now, she had to stay focused on her goals. Reaching for the yellow legal pad near her keyboard and her favorite pen, she jotted down her plans.

Take care of Gramps.

Finish school.

Win the lottery.

Dreamy nibbled on her bottom lip and tapped her pen on the notepad as she reviewed what she'd written. Not totally satisfied with the order of items, she circled *win the lottery* and then drew a line, placing it at the top of the list.

"That's better." She smiled and went back to working on the report. Once she won the lottery, her life would be perfect.

She couldn't wait.

Chapter Two

KARTER REDFORD ROCKED BACK IN HIS LEATHER DESK CHAIR before swiveling around to stare out the large window behind him. The Los Angeles skyline with the Pacific Ocean in the distance greeted him. But today the view didn't offer the peace it usually brought. The scenery was what sold him and his brother on purchasing the one-thousand-foot-high skyscraper years ago, but at the moment, its panoramic beauty wasn't enough of a distraction to clear his mind.

Delton was gone.

It still didn't seem real. Karter had attended his friend's funeral two days ago, thinking that once Delton was laid to rest, then his death would become real. It hadn't. Karter still couldn't wrap his brain around the fact that one of his best friends since college had breathed his last breath.

Forty years old.

That was too young to die. Delton should've still been around giving Karter hell or cracking inappropriate jokes over dinner.

They had plans to open a resort in Cabo San Lucas within the next five years. That, along with other plans, would never happen.

It was too late.

Now all Karter was left with was melancholy that weighed him down like a suit of steel armor, and he couldn't seem to get out from under it.

You're next if you don't make some changes.

Karter ran his hands down his face and huffed out a noisy breath as the words of his brother, Randy, boomed inside his head. He was right. There was a good chance that Delton's heart attack was a result of the stress that came with working sixteen-hour days for weeks at a time over the last few years. Which was something Karter could relate to. All he did was work. Sure, he had a biweekly dinner with a few friends, and he attended various events on occasion, but that was it. As a venture capitalist, his whole world was basically centered on his career.

I have to make some changes.

And he needed to make them sooner rather than later. Life was more than closing deals and amassing millions. He knew that, but knowing it and doing something about it were two different things. What he needed was a social life. Or hell, even a hobby or two to balance his workaholic behavior would help. Otherwise, he was going to end up just like Delton.

"Okay, Karter. The contract is all set and ready for your signature," his assistant, Gloria, said from behind him.

He'd been so caught up in his thoughts, he hadn't heard her enter the office. He spun the chair around to face the desk before giving her his attention. No one would ever believe that she was in her midsixties. The saying "Black don't crack" immediately came to mind when he stared into her terra-cotta-toned face. There wasn't a wrinkle in sight, and her youthfulness showed in her stylish short hairstyle, along with the cream-colored blouse and black pencil skirt. Three-inch black pumps rounded out the outfit.

"I flagged the sections that Robert suggested you reconsider," she said.

Karter accepted the document and flipped through a couple of pages. Robert Schwartz, his longtime attorney, was merciless when it came to contracts. Something Karter usually appreciated, but this wasn't one of those times.

Karter was always looking for the next best deal, or he was being sought out to provide capital to a company or for a project. Occasionally, an opportunity showed up that didn't look great on paper but had something that made him take a bigger risk. That was the case with John and Lorraine Miller's *Taco Grub* food truck. Though their food was amazing, they hadn't made a profit in three years, and their desire to move into a restaurant was a long shot. Yet, Karter wanted to take a chance on them and help them reach financial independence.

Growing up with an A-list actor for a father and a socialite mother, Karter lived in two worlds. One being that of the rich and famous. The other—where he was most fulfilled—involved helping the less fortunate, backing start-up companies, and investing in cutting-edge ideas.

He wanted to invest in the Millers. He still remembered the first day he'd met the owners and they told him about their business. There had been something special about the couple that immediately caught Karter's attention. He liked them. He liked their determination, their tireless work ethic, and the fact that they truly believed in their business. More than that, he liked their relationship.

His parents had been together forever, but they never had that passionate, *I can't live without you* type of love. But John and

Lorraine had been married for almost forty years, and their love for each other shined like a beacon in the night, lighting up the darkest sky. What they felt for each other was palpable, and anyone in their presence for more than ten minutes would be able to see and feel how much they adored and respected each other. It was in the way they gazed into each other's eyes and the smiles they shared. Add that to the way they touched each other—a gentle hand on the arm, or the way John pushed hair from his wife's face spoke volumes. They were a couple who were still madly in love with each other.

That was the type of relationship Karter wanted. Actually, it was the type of relationship he had a few years ago until it went to hell.

Karter shook those thoughts free, not wanting to walk down that rocky memory lane. Granted, back then he had vowed to never give his heart to another woman, be a bachelor for life. He didn't want the drama and demands that came with romantic relationships.

Though he kept reminding himself of that, lately something had shifted inside of him. He wanted what his closest friends had found—a woman to look at him as if he hung the moon. A person who was not only supportive and encouraging, but also a partner he could share his life with.

"What you put into life is what you get out of it."

The words of the legendary Clint Eastwood—a friend of his grandfather's—floated around in Karter's mind. He needed to think about what he really wanted. His career and financial life were on point, but his social life was in the toilet.

He sighed and set the document on the desk. "I'll take a look at this, but I'm pretty sure I want to keep it as is."

Gloria gave him one of her *I'm proud of you smiles.* "I hope so. I think it's sweet what you're doing for John and Lorraine. They walked out of here pretty excited the other day with the ideas you shared with them. You were their last hope. You're a good man, Karter Redford."

The left corner of his lips kicked up, and his chest puffed out a bit. He was close to Gloria's kids' ages, and at times she treated him like one of her sons more so than her boss. Nonetheless, she had a way of making him feel great about some of his decisions.

"I'm glad you think so, and I'm happy I can help them."

"Me too." She exited the office leaving Karter to review the contract.

He had barely gotten through the first page when he heard his brother's voice in the outer office.

"Is Mr. Grumpy in?"

Karter closed his eyes and rubbed his temples. He hated when Randy called him grumpy. Just because he didn't go around whistling show tunes all day or participating in idle chitchat didn't mean he was grumpy. Or boring as he was sometimes called. He was just more serious than certain members of his family. Namely Randy Redford.

"How's it going, my brotha?" Randy said as he strolled in, closing the door behind him.

People had often talked about how much they looked alike. Karter could see the resemblance a little. Their reddish-brown skin and light brown eyes were inherited from their mother. But thankfully they had their father's height at over six feet tall. While Karter also had his dad's wide shoulders and muscular build, Randy had more of a runner's body, fit and lean.

His brother sat in one of the guest chairs, then propped his feet up on the desk as if he didn't have a care in the world. Light blue socks with bold, black words that read *I Kicked 2020's Ass* peeked from under his dark blue jeans.

Randy was two years older, and he and Karter were as different as stocks and bonds. His brother's laid-back style of dress, including his sock choices, were glaring proof of that. Karter believed in looking the part of a successful businessman with designer suits, ties, and footwear. Unlike Randy, who usually could be found wearing Henleys, blue jeans, and Chucks on his feet. No one would ever guess by looking at him that he was wealthy.

Like Karter, Randy hadn't been interested in becoming a Hollywood actor like their father and grandfather. He was an artist, preferring to spend his time painting. Everything from abstracts to portraits, Randy was one of the most talented people Karter knew. He was also a pain in the ass.

"Get your feet off my desk." Karter swiped at his brother's size twelves and knocked his feet to the floor. "Why are you here? Don't you have a client you could be harassing instead of me?"

"He just left. So I figured I'd stroll upstairs and bug you." As part owner of the office building, Randy set up his studio in a huge space two floors down. "What are you up to?"

Karter glanced at his platinum watch. "Actually, I'm getting ready to head out shortly. Morgan begged me to meet with the owner of a fairly new tech company who's looking for funding."

"I thought you said you weren't investing in any more technology companies."

"I've learned to never say never. Besides, you know how hard it is to say no to her."

Randy nodded. Morgan was twelve years younger than him and ten years younger than Karter. She was one of the sweetest and kindest people on the planet, but also spoiled.

"Speaking of Morgan, how's the roommate situation going? I heard she moved in with you instead of going back to Mom and Dad's place."

"Yep, that's true, but I rarely see her."

After traveling around Europe for the past couple of years to *find herself,* Morgan had returned to the States a few weeks ago. He wasn't sure if she had *found herself,* but considering she still didn't know what she wanted to do with the rest of her life, he'd guess she hadn't.

Karter's Hollywood Hills home was over seven thousand square feet with six bedrooms and nine bathrooms, and was barely lived in. He didn't have a problem with Morgan camping out there until she decided next steps, and his housekeeper was thrilled to have someone to fuss over.

"Did you hear that Morgan brought me a gift?" Karter said dryly.

"What, booze? An antique desk globe? A travel neck pillow?"

Karter frowned. "Not exactly."

He lifted his cell phone from the desk and scrolled through his photos. Once he found what he was looking for, he turned the device around so that his brother could see the screen.

Randy stared for a moment, then burst out laughing. "A *dog*? Let me get this right. She bought *you,* Mr. I Can't Be Bothered With Anything Because I Work twenty-four-seven, a dog?"

Karter ignored the jab. "Yes. A rescue puppy. His name is Melvin."

"*Melvin?* His name is Melvin? Not Max, Bo, or Lucky, but . . . *Melvin?* Seriously?" Randy howled, laughing so hard he practically tumbled out of the chair.

"Damn, bro. It's not *that* funny."

"Yes. Yes, it is." Randy swiped at the corners of his eyes. "Let me see the photo again. What type of name is Melvin for a dog? Then again, his puppy dog eyes do look a little too serious to call him Lucky."

"I agree. I tried calling him Mel, but he only responds to Melvin."

This time Randy did fall out of the chair and landed hard on the carpeted floor, laughing. It took a full five minutes for him to pull himself together and reclaim his seat.

Karter held out his hand. "Just give me my phone back."

Randy slapped it into his hand. "Anyone who knows you knows that the last thing you want or need is a pet. And that's a classic Morgan move. She thinks just because she doesn't do anything but shop all day and drink foo-foo coffee that everyone has the luxury of sitting around doing nothing. Unless you call traveling around Europe working."

Karter didn't bother agreeing or disagreeing with his brother's assessment of their sister, but he had to admit that he'd seen a change in her. She might not have any immediate plan for what she wanted to do with herself, but she had returned home a different woman. Gone was the little girl who was all about *me, me, me*, and in her place was a young woman who was more thoughtful and a lot less self-centered.

"She claimed the dog would help me get out of the slump I've been in. According to her, I'm dealing with high-functioning depression."

Randy's eyebrows lifted slightly, and he nodded. "I don't usually agree with her on anything, but on that, I think she might be onto something. You haven't been yourself since Delton died."

"I'm not depressed," Karter defended. Sure, there was a hollowness deep inside of him that he didn't know if he'd ever fill, but he wouldn't say that he was depressed. "I've just been doing a lot of thinking."

Randy waved him off. "If you say so, but I think a dog might actually do you some good," he said. "It'll force you to leave this place at a decent hour and help you focus on something other than work. Besides, the companionship would be good for you. Unless of course you have a woman in your life."

"I don't have time for a dog," Karter said quickly, ignoring the last part of Randy's comment. "My lifestyle isn't conducive to a three-month-old beagle puppy. And if it weren't for Nana, I would've insisted Morgan find another home for the dog."

His housekeeper, a woman who had been their nanny growing up, was in love with Melvin. The dog could do no wrong in her eyes, even when he destroyed one of Karter's brogue wingtips. Of course, it had to be his favorite pair of shoes. Karter had been livid until the dog stared up at him with those damn puppy dog eyes. It had been impossible to stay mad.

His intercom buzzed and he pressed the red button on the desk phone. "Yes?"

"Karter, don't forget your meeting with Mathison Technology. Najee is waiting downstairs for you whenever you're ready," Gloria said of his driver.

"Okay, thanks. Let him know I'll be down in five minutes."

Randy stood but planted his hands facedown on the desk and looked at Karter seriously. "So how are you really? You were pretty shaken up after the funeral."

Karter stuffed his cell phone and keys into his pocket before grabbing his laptop bag. "I'm better. I have moments when I pick up the phone to call him, then remember that he's gone. It's weird, man. I never thought that the last time I talked to Delton would've been the last time."

Randy nodded. "Yeah, I know. I went home that afternoon and couldn't stop hugging Bethany and the girls," he said of his wife and kids. "Delton's death was a reminder that we shouldn't take anything or anyone for granted."

"True," Karter said as they left his office.

He vowed in that moment that starting immediately, he was going to take stock of his life and make some changes. He just wasn't sure exactly where to start.

A SHORT WHILE LATER, KARTER STROLLED INTO THE OFFICE building that housed Mathison Technology, immediately impressed with the modern design and its black-and-white decor. Based on all of the glass, marble, and intricate artwork wonderfully displayed, no expense had been spared.

He moved farther into the lobby, the wide-open space inviting and busier than he expected for that time of day. Professionally dressed people milled about, while a few others stood at the receptionist counter waiting for attention. He fell in line after the last person, his gaze still taking in his surroundings until it locked on a woman a few feet away.

Karter studied her as she leaned against a wall, chatting and laughing on her cell phone. She was hard to miss. Her bold, colorful attire stood out like a neon sign, especially against the backdrop of the professional setting.

He continued to stare, unable to pull his attention away. There was something so familiar about the woman. Yet he was sure they'd never met. No. He would've remembered someone like her. Eccentric. Captivating. Beautiful without even trying.

His gaze did a slower sweep down her curvy body, admiring the way her flamboyant outfit hugged her enticing figure. It made a statement about her personality. Bold. Secure. Lover of life. It was clear she didn't give a damn what anyone thought. Otherwise, she would've thought twice before walking out of the house looking like that. No doubt she was definitely her own person if her style was any indication.

His eyes traveled back up her body. Her straight, jet-black hair was tucked behind her ears and flowed down her back giving him an unobstructed view of her golden-brown face.

Normally, women as young as she appeared, maybe in her mid-to late twenties, and dressed the way she was didn't snag his attention, but she had done just that.

She laughed into the phone, and a strange sensation fluttered through Karter's body. He recognized that laugh. That soulful chortle that sent prickles of desire racing over his skin. He'd heard it a couple of times over the last two weeks.

But . . . it couldn't be. No way that was Dreamy Daniels, Mathison's secretary.

Karter had spoken with her a couple of times when she'd called the office with information that he had requested. He remembered her voice because it had a sultriness to it that immediately made him think of a phone sex operator. Not that he had experience talking to one, but he assumed that's how one would sound if he had ever called. Dreamy also had the wit of a woman twice her age, and a whimsicality that could be felt through the phone line.

He continued staring and, as if feeling his gaze on her, the woman turned. Their eyes locked . . . and then she smiled. The intensity of that small gesture was like taking a punch to the gut, the air bursting from his lungs.

No introductions were necessary. He couldn't explain it, but something deep down inside told him what he already knew.

That's Dreamy.

Chapter Three

DREAMY ENDED THE CALL WITH HER COUSIN AFTER BEING DIS-
tracted by the handsome man who'd been staring at her for the last
few seconds. At first, she'd done a double take, thinking he was the
actor Laz Alonso, but when he smiled, she realized he wasn't. But
still, this guy was a walking billboard for all things powerful and
sexy.

She sent her sparkliest smile in his direction, and he slowly returned it. Yet, he looked familiar. She just couldn't place where
she'd seen him before. She often spotted famous stars moving
around the city incognito with their various disguises.

However, this guy wasn't hiding anything. Not his good looks
or his appreciative gaze that was still taking her in. If his delighted
attention was any indication, her outfit wasn't as outlandish as Mariana made it out to be.

Remembering why she was in the lobby, Dreamy glanced at her
watch, noting that Mr. Redford should be arriving in a few minutes. Instead of waiting for Suzanne, the receptionist, to call upstairs, Dreamy had come down early to wait for him.

She leaned her shoulder against the wall and glanced out the window, glad she didn't have class later. Night school might be a pain, but at least it allowed her to work a full-time job during the day.

Just one more semester, then she'd be free.

"Dreamy."

Dreamy startled and turned her attention to Suzanne.

"Mr. Mathison's five thirty appointment is here," she said, and nodded toward the man standing at the counter. The gorgeous Laz Alonzo look-alike.

Her mouth went dry.

Good Lord. That's Karter Redford?

He was so not what she was expecting. She assumed he'd be some old guy with gray hair, glasses hanging low on his nose, and a scruffy mustache. Instead, she got tall, dark, and hot as Hades. Yes, this man appeared to be older than her, but there was nothing scrawny about him. His broad shoulders and fit body were encased in a dark, three-piece suit that looked as if it had been tailored specifically for him. His appearance, including his perfectly shined shoes, screamed wealthy.

"Dreamy?" the receptionist prompted.

"Oh. Yes. I'm sorry," she hurried to say as she approached the long, marbled desk. As she turned to the gentleman, who was more mouthwatering than she'd originally thought, her words lodged in her throat.

She subtly inhaled, taking in his intoxicating cologne, a combination of patchouli and sandalwood that enveloped her. Every coherent thought fled from her mind, and it was taking all of her self-control not to leap into his arms, bury her nose in that area between his neck and shoulders, and inhale again deeply.

"Hello, Dreamy."

Oh. My. God. That voice.

It was even deeper than it had been on the phone a couple of days ago.

An erotic tingle scurried over her skin, and goose bumps flared on her arms. The way he uttered her name was like . . .

Wait. What the hell was she doing? She shouldn't be acknowledging how gorgeous this man was or marveling at his sensual voice. She was done with men. Wealthy or broke, she wanted nothing to do with any of them. Especially one that probably traveled in the same circles as her ex, Brandon.

Not cultured. Not sophisticated. Not educated enough. His words rattled around in her mind before she shook them free.

"Excuse me," a woman said from behind them.

Dreamy and Mr. Redford turned, realizing they were holding up the small line that had formed. They eased away from the counter.

"Mr. Redford, I'm glad to finally meet you."

"Same here, and please, call me Karter. It's a pleasure to meet you, Dreamy." His light brown eyes twinkled, and if he were anyone else—not some insanely wealthy man—she would've thought she saw interest in his gaze.

No way. There was no way in hell he would ever be interested in someone like her. He probably paid more for his suits than she made in a year. What could he ever see in her? But knowing that didn't stop butterflies from exploding inside her stomach. This virile guy was all man and had excitement roaring through her veins.

She glanced away, trying to normalize her breathing as she ran her sweaty palms down the sides of her floral pants. Karter . . . no, Mr. Redford, was so damn distracting. She needed to get him to a bedroom . . . er, a conference room pronto. Goodness, he had her all screwed up. The best thing she could do for everyone involved was hand him off to Gordon as quickly as possible.

"We can take the elevator up," Dreamy finally said, hoping her professionalism was soundly in place. "Follow me, please."

Squeak. Squeak. Squeak. Her shoes screamed with every step.

Oh. Dear. God. Marianna was right. Her shoes sounded like she was stomping on kittens.

She prayed a black hole would magically appear and swallow her up. It was probably too much to hope that Mr. Redford couldn't hear them, but there was no way the irritating noise wasn't audible.

Just before they stopped at the elevator, he looked around as though alarmed. Finally, he asked, "Are those your shoes making that sound?"

"Yes," Dreamy said without missing a beat, her head held high as if squeaky new shoes were the norm. "I'm field-testing a shoe lubricant. Clearly, the scientists need to tweak whatever formula they used."

Karter stared at her for the longest time, as if trying to determine whether she was serious, and then burst out laughing. He didn't hold back. His hand rested on his chest as he fought to pull himself together. Just when she thought he had recovered, he started up again.

Dreamy smiled, glad the elevator had arrived. Not much embarrassed her, or made her nervous, but around this man, she was experiencing both.

Just breathe. Slow and steady. Just breathe.

Telling herself what to do and actually doing it were two very different things. Her pulse pounded loudly in her ears, drowning out her chant. How could she breathe when she was standing side by side with a multimillionaire who looked as if he should be on the cover of *GQ*? He had such a commanding presence. One that was alluring, yet authoritative. A presence that sucked the air right out of the small space of the elevator.

Everything about him had her on edge. Not necessarily in a bad way. No, more like he was so appealing, just standing next to him had her body pulsing with a desire she had never experienced, especially with the men she normally dated.

"I have to admit," Karter started, his head tilted slightly as he studied her, "you're not at all what I expected."

Dreamy didn't dare ask what he'd been expecting. He'd probably been imagining some tall bombshell with big perky breasts, an hourglass figure, and long legs that went on forever. When in fact she was an ordinary-looking five-six woman who barely filled a B cup, and had a little belly she couldn't get flat. Add that to her curvy hips that didn't quite go with her skinny bird legs, and you had an ordinary woman.

Instead of responding to his comment, Dreamy changed the subject. During the short ride, they chatted about the building, the businesses that were housed there, and how long she'd been working at Mathison Technology. Once they were on the top floor, she led him to the conference room. When they walked in, Gordon was pacing near the projection screen. Even though his knowledge of technology was endless, he'd been on edge most of the day.

"Mr. Mathison, this is Karter Redford. Mr. Redford, Gordon Mathison." Dreamy headed to the door, glad she had brought coffee and water in before she'd gone downstairs. She couldn't wait to get away from both men for two very different reasons.

Gordon was a pain in the ass. Mr. Redford, on the other hand, had all her girlie parts on code-red, high alert. But he was so far out of her league, she shouldn't even be imagining herself being with him. In his presence, she was painfully aware of their differences. He was well spoken, too good-looking, too smart, too wealthy, and too old. He had at least ten years on her.

Yep. Way out of my league.

Crap. She had to stop thinking about him as a man. He was a

potential investor, and possibly the answer to her getting a much-needed raise. Nothing more.

She tiptoed carefully toward the door, barely letting her heels touch the floor, hoping to quiet the screeching whine of her new shoes.

Gordon cleared his throat. "Dreamy, I need you to sit in on this meeting."

Her heart kicked against her ribs and then plunged to her feet. *Ah, hell.*

Chapter Four

KARTER PUSHED HIS SEAT BACK FROM THE POLISHED MAHOGANY conference room table and crossed one leg over the other. Thirty minutes into the meeting, and he was impressed with the sentient computer proposal. Their hypothetical machine, a form of artificial intelligence, would be able to simulate human behavior and skills.

If Karter decided to work with them, he'd already thought about using money from his innovation account to fund the project. Despite the fact that some of their financial information was lacking, Mathison Technology had the potential for long-term growth.

Unfortunately, Karter had picked up on a glaring issue that had nothing to do with the new sentient computer or the company's finances. Gordon Mathison. The man was a control freak and an asshole.

He blamed everything that went wrong with his presentation on his secretary and other members of his staff. A man who complained about even the smallest detail, like not having a pen *and* a pencil at his disposal, was a loser in Karter's book. Karter was the type who owned up to his mistakes or problems, as any good leader should, and that's what he expected of people he worked with. Instead, what he was seeing from this guy was that if there ever were an issue, it was everyone else's fault but his.

He also treated his staff like servants, not colleagues. One minute he'd asked Dreamy to get him some information, but just as quickly, he changed his mind and told her he'd do it himself. That happened three times in the last half an hour. The stress radiating off the guy was palpable, and the tension in the room between him and Dreamy could be cut with a chainsaw.

Gordon sat at the head of the table like some king of coding, periodically mumbling under his breath about incompetence. Dreamy sat to his left, which put her directly across from Karter.

"Tell me a little bit about your staff and the team who would be working on this project," Karter said to the owner.

With a smug expression, Gordon folded his arms across his scrawny chest. "Mr. Redford, I assure you, the staff is top notch. I picked them myself. You don't have to worry about them. They do what I tell them to, and I can guarantee that you'll be pleased with the product."

Karter stared at the man for a moment before stealing a glance at Dreamy, who was staring down in her lap while slightly shaking her head.

"Gordon, I don't just invest in companies and projects," Karter said, needing to make a few things clear to this pompous jerk. "I also invest in people. So when I ask you about—"

"Mr. Redford, I think you would be impressed with the team of people working for Mathison Technology," Dreamy interrupted as she reached for her boss's computer. "Do you mind?" she asked Gordon, but didn't wait for him to answer before sliding his laptop in front of her. She clicked a few times before turning the screen for both him and Mathison to see. "I recently updated our website to include our staff members and a brief description of their impressive experience."

"I didn't tell you to do that," Mathison said, frowning, but didn't take his attention from the screen.

"No, you didn't, but we have an incredible team who should be showcased," Dreamy explained, and proceeded to tell both men about the individuals who worked for the company.

Karter listened as she discussed a few of the staff members and the roles they played. She then pointed out those who were slated to work on the project. He was impressed not only with what he was hearing but also with her initiative. Considering the friction between her and Mathison, Karter was more than a little surprised that she'd go beyond the call of duty for the man.

"Oh, and I guess I should've started with the project manager, Samantha," Dreamy continued, and pointed with a manicured finger at a photo of a woman with straight blond hair, stylish glasses, and a dimpled smile. "Sam has been with the company for three years, and she's brilliant. She used to work in Silicon Valley and was instrumental in the development of a portable heart attack detector.

"This guy right here is Carl," Dreamy said after scrolling down and stopping on a picture of an older black man with a bald head and dark, bushy eyebrows. "He's a software engineer who has worked in the tech industry for almost twenty-five years. He's one of our newest hires and a super-nice guy."

As she continued going through the list, admiration sounded in her tone as she not only described their role at Mathison Technology but spoke highly and personally of each of them, adding in a few interesting tidbits. Karter was quickly learning that Dreamy was more than just a secretary. He wouldn't be surprised if she was the backbone of the company. Where Gordon lacked people skills, she clearly made up for it by knowing the ins and outs of the company and its employees. Or she was just putting on a good show. But he had a feeling that what you saw with Dreamy was what you got.

"I'm sorry, I didn't mean to keep going on and on." Dreamy nibbled on her lower lip and cast a shy smile in Karter's direction as she eased the laptop back in front of Gordon.

"Actually, that's exactly the kind of information I need to know. Thank you. It's clear that you know the staff well," Karter said to her, but gave Gordon a pointed look. The man was too busy sifting through a file folder to even notice.

"Dreamy, where are last quarter's numbers that I asked you to bring in?" Mathison asked. "The accountant assured me that you would have them this afternoon to put with the rest of the material."

"When I offered to print them out, you said you'd do it. So I emailed the documents to you hours ago," she said.

"No, you didn't. I don't have them."

"If you check your email, I'm sure you'll find the information." Though the words were spoken calmly, there was an edge to her tone. Her chest heaved and her jaw was clenched tight enough to crack teeth. If she was trying to remain calm, it wasn't working. The grip she had on her pen tightened, and at any minute she or the pen would snap.

Karter had watched her and Gordon interact. Dreamy seemed competent and had an explanation for everything she did or didn't do. On the other hand, there was Gordon, the poster boy of an arrogant, absentminded professor. He could recite everything from the smallest detail about the new technology, but he wasn't good at making eye contact. He also seemed to be lousy at delegating. And so far, the few people who had been in and out of the conference room at Gordon's request all walked out rolling their eyes or mumbling under their breath.

Mathison shook his head, and a low growl sounded in his chest. "I don't recall saying that I'd print anything out. I need those numbers. You should've just printed them instead of—"

Mathison startled when Dreamy shot out of her seat, a smile that could make the Joker's smile look tame plastered on her gorgeous face. "I'll go and get that information for you."

Squeeeeeeak, squeeeeeeak, squeeeeeeak.

"What in God's name is that noise?" Mathison barked, his face twisted in a scowl.

"My shoes," Dreamy said simply.

The sound followed her out the door, and Karter struggled to keep a straight face. He didn't know what was more entertaining, the fact that her shoes sounded like she had chew toys built into the heels or that despite the noisiness of them, she walked with confidence. She carried herself proudly with her head held high, even though she walked to a different, albeit noisy, beat.

Clearly, the woman could hold her own with anyone if the way she'd handled herself throughout the meeting was any indication. Dreamy had a way about her . . . a way that made him take notice. No one would claim that he was easy to impress, but that was exactly what she had done.

Within seconds, she was back. "Here you go." She handed Mathison the document. "Will there be anything else?"

"Not at the moment. You can leave." Mathison waved her away, his attention on the documents. "Close the door behind you."

She glanced at Karter, her expression unreadable before she turned and walked back across the room. He couldn't stop his gaze from following the gentle sway of her hips. *Left. Right. Left.* His body hummed as he zeroed in on the way the bold, floral pants hugged her shapely butt and molded over firm thighs and toned legs. The woman stirred something so primal inside of him that it was taking a Herculean effort not to follow her out of the room.

What the hell?

He sat up straight, surprised at the route his thoughts had taken. Clearly, he needed to get laid or at least get out more. Dreamy wasn't his type. She was way too young. Too eccentric. Too . . . everything. But maybe that's what he liked from the moment she'd caught his attention in the lobby.

"It's a good thing she's worked for me for almost a year," Mathison grumbled, disdain dripping from his words. "Otherwise, I'd get rid of her. She's starting to drop the ball just like my past assistants."

Surprise yielded quickly to disgust, and Karter sat forward. A protectiveness for Dreamy he couldn't quite explain sparked, and he glared at the condescending bastard.

"She is the *only* reason I'm still sitting here," Karter snapped. "I suggest you keep her around as long as you can. The artificial intelligence device is brilliant, but without her by your side, I doubt you'll raise enough money to buy a cup of coffee."

Mathison's brows bunched together as he glared. "What are you saying?"

Karter wanted to tell him that it meant he was an ignorant asshole. Instead, he asked, "What's your turnover rate like? Fifty, sixty percent? If the way you treated Dreamy and the woman who was in here earlier is any indication, I'd say that you don't have a good relationship with the members of your team."

Mathison went rigid, and his gaze dropped as he took his time responding. "My relationship with my staff should be no concern of yours. As long as I can deliver what I promise, and make a profit for our companies, that should be all that matters."

"That's where you're wrong." Karter reined in his temper and stood as he fastened the buttons on his suit jacket. "Mr. Mathison, I suggest you get your business in order before you continue seeking investors. Good luck to you. You're going to need it."

"Wait." Gordon stumbled out of his chair, knocking a few sheets of paper to the floor. "Does this mean that you're not going to invest in my idea?"

Karter studied the man whose green eyes pleaded for a chance. "I like the direction that you're going in with this idea. There's real promise there, but I'm concerned about how you operate your business. Mistreating your staff is a great way to sabotage the success of your company."

"I . . . I'll"—he ran his fingers through his dark hair—"I'll work something out. I really believe in this new product. Whatever it takes to get the financial backing, I'll do it."

Karter nodded, but he wasn't sure if the guy was someone he wanted to work with. "Let me think about it. I'll be in touch."

Chapter Five

DREAMY POUNDED A FIST ON HER DESK, RELEASING THE ANGER bubbling inside of her like a roaring tornado twirling across a flat terrain. She marched back and forth in the tight space behind her desk, trying to tamp down the need to throat punch her boss.

She wasn't a violent person, but Gordon would deserve anything she hurled at him for embarrassing her in front of Mr. Redford. It was bad enough he didn't let her do her job without questioning every . . . damn . . . thing, but making her look incompetent? He'd gone too far.

"That *asshole!*"

He was lucky that she needed this job. She just had to hang in there for another semester, when she'd finally graduate with her degree, or until she won the lottery. Then she'd tell him what he could do with his maniacal, micromanaging behavior and his job.

With a noisy huff, she dropped into her chair and propped her elbows on the desk. Covering her face with her hands, she took several deep breaths to get her nerves under control and to fix her jacked-up attitude. No way was she allowing Gordon's behavior to dictate how she conducted herself.

Gordon had been an insensitive jerk since her first week on the job and could benefit from sensitivity training. No one could deny that he was brilliant at what he did. Outside of that, though, he was a disrespectful, narcissistic, egotistical jerk. She and the staff deserved to work in a great environment where their skills could shine without his coldness. There was too much talent in the company for any of them not to be recognized, which was why she'd enjoyed telling Mr. Redford about everyone.

What am I going to do about Mr. Asshole?

"Are you okay?"

Dreamy startled at the deep voice, and jerked her head up. Karter stood in front of her desk, and his intense eyes held a concern that probably should've been reserved for someone he actually knew. Yet here he was.

She leaped from her seat and ran her fingers through the long strands of her wig, hoping it hadn't shifted on her head. She pulled her shoulders back and stood tall. "Oh, yeah. I'm fine. I was just . . . just pulling myself together," she said honestly, and let her shoulders droop.

"Is the meeting over?" she asked, which was clearly a dumb question if he was standing in front of her desk. "What did you think of the sentient computer idea?"

"I think it's magnificent. Based on my research and what I know about Mathison Technology, it'll be a nice addition to the company's product line."

Dreamy smiled, feeling encouraged that the tech company might get the funding it needed. Meaning she'd also get the raise that Gordon promised. Assuming he kept his word. If he didn't, she would have no other choice but to leave. No way was she going to keep putting up with his shit if it didn't come with more money.

But more than that, even if she didn't stay with the company, she wanted to see it succeed mainly because of those who worked for Mathison.

"Well, I'm glad you're going to invest in—"

"I didn't say *that*," Karter said. There was no warmth in his tone, and his uninterested expression spoke volumes.

They'd blown it. No, Gordon had blown it. Dreamy shouldn't be surprised. No doubt Mr. Redford had felt the discord that filled the room. She had hoped that he'd overlook it and base his decision solely on the product.

Guess not.

"Mr. Redford . . ."

"Karter, please," he said with a slight smile.

"Okay . . . Karter, is there anything I can say or do to persuade you to consider taking a chance on Mathison Technology?"

Like kiss the ground you walk on . . . have your babies . . .

One tempting idea after another flooded her mind, but no way would she voice any of them. She had already embarrassed herself enough with her squeaky shoes and flower garden outfit. No sense in adding to that list by saying something crazy or sharing inappropriate thoughts.

Karter's head tilted slightly as he studied her.

Wait. I didn't say any of that crap out loud . . . did I?

No. No I didn't, but . . .

Dreamy tried not to fidget under his perusal, but there was something about the man that made her all flustered. It was more than the fact that he was wealthy. It was . . . everything. It was his cool, calm demeanor that was present throughout the meeting. His good looks. His scent. His powerful presence . . . Everything about him messed with her sanity. It didn't help that he had the social grace of the Duke of Sussex and the seductiveness of Idris Elba. The man was damn near perfect. The total package.

And, God, he smells so good.

She cleared her throat as if that would help steady her breathing. "Why are you looking at me like that?" she blurted before she could pull the words back.

Suddenly, the intensity in his gaze morphed into a softer expression, and the left corner of his sexy mouth lifted slowly into a crooked grin.

"You fascinate me," he said. "I have a lot of respect for people who look out for others the way you did with your co-workers. Clearly, you admire their accomplishments as well as their contributions to the company."

I fascinate him?

Now that's one Dreamy hadn't heard before, and damn if it didn't make her feel as if she could conquer the world. If she weren't taking a break from male species, she might invite him out for a drink. Then again, she probably couldn't afford whatever top-shelf booze he usually drank. Besides, a man like him probably didn't respond well to pushy women. But more than anything, he was at such a different place in life and so far out of her league.

She needed to just stay focused and help get the needed funding.

"Gordon Mathison has developed numerous cutting-edge products, and I have no doubt his latest idea will be just as magnificent," she said. "He might own the company and be brilliant, but as far as I'm concerned, his success is due to the talent of his team. His accomplishments are a result of the group effort."

They needed this man's money. Hell, Dreamy needed that raise. She was about ready to say anything.

"Karter, I hope you decide to invest in the company. I'd hate for you to miss out on a good thing—I mean, a good opportunity."

Another smile crept over his mouth, and Dreamy could've sworn that his gaze swept up and down her body with interest. Similar to the way he'd checked her out in the lobby.

"Yeah, I'd hate to miss out on a good thing too." Karter's words were spoken quietly, but she didn't miss the suggestiveness behind them.

Was he flirting? And how sad was it that she wasn't sure?

Dreamy swallowed. Her heart pounded a little faster as she forced herself to stand still when he appeared to move a little closer. She didn't much like people invading her personal space, but the burst of desire that this man had awakened within her was hard to ignore.

Karter towered over her by at least nine inches, and Dreamy had to lean her head back to meet his gaze. The tenderness in his gorgeous eyes, which were almost hazel, was nearly her undoing. An overwhelming longing gripped her, making her want to wrap her arms around his neck and taste his delectable lips.

But she wouldn't.

She couldn't.

But damn if she didn't want to.

Frozen in place, she willed her arms to stay at her sides. It would be a bad idea, a very bad idea, but curiosity was getting the best of her. How would his lips feel against hers? Soft? Hard? And what would he taste like? Mint? Cinnamon? Or how would he . . .

"Why are you pitching so hard to make this deal happen?" Karter asked in a low voice.

Her thoughts screeched to a halt. His words were like a cold bucket of water poured over her head as he reminded her of why he was there. Mathison Technology needed not only his investment in the company, but his expertise to take the business to the next level.

"I believe in the technology," Dreamy squeaked out, then cleared her throat as she got her outlandish thoughts under control and her professional demeanor back in place. "I also believe in our team. Before you make a decision, would you be willing to meet with those who'll be working on the project?"

Again, he eyed her. Dreamy had no clue what he was thinking, but she stood her ground, praying the company hadn't missed out on his investment.

"I hope Gordon Mathison appreciates what you bring to this organization," he said. "But based on what I saw of the guy, I'm sure he doesn't. Which is a damn shame."

Dreamy blinked several times. What the heck could she say to that? If she was honest, she'd tell him that her boss didn't think much of her, period. Instead, she didn't say anything.

"Sure. I'll meet with the team." Karter moved closer. "Set it up and call my assistant with a date, but I have one condition."

Dreamy's brows dipped into a frown. "And that is?"

"You have to be at the meeting too."

"But . . . but I'm not really part of the team. I just—"

"It's because of you that I'm still considering investing. If you're not there, then there's no deal."

Dreamy hesitated for a minute, surprised by his admission. Gordon would probably have something to say about her being at the team meeting, but . . . "I'll be there."

Chapter Six

"AND *THEN* HE SAID, *IF YOU'RE NOT THERE, THEN THERE'S NO deal*," Dreamy practically screamed the last part, still feeling some kind of way at her brief interaction with the multimillionaire. "It's because of me we have a second chance to pitch. Can you believe that?"

"Of course I can believe it," her cousin, Jordyn, said and moved over to the stove. "That low-life ninny who you refer to as your boss is a joke, no matter how often you call him brilliant. But Mr. Multimillionaire spent less than an hour with you and saw what everyone at Mathison knows—you run that place."

Dreamy grabbed the rest of the dirty dishes from the fake granite countertop and placed them in the sudsy water. They had just finished eating dinner, and she was washing the dishes by hand since the dishwasher had died the week before.

"You're wasting your time and talents at that place," Jordyn continued. "You should've left the week you started."

"Jay, don't start," she said. "It's not like I'm staying with the company for the rest of my life. Despite Gordon's faults, Mathison pays better than other companies I've worked at, and I can practically walk to school from there. Right now, it's convenient in more ways than one."

"I still think—"

"Besides, I don't look at working there as wasting my time," Dreamy interrupted as she continued with the dishes. "I work around awesome people, and I learn something new every day. Skills that I'll be able to take with me on my next venture. We all can't be interning at our dream job and be months away from becoming a lawyer."

Jordyn was two years older, movie-star gorgeous with a body that would make any man take a second and third look, and she was in her last year of law school. Her cousin had always excelled at everything she did and made adulting look easy, but Dreamy knew it hadn't been.

While Dreamy's mother, Tarrah, had left Dreamy on her grandparents' doorstep, Jordyn had been raised by her parents until tragedy struck. Her mother, who had battled depression for years, took her own life when Jordyn was seven. From there, her father, Tarrah's brother, raised her, but he died from an accident at work on a construction site when she was in high school. Jordyn had been devastated, but she hadn't let her grief keep her down. She'd always wanted to be a defense attorney, and soon she would realize her goal.

They both were only children, but when Jordyn came to live with their grandparents, she and Dreamy had been raised like sisters. They'd been tight ever since. Her cousin was her role model, her confidant, and Dreamy trusted her opinion, but . . .

"Working at Mathison Tech is just a stepping-stone for me," she said, wanting to assure her cousin that she wasn't planning to stay there forever. "I have huge goals, and I plan on accomplishing every single one."

"I have no doubt," her cousin said absently.

Dreamy dried her hands and leaned against the sink, watching as Jordyn vigorously scrubbed the stove top trying to loosen the stuck-on tomato sauce. Her curly hair swayed back and forth with each stroke. She had cooking duty this week, and tonight had prepared spaghetti and meat sauce, a salad . . . well, lettuce and dressing. And since they didn't have any fancy bread, her cousin had served up wheat toast.

They alternated household duties. Tonight, Dreamy was responsible for cleaning the kitchen, and when her cousin offered to help, she didn't turn her down.

"So tell me more about cutie-pie Karter with a K," Jordyn said. "I've heard of him and about some of the companies he's invested in. He's a friend of one of the partners at the firm."

Dreamy had given Karter the nickname and smiled at her cousin's use of it. Cutie-pie Karter with a *K* was so fitting. She had to keep herself from sighing as she recalled how gorgeous he was.

"I didn't know much about him until after he left the office. I was shocked when he showed up looking like a fantasy come to life. It's definitely not good to judge someone without getting to know them first. Gordon had gone on and on about this venture capitalist, a man who could change the trajectory of a company with a snap of his fingers. I guess he knows someone who knows Karter or something like that, but I assumed the venture capitalist was some old geezer with a boatload of cash. Then Karter showed up."

Dreamy fanned herself, thinking about his handsome face and muscular build.

"Girrl, that man is the total package, and he has the most gorgeous light brown eyes I've ever seen. The moment he left the office, I googled him. I know I called him old, but only because he's ten years older than me. He's really not *that* old and looks good to be almost forty. Oh, and I found out his father is *Marcus Redford*," Dreamy squealed, still shocked by that information.

Jordyn shrugged and kept scrubbing. "So what? His father is a big-time movie star. Who cares?"

"*Seriously?*" Dreamy grabbed her cousin's arm, forcing her to stop cleaning and look at her. "Are you seriously saying that having a superstar father is not a big deal?"

Her cousin threw up her hands. "Okay, fine. That is pretty cool, but still. He's just a guy, Dreamy. A rich, good-looking guy. The way you've been going on and on about him, one would think he was God himself. But if you two started dating, now *that* would be something to squeal about."

"Ha! Yeah, like that would ever happen."

Dreamy hadn't been able to stop thinking about the guy since he'd left her standing in awe by her desk. She liked what little she knew of the man and had even fantasized about what it would be like to really get to know him. But then she reminded herself of how far out of her league he was. The thought had brought her crashing back to reality.

"Actually, you would probably be a better fit for him than me," Dreamy said, thinking that maybe she should introduce her cousin to Karter. "You're cultured, smart, and know how to carry yourself around the rich and famous. When you're not slumming around in jeans and T-shirts, you even clean up good."

"I clean up well," her cousin gently corrected.

The comment stung, but Dreamy would rather be corrected by her than someone else. English might've been her native language, but she was good at butchering it.

"Clearly, Karter is more into the cute, bubbly, quirky type," Jordyn said.

"What do you mean by 'quirky'?" Dreamy asked, sounding a little more defensive than intended.

Her cousin leaned a hip against the stove and folded her arms across her chest. "Unconventional. Eccentric. March to your own beat. You're a lot like Gramps."

"Oh, that's just great," Dreamy grumbled.

"That's not an insult," her cousin insisted. "What's wrong with you tonight? You're usually not this insecure."

"I know." Dreamy hated when moments of self-doubt crept in. She loved the person she was, but every now and then she fell into the comparison trap. Comparing herself to those around her and even to people she didn't know. But she had to stop.

I am beautiful. I am confident. I am lovable. I am a lottery winner.

She straightened her shoulders and lifted her chin. "Forget what I just said. That was just a moment of weakness. I'm more than enough for *any* man, even cutie-pie Karter with a *K*."

"That's what I'm talkin' about. Know your worth, girl!"

"I do, but remember, I'm taking a break from men. So nothing could happen between me and Karter even if there was a chance."

"I hope you're not still hung up on that idiot Brandon. That dude might be a lawyer, but he's so stupid, he probably can't find his way out of a wet paper bag loaded with holes."

Dreamy laughed, knowing her cousin was just trying to be funny. Brandon might be a lot of things—shallow, conceited, self-centered—but stupid wasn't one of them.

"You know what? Once I win this money—"

"Ahh, hell. Not that crap again." Jordyn tossed the dish towel on the counter, then stomped out of the kitchen. She headed to the living room with Dreamy right on her heels.

"Jay, I'm serious. You should start pooling your money with me and Gramps. Tonight's the night. We're going to be millionaires in a few minutes."

"Yep, sure you will." Jordyn sat on the navy-blue threadbare sofa and grabbed her laptop from the coffee table. "You say that every week. Yet here we are hanging out in a run-down house with bars on the windows and peeling linoleum, hoping the power company won't turn the electricity off just for the hell of it."

"Geez, I forgot to pay one time, and you're still afraid we'll end up in the dark."

Dreamy dropped down on the sofa next to her and released a long-drawn-out sigh. Her cousin normally wasn't a Debbie Downer, but lately, she'd become more of a realist, and understandably so. It was getting harder and harder to keep up with the bills.

"Besides, if I wanted to throw money away," Jordyn continued, not taking her eyes off the laptop screen, "I'd just shove it into a shredder at work and watch it disappear. Or give it to Gramps and let him smoke it."

"Whatever." Dreamy grunted but it sounded more like a snort since she was trying to keep from laughing, not wanting to encourage her cousin's sarcasm.

"Ugh, Gramps!" Dreamy shrieked when she looked up to find him standing in the opening to the living room with nothing on but tighty-whities.

She shielded her eyes, then turned her head. She and Jordyn had been trying to convince him to embrace boxer shorts, but Gramps insisted on the briefs that were snug enough to cut off circulation.

Hoping her grandfather had gone back to his room, she chanced a glance.

Nope, still there.

"I thought we agreed that you wouldn't walk around the house in your drawers," she said.

"I ain't agree to nothin'," he said, his legs spread apart and hands on his hips, looking like a wrinkly Captain Underpants.

Jordyn groaned and dropped her head back against the sofa.

"Gramps, we talked about this. You can't be walking around half-naked. We don't wanna see all that. What if we had company?"

"Do we?" he asked, looking to his left, then to his right as if actually expecting to see someone.

"No, but what if we did? No one wants to see your goodies hanging out," Jordyn said.

"Do we have a frozen banana?" he asked, ignoring them. "And I need whip cream and some nipples."

Dreamy gasped.

"What?" Jordyn screeched.

"Oops, did I say nipples? I meant cherries." He started strolling away as quietly as he had entered.

"Oh my God. I just can't with him." Dreamy laughed and cringed at the thought of what he could be doing in his bedroom. Sometimes it was best not to ask. "You know what? I'm going to let you deal with *your* grandfather. You probably should see if he snuck a woman into his room. I'd check, but I don't want to miss the Powerball drawing."

Jordyn set her laptop back on the table in front of the sofa. "Oh yeah, wouldn't want you to miss out on seeing every number *but* yours drop."

Dreamy waved her off and grabbed the remote, turning to the station that aired the drawing. She glanced down at the ticket that held six numbers she knew by heart, numbers they played every week, and hoped for the best.

"Good evening, America, let's play," the announcer said as one of the balls rolled out of the hopper. "First number up is twenty-three, followed by fourteen."

"Oh my God. We have two of the numbers. Come on. Come on," she said to the television, excitement blossoming inside of her as she sat on the edge of the sofa.

"The next number is . . ."

Dreamy startled when everything went black. The room. The television. Even the raggedy refrigerator had stopped humming.

"What the . . ."

"Damn it, Dreamy!" Jordyn yelled from the back of the house. "Did you pay the electric bill?"

Oh crap.

Chapter Seven

THE NEXT AFTERNOON, DREAMY MARVELED AT HOW GREAT HER day was going despite the night she'd had. Thankfully, the electric company hadn't been the cause of their being plunged into darkness. Instead, a palm tree in the neighborhood had fallen on a power line up the street. The Santa Ana winds had been strong for the last couple of days, and luckily only one tree had toppled.

At least their dilemma hadn't been due to an unpaid bill or old circuit breakers in need of updating. The house was in dire need of electrical work, as well as a new roof, but she and Jordyn were hoping for a little more time to scrape money together.

All the more reason why Dreamy needed to win the lottery, or at the very least, finish her degree and get a better-paying job. But if—no, when—she won the lottery, all their problems would be solved. She hoped.

Last night, they matched three of the numbers from the Powerball drawing. It was only a matter of time before she and Gramps would get all six numbers and cash that fat check. She was ready for a win. She needed a win. Not only a lottery win, but a win in life, period.

Dreamy's attention returned to the email she was drafting, but she glanced up and spotted Gordon through the glass wall. He was marching toward their suite of offices, and his normally pale face was red as if he was about to blow. He jerked the door open and stormed inside.

"In my office. Now!" Without a backward glance, he stomped past her desk and down the carpeted hallway.

Sigh. Just when her day was going so well, but no way was Dreamy allowing him to ruin her good mood. She stood and picked a loose thread off her hot-pink blouse. She had toned down her outfit today in case she'd had to meet with Samantha, Fiona, and Carl in person. Wearing the pink blouse and winter-white pants had been a good choice. She managed to look professional without having to appear drab in dark colors the way so many others dressed. But she ended up not having to have a face-to-face with any of them. Instead, they communicated via a conference call regarding the upcoming meeting since one of them had been working from home.

Dreamy grabbed the electronic tablet from the corner of her desk and took the short walk to Gordon's office. Her shoes, a multi-color pair of two-and-a-half-inch heels, were super comfortable and as quiet as if walking on pillows. Still horrified by her appearance and footwear choice from the day before, Dreamy planned to make sure the next time Karter saw her, she looked and sounded like a professional.

She strolled into Gordon's office. "I have some great ne—"

"Who do you think you are setting up meetings with my management team behind my back?" he snapped.

Dreamy pulled up short in surprise. Gordon stood in front of his desk with his arms folded across his chest. If looks could kill, she'd be splattered against the wall across from him.

"First you embarrass me in front of Karter Redford. Now you're setting up meetings with *my* managers? You're just a secretary. You do what *I* tell you to do!"

Dreamy gritted her teeth and gripped the tablet to keep from hurling it across the room. She'd always been good at throwing a Frisbee. If she aimed just right, she could nick him right in his Adam's apple. That would probably be better than the throat punch she'd entertained giving him the day before.

"First of all, I would think you'd be happy that there's still a chance to get Karter to invest. I set that meeting up at *his* request. You haven't been answering your phone. Otherwise, I would've given you a heads-up.

"Secondly, I'm not sure what *you* did to screw up the meeting after I left the room yesterday, but he wasn't going to fund the project," she lied, sort of.

Karter hadn't exactly said that, but Dreamy could tell that he was wavering toward a big fat *no*. She couldn't much blame him. Besides explaining how the artificial intelligence thingy would be different from anything on the market or in the works, Gordon hadn't done much more to convince Karter to take a chance on him.

Dreamy explained the conversation she'd had with Karter the day before. Surprisingly, Gordon listened without interrupting. She knew how much he wanted that funding, especially with Karter's investment history. During her research, she had learned that he had invested in a few tech companies that tripled their profit within three years, thanks to his help. That's the type of support Gordon needed whether he wanted to admit it or not.

"*Karter?*" Gordon finally spoke, and frowned at her. "Since when do you start calling potential investors by their first name?"

Dreamy shrugged. "He told me to call him Karter. I don't think he's that formal. So I—"

"I don't pay you to think, and I don't appreciate you going behind my back talking to him and setting up meetings with my leadership team. You can cancel that meeting. I'll be discussing the project with Mr. Redford alone."

"But he said—"

"You can leave now."

"You're making a huge mistake," Dreamy insisted. "Karter made it very clear that he wanted a meeting with all of you, and he wanted me in that meeting."

"I'll handle Mr. Redford." He shooed her away with a wave of his hand. "Close my door on your way out."

Dreamy huffed and stormed out of the office, slamming the door behind her. Why did she care? If she were a mean-spirited person, she'd call Karter and tell him to take his investment and give it to a more deserving company.

When she made it to her desk, she banged down the tablet and grabbed her purse from the bottom drawer. It was only a few minutes before her workday ended, but if she stuck around there much longer, there was no telling what she'd end up doing.

She shut down her computer and decided at that moment, she was going to be sick for the next couple of days.

Just a secretary my ass. Let's see how he manages without me for a while.

KARTER STEPPED OUT OF HIS OFFICE BUILDING JUST AS A WARM breeze kissed his face. The weather in Los Angeles was unseasonably hot for October, but he welcomed the heat after being cooped up in his office for much of the day. With sunglasses covering his eyes and a bottle of water in his hand, he headed to his luxury black SUV, not surprised to see Najee holding the back door open.

"Good evening, Mr. Redford," Najee said. For over ten years, the retired Marine had chauffeured Karter through LA's busy streets and freeways. But Najee was more than a driver. He was a friend and had been a trusted confidant. A sounding board when needed.

Tall, broad, and capable of killing a man with his bare hands, he also doubled as personal security.

"How's it going, Najee?"

"All is well, sir."

It didn't matter how many times Karter told him not to call him sir or boss, and that it wasn't a requirement to wear a suit; Najee insisted.

Thanks to some great investment tips Karter had given him, Najee could've quit the driving gig years ago. He had amassed enough to move him and his wife to a small exotic island and spend their days sipping fruity rum drinks. Instead, he chose to work, always making himself available to Karter.

Karter removed his sunglasses and climbed into the back of the vehicle. The soft, butter-like leather seat enveloped him, and instantly some of the tension from the day fell away. He settled in for the hour-plus drive to Orange County, where he was meeting his best friends for dinner. Normally, he preferred driving himself, except during rush hour, which seemed to be all day in LA.

He laid his head against the seat and closed his eyes. Immediately, Dreamy came to mind. It had been three days since his meeting at Mathison Technology, and Karter couldn't stop thinking about the eccentric woman. He still couldn't explain his fascination with her, except that she was like no other woman he'd ever met. Which was probably why he was disappointed that she hadn't called to request a new meeting. He wanted to see her again. He missed her sense of humor, her lively personality, and, hell, even her squeaky shoes.

A smile kicked up the corners of his lips at the thought of her overly bright stripes and flowers, and the lubricant that she claimed to be testing.

Karter chuckled. Dreamy was refreshing, and she had pushed hard for the company to get another chance to pitch. So why hadn't she called? Instead, his assistant, Gloria, had received several calls from Gordon Mathison, asking—no, demanding—Karter return his call.

His cell phone chirped, pulling him out of his thoughts, and he removed it from the interior pocket of his suit jacket. Glancing at the screen, Karter read the text from Gloria.

She called! You have a meeting at Mathison's Friday morning at 10.

He smiled as he sent Gloria a thumbs-up emoji.

What he really wanted to know was why it had taken Dreamy so long to contact his office.

He set the phone next to him and settled back against the seat. He glanced at the back of Najee's shiny, dark bald head. "Hey, Najee. Have you ever met a woman who you just couldn't stop thinking about no matter how much you tried? One who made you act out of the norm?"

The older man glanced at Karter through the rearview mirror and flashed him a white, toothy grin. "Yep, about thirty years ago, but I remember that night like yesterday," he said, a hint of his South African accent coming through the humor in his tone. Najee had moved to the United States when he was twelve. Yet, during certain conversations, ones that held emotion, his accent was more prominent.

"Why do I feel there's a deeper story here?" Karter said on a laugh.

Najee chuckled as he crept through traffic. "It is. I had just returned from my first tour of duty and stopped in a neighborhood bar. I took the only available bar stool next to a nice-looking curvy woman. I typically gravitated to petite, demure, professional women. This woman was none of that. She filled out a T-shirt that read *I Eat Chumps like You for Dinner*, and was yelling at the TV behind the bar at some Laker player's boneheaded foul. Mind you, I'm a Clippers fan. I might've mentioned something about the Lakers being the weaker team. And she might've *accidentally* thrown a drink in my face."

Karter's brows shot up. "Really?" Najee was a tall bear of a man with intense dark eyes and a lethal quality that would scare the devil out of a sinner. But a woman challenging him? Karter couldn't imagine it. "What'd you do?"

"I married her. Best decision I ever made."

Karter laughed. He'd never heard the story of how Najee and Cassandra met, and before he could ask more questions, his cell phone rang. He picked it up and glanced at the screen.

Mom.

The groan that rippled inside his throat seeped out, and annoyance galloped through him, piercing several nerves along the way. Instead of answering, he silenced the phone. He had talked to her the day before. Actually, she had done most of the talking. The topic of conversation—Angelica Montgomery. The woman his mother wanted him to marry and have six beautiful babies with— her words, not his.

Clearly, they were tag teaming him. Angelica, a lingerie model, social butterfly, and his ex-girlfriend, had been blowing up his phone for the last few days. She, much like his mom, wouldn't be ignored for long. If he didn't respond soon, Angelica would appear at his office or, worse, on his doorstep. At least at work he could have security toss her out.

Karter's phone rang again, and he ignored it. Five minutes later, the insistent ringing sounded again. "This is getting ridiculous," he grumbled. Glancing at the screen, he wasn't surprised to see that it was now Angelica. "Hello."

"Hello to you too, love. You don't have to sound so thrilled to hear from me," she said sarcastically, her whiny, childlike squawk grating on his nerves.

"What do you want, Angelica?"

"First, I would like for you to start returning my calls. Secondly, I want you to be my date for—"

"No and no."

He ran his free hand over his head and let it slide down to the back of his neck, rubbing away the building tension.

"At least let me finish explaining before you say no."

Karter stared out the tinted window as the vehicle crept through traffic, and Angelica yammered on. Too bad it hadn't been Dreamy calling, he thought, then frowned. He needed to stop thinking about her since there was no way he could mix business with pleasure. Sure, he'd wanted her to call regarding the meeting. And yes, he was looking forward to seeing her again, but that was it. It was business, and he'd do well to remember that.

Still, he was sure conversation with her would be more interesting than the person currently on the other end of the line talking his ear off. He didn't know Dreamy, but she didn't come across as some spoiled, self-centered attention junkie who sucked the joy out of every life-form in the room the way Angelica did.

"Are you listening to me?" Angelica's voice rose with every syllable. He hadn't heard everything she said. Yet he'd heard enough.

"As far as I'm concerned, there's nothing to discuss." Karter yawned loudly, not bothering to excuse himself. "Whatever you want, the answer is still no. Now stop calling."

"I need a date for my parents' annual fundraiser," she said as if he hadn't just spoken. "And I want you. Besides, your mother assured me that you were attending and that you didn't have a date. It only makes sense that you and I go together."

Karter's brows drew into a frown. "Why would that make sense? Again, you and I aren't a couple."

"That might be true, but since neither of us are attached, we might as well go together. Besides, we look really cute together. Wear the navy tux. It will be perfect with the couture gown Vicky, as in Victoria Beckham, is designing for me. The photographers will go crazy. We'll probably end up on the covers of all the tabloids."

Karter grunted. The Montgomerys' star-studded fundraisers were legendary. The event always included food catered by some famous chef and entertainment that could rival Coachella. No doubt the media would be in attendance. And, of course, photo ops at the event would be the only thing that mattered to Angelica.

I don't know what I ever saw in her.

He closed his eyes and pinched the bridge of his nose. That wasn't true. Karter knew exactly what had drawn him to her. Gorgeous women had always been his kryptonite. He'd seen her beauty, but soon determined it was only skin deep. Immediately he recognized her selfish ways and prima donna attitude. They had dated for six months. That was five and a half months too long. If only he had walked away sooner.

She'd been the first woman he had gone out with after his failed engagement almost two years ago. Karter hadn't been looking for anything serious or long term. So in that sense Angelica had been perfect, but in every other way that mattered, she wasn't.

He wanted a special woman. Not the *proper* women his mother kept pushing on him at every turn. And by proper, she meant wealthy, self-absorbed, and presentable to the social set. Whereas Karter wanted someone beautiful inside and out. Someone who challenged him to be a better man, and a person who could hold his interest.

"Karter? Are you still there?" Angelica's voice pulled him back into the conversation.

"Yeah, I'm here, but I'm not going to the fundraiser with you, or at all, for that matter. You're resourceful. I'm sure you'll be able to find someone else." *Let some other poor sucker put up with you for the night*, he wanted to say, but kept that suggestion to himself.

"Are you seeing someone else?" Her accusatory voice rose an octave. "That's it, isn't it? That's why you haven't returned my calls."

There was a huge part of him that wanted to say yes. Then maybe she'd back off, but it wouldn't matter. Angelica was going to think whatever she wanted to think, and do whatever the hell she wanted to do.

"Who I see or don't see really isn't any of your business."

"So, there is someone else."

Why did he attract only high-maintenance women who wanted him only for his money or his connections? He was so sick of people using him. It had started in high school, when some of the girls found out his father was Marcus Redford, an actor who had been in more movies than Karter could count. Needless to say, Karter had gotten more attention from the female population than he asked for, and it got harder and harder to determine who liked him for him.

"Bye, Angelica," he said abruptly. He disconnected the call and then blocked her number, something he should've done a long time ago.

When it comes to women, I definitely need to be more discerning going forward.

Chapter Eight

KARTER GLANCED OUT THE WINDOW AS NAJEE EASED UP THE circular drive that would take them to the Bluffs restaurant. On a clear day, the eatery offered hilltop views of the California coastline starting at Newport and extending to Catalina Island.

None of that mattered as tension suddenly clawed through Karter's body. For years, he and his best friends met at the restaurant for dinner every other week. It was a bit of a drive for all of them, but the location gave them the temporary escape from the city that they all craved.

"Najee, you're welcome to join us," Karter said as he unfastened his seat belt. He extended the invitation on occasion, but felt led to do so even more today. Today was the first time that it would be just three of them at the table. There would be a vacant seat—Delton's seat—and he wasn't looking forward to the awkwardness and sadness that it might cause.

Karter inhaled deeply, then released the breath slowly and willed himself to settle down and redirect his thoughts. Yes, Delton would be missed, but he would definitely be remembered.

Najee glanced over his shoulder. "No, but thanks. I need to make a couple of runs while you're here, but I'll be nearby. Just text me when you're ready to leave."

Though it wasn't necessary, Najee hurried out of the vehicle and strolled around the front of the SUV to open the back door.

"Thanks, man. I'll see you in a few," Karter said as he stepped out and buttoned his suit jacket.

A valet pulled the restaurant door open. "Good seeing you again, Mr. Redford."

"Thanks, Fred. You too."

"Good afternoon, Mr. Redford. Your usual from the bar?" The hostess, Sabrina, asked when he strolled in.

"That would be great. Thanks."

Karter moved down the dimly lit hallway that led to the main dining room. He and the guys had a standing reservation and occupied one of the tables in the back of the restaurant near a huge window.

It was weird how his pulse amped up with each step he took. Knowing that Delton wouldn't be joining them ever again was going to take some getting used to. He was the comic relief that their small group counted on to keep things light when they started talking business. Death might be a part of life, but knowing that still didn't make it easy.

"You're late," Avery said, and stood. "We were just about to start without you."

"Yeah, right. I'm not even a minute late and, knowing you, you probably just walked in," Karter said as he grabbed hold of his friend's extended hand, and they pulled each other into a one-armed hug.

Avery, his best friend since grade school, could've easily doubled for Michael Strahan from his large build to the slight gap between his front teeth. Unlike Strahan, though, Avery hadn't played professional football. Instead, he was more of a brainiac than an athlete and had made his millions in the medical field.

Karter gave Lawrence, who was the quieter of his two friends, the same affection, greeting him with a man hug. The two of them had met during their freshman year of college. While Karter had majored in business, Lawrence had been an engineering student and had gone on to own one of the largest engineering firms in LA.

As soon as Karter sat down, their usual waiter greeted him and set a two-finger glass of Johnnie Walker Gold in front of him.

"Thanks, Ford."

"How about a toast?" Lawrence said, his blue eyes twinkling while his lips twitched as if trying to hold back a smile.

Normally, Delton was the one toasting everything from botched haircuts to the birth of one of their kids. Seemed Lawrence planned to pick up where their friend left off.

Karter lifted his glass, and no one spoke for a few seconds. It was clear that they were all feeling some of the same emotions as they sat in silence for a moment.

"Here's to expensive whisky and fine wine. Here's to Delton the asshole, who will be with us in spirit until the end of time," Lawrence said with a crooked grin, and they all laughed.

That was the exact toast Delton would've made if one of them were no longer around. To him, everyone was an asshole.

Lawrence sobered and pushed his blond hair, which was longer than usual, out of his face. "Here's to Delton."

"To Delton," Karter and Avery said in unison, and they clinked glasses.

"How's everyone's week been?" Avery asked, and with that, conversation flowed.

For the next forty-five minutes they ate and discussed all that was going on in their lives. As Avery and Lawrence chatted about their wives and kids, a sudden pang of envy pierced Karter's chest.

Jealousy?

That was new, and why now? They talked about their families all the time, and it usually didn't bother him. But at the moment, he wanted to talk about anything but their intimate relationships.

It didn't make sense. He'd been the best man at Avery's wedding, and a groomsman at Lawrence's. Karter couldn't understand the bitterness flowing through him. He was happy that his friends had found and married the women of their dreams. Heck, he was even the godfather to Avery's three kids. There was nothing to be jealous of.

Karter stared down at his plate. He had almost finished eating, but still had a little miso-marinated sea bass and rice left. Granted, Delton's death had him reevaluating his life, but was he *really* ready for what his friends had—a wife and family? His whole world would change into something he knew nothing about. The days of being responsible only for himself would be over. Could he really handle having a wife and kids depending on him for everything?

He had always imagined settling down someday, but was it time? How would he know? The years had flown by, and there hadn't been a certain age that he had identified to settle down. But like Randy said, he wasn't getting any younger.

"When are you going to start dating again?" Lawrence asked Karter as if reading his mind. "You haven't mentioned a special someone in a long time. If you're ready to put yourself back out there, my wife has a friend who—"

"No," Karter said quickly and glared at his friend. "Clearly, you have forgotten about the woman you set me up with a few years ago. You remember? The one with the high-pitched annoying voice that sounded like a cartoon character. I took her to one of my favorite restaurants in Santa Monica, and she talked loud enough the wake up the dead. Oh, and don't even get me started about her laughing snort. The maître d' offered to pay *me* to get her out of there. I've never been so embarrassed in all of my life."

The guys laughed so hard, the ruckus caught the attention of other diners. Lawrence was the first to regain his composure.

"Okay. I'll admit I'm bad at matchmaking, but McKenna has hooked up several couples who are still together years later. Give her a chance to match you up before you say no."

"I already said no." Karter pushed his plate away and wiped his mouth with the black cloth napkin. "I mean no disrespect, but I'm done hooking up with one superficial woman after another. That's not what I'm looking for right now. Actually, that's not what I'm looking for ever."

"Then what are you looking for?" Avery asked with a bite in his tone as his dark gaze zeroed in on Karter. "Man, you've been finding every excuse not to settle down. Let me tell you. Work can't keep you warm at night."

His friend was another one who'd been telling Karter that he worked too much and needed to find a nice woman to fill some of that time.

"I'm looking for someone . . . different. Someone who isn't cut from the same cloth as the women I tend to gravitate to. Someone who's . . . who's . . . unique," he said again, unable to come up with a better word.

"So basically, you don't know what you're looking for," Avery cracked, and Lawrence chuckled. "You're going to mess around and life is going to pass you by before you really start living it."

"My life is fine just the way it is," Karter countered.

"Is it, though? Is it really fine that you're going on forty, and you haven't been in a serious relationship since Angelica? Assuming we can even consider that disaster a serious relationship."

Karter was surprised that Lawrence had a lot to say today. Normally, he'd just listen to the rest of them talk, only adding to the conversation periodically. It could be that Delton used to dominate most of their discussions. Mr. Funny Man always had something to say or talk about, never failing to keep them laughing about one thing or another.

But right now, Karter wasn't laughing. He picked up the glass of Johnnie Walker, his second one, and took a generous swallow. "You're right. Angelica doesn't count."

Avery pointed his fork at Karter. "I would say your last *real* relationship was Valerie. You haven't been the same since you broke off the engagement."

Karter shook his head. "Oh, hell no. I'm not about to sit here and let you guys dissect my dating life." *As pitiful as it was.*

Valerie had been one of his biggest mistakes. Intelligent and sexy, she had the most gorgeous hazel eyes he had ever stared into. It had been love at first sight for him, and in addition to the movie-star good looks, she was a fierce businesswoman. An up-and-coming interior designer, Valerie had made her first million by the time she was thirty. Her ambition to succeed was something they had in common.

It wasn't until after they were engaged that he started seeing how the perfect picture she had painted of herself started chipping away. It was little things at first. Rudeness to servers at restaurants. Excuses not to travel with him to check out potential investment opportunities. Shortness with his assistant, Gloria. But it was her lack of compassion for those less fortunate that had him questioning his decision to marry her.

Karter still couldn't figure out how he had missed all of the signs. Valerie was all about Valerie. It really became apparent a few weeks out from their wedding date. Arriving home early one evening, he overheard her talking on the phone with her best friend. She was boasting that she'd made a ton of connections, thanks to him and his family and that soon she wouldn't need him. She'd planned to stay married a few years, get what was promised to her through the prenup, and then move on.

Needless to say, they never made it to the altar, and considering how easy it had been to move on, Karter wondered if he ever truly loved her. Or maybe he had loved the idea of being in love. Either way, he vowed then never to let a woman get that close again. Yet, here he was thinking that maybe he did want a chance at something more, and that if there were a next time, he would go into a relationship with his eyes wide open.

Next time, I'll choose better, he thought, and finished off his drink just as an image of Dreamy Daniels popped into his head. He shook the vision from his mind.

I can't mix business with pleasure.

He would keep reminding himself of that until it sunk in. He just hoped he remembered it the next time he saw her.

Chapter Nine

DREAMY SET THE COFFEE CARAFE ON THE REFRESHMENT TABLE
next to the mugs and stepped back. Picking up pastries on the way
to work had been a last-minute decision but a good one. Cheese
Danish, bagels, vanilla cream puffs, and chocolate puff pastries—
her favorite—were on display.

Yep, a continental breakfast was a great idea.

She headed for the door, but slowed and swept her gaze over the
whole conference room, making sure everything was in place. Satisfied with the setup, Dreamy returned to the front of the office
suite.

"Wow, nice outfit," Samantha said, smiling as she strolled in
looking as pulled together as usual.

Dreamy beamed at the compliment. "Thank you. I figured I'd
try to blend in today."

She glanced down at her attire, happy that she had chosen the
short tan suit jacket, borrowed from Jordyn. She would've been up
shit creek if it weren't for her cousin, who owned a decent amount
of professional attire. Unlike Dreamy, whose wardrobe looked

more like a bag of Skittles exploded in her closet, leaving behind every color of the rainbow. Jordyn typically preferred muted colors, like the brown skirt Dreamy borrowed this morning. At least the lacy tan camisole and the straight, shoulder-length bob wig was hers. That, as well as the sky-high brown snakeskin peep-toe heels. The non-squeaky edition.

"Well, you did good." Samantha glanced around, as if looking for someone, before moving in closer. "I want to thank you for getting us this chance to speak to Mr. Redford. I know if it weren't for you, this meeting wouldn't be happening."

Dreamy nodded. After she'd pretended to be sick for two days, Gordon called to apologize for being a total douchebag. He also begged her not to quit and promised that a raise would show up on her next paycheck whether Karter invested in the company or not.

Shock didn't begin to describe her reaction. Dreamy had been more than a little curious to find out what had sparked the sudden change in his attitude. It wasn't until she returned to work and learned that Karter wouldn't take Gordon's calls that she realized what had prompted her boss's desperation.

"I'm glad I could help," she said to Samantha.

"Yeah, me too. Okay, I'll be in the conference room if anyone is looking for me."

Joy bubbled inside of Dreamy as her co-worker strolled away. It felt good knowing she'd made a difference, and everyone recognized it. The day Gordon went off on her, she'd been tempted to do more than call in sick. Quitting had been at the top of her list of things to do. But if she had learned anything from her grandfather's speeches while she was growing up, it was to never quit a job before you had another one.

But as soon as I win the lottery . . .

She tidied her desk while thinking back on her days off that had been extremely productive. Her business plan was coming along, and she was getting more excited about the idea. It might've started as a class assignment worth forty percent of her midterm grade, but Dreamy was taking it seriously for another reason. This was her future that she was working on, and she had every intention of seeing her ideas through.

Jordyn had recently told her about mentors who volunteered weekly at the community center. They offered advice to entrepreneurs and those looking to start businesses. That was exactly what she needed. The opportunity to talk to someone who'd been where she was trying to go. She planned to go armed with her draft business plan, hoping she would get help on the parts she was struggling with, like marketing ideas and budgeting.

Dreamy grabbed her notepad and pen before glancing at her watch, wondering when Karter would arrive. He wasn't late, but she was eager to see him again. He had definitely left an impression on her. So much so that she had dreamed about the guy every night since meeting him. Not sweet, innocent, black-and-white dreams either. Instead, they were hot, colorful and, probably to some, inappropriate fantasies that had her tossing and turning much of the night.

She could still envision him strutting around in her bedroom—naked. And then there was the dream where he was stretched out on the hood of her hooptie—naked. But her favorite had been the one where he'd danced on her kitchen counter—naked. Each vision had been a beautiful sight to behold, but they also left her hot, bothered, and horny as hell.

"Hello, Dreamy."

Dreamy's breath caught, and she whirled around, only to come face-to-face with the object of her nightly . . . and daily fantasies.

Cutie-pie Karter with a K.

Her gaze traveled the length of him. His close-cropped hair was freshly cut, and his full beard—trimmed to perfection—only enhanced his handsome face. His appearance the other day made him appear strong and powerful. Today, though? *Whew*, the man was absolutely scrumptious. Impeccably dressed in a slate-gray suit perfectly tailored to his muscular body, he looked as if he had just left a photo shoot.

Did he dress himself? Or did he have a butler who picked out his clothes every morning? The light gray shirt paired with the burgundy, gray, and black tie accented the expensive suit to perfection.

Had he taken extra care with his appearance to impress her the way she'd done for him? She sighed at the thought. *Probably not.*

"Good morning, Mr. Red . . . I mean, Karter," she finally said. "I'm glad you were able to make it."

She didn't miss the way his appreciative gaze slowly glided down her body, lingering on her legs, and inched back up again. Any other time, she might've taken offense at his blatant interest, but their mutual attraction was hard to ignore. And today, the vibe between them was popping and crackling like Rice Krispies on steroids.

When his attention returned to her eyes, the left corner of his full lips quirked up.

"It's good to—"

"Mr. Redford, welcome back," Gordon said enthusiastically as he blew into the space like a heavy gust of humid air. "Come on back. We're ready for you."

Karter started to walk away with Gordon, but stopped and glanced over his shoulder at Dreamy. "Are you coming?"

Damn. He asked her the same thing last night in her dreams. Or maybe it was *Come for me.* Yeah, that was it. *Come for*—

"Dreamy?"

Her gaze snapped to his. "Uh, yeah. I'm right behind you."

Thirty minutes into the team's presentation, and Dreamy was impressed. This time, Gordon seemed perfectly content letting the team present. Samantha had taken the lead, but the agenda also included short presentations from Fiona and Carl. Dreamy's only complaint—it was hard to focus with Karter sitting on the other side of the conference room table.

Why'd he have to choose the seat directly across from hers? She had already lost sleep in anticipation of this meeting. The last thing she needed was his distracting her any more than he already had.

Carl stood at the front of the room next to the large screen. Each time a question was posed, he'd use a long pointer to draw their attention to the screen. Dreamy didn't know what type of software he was using, but found it fascinating that he was able to create an animated version of the proposed machine. His software engineering background was on full display, showing his range in design and knowledge.

She only wished he'd use terminology that she could under-stand. Was she the only person who didn't know what *admissible heuristic* was, or how algorithms worked? Her lack of knowledge in the field was probably why she kept drifting in and out, daydream-ing about everything but the presentation.

"I like the ideas you've come up with, and it's apparent that you and your team have thought of everything. But have you consid-ered that something like this used in the medical field to assist with image analysis will . . ."

With his thought-provoking questions, clearly Karter wasn't having any trouble following along.

Smiling to herself, Dreamy propped her elbow on the table and rested her chin in her palm as parts of last night's dreams entered her mind.

Dirty dancing on the conference room table, Karter moved as if he were the main feature at the Baloney Pony Strip Club. Stripping away one garment after another, he had already shed his tuxedo jacket and shirt, leaving him in a platinum bow tie. Next went the pants.

Good Lord.

Her eyes almost popped out of her head. A matching G-string. Yes! The little strip of material barely contained his long, thick package and should've been required attire on a daily basis. Dreamy wanted to shed her own clothes on principle alone.

He was fine in clothes, but practically naked? Damn. God had truly done his best work when he molded this beautiful specimen of a man. The corded muscles in his arms and legs were even more pronounced as he seduced her with his dance moves. He swayed and gyrated to "Pony" playing through the speakers, and Ginuwine singing about her riding it without falling off had her rocking in her seat.

Karter might not need her dollar bills, but she stuffed them into his G-string, copping a feel in the process. She teased, squeezed, and licked . . .

"Dreamy? Dreamy!"

Dreamy startled, vaulted out of her seat, and banged her thigh on the edge of the conference room table. "Ouch! Son of a . . ." Her words trailed off as she glanced around the table at the stunned faces. Warmth spread to her cheeks, and the sickening feeling that she might've been acting out her daydream clawed through her body.

Had she said anything? Hell, had she done anything?

Her face heated as every pair of eyes were on her. By the looks of their expression, she'd done or said something, but what?

She replayed the last part of her daydream through her mind and recalled stuffing money into Karter's G-string just before she licked . . .

Oh. My. God. Just strike me down now.

Chapter Ten

KARTER HAD NO IDEA WHAT HAD BEEN GOING THROUGH Dreamy's mind, but he'd pay a million bucks to find out. Whatever it was must have been X-rated because the horror on her beautiful face—priceless.

Though he was concerned with how hard she'd banged into the table, her expression registered more shock than pain. And sad to say, it was taking everything within him not to burst out laughing. He wouldn't . . . at least not right now. He didn't want to embarrass her any more than she'd embarrassed herself. But it wasn't helping that Samantha and Fiona were snickering behind the tablets covering their faces.

It all started when the software froze and Carl had to stop his presentation. While he worked to fix it, Samantha and Fiona shared other elements of the project. Karter had noticed Dreamy staring off into space. Various emotions flitted across her face, and he'd wondered what was going through her mind. He tried to discreetly pull her into the conversation. Only he had no idea she'd practically leap out of her skin at the sound of her name.

"Are you okay?" he mouthed, and Dreamy gave a slight nod.

Rubbing what was sure to become an ugly bruise on her thigh, she eased into her seat. Adjusting her jacket, which barely covered the lacy thingy beneath it, she picked up her pen and twirled it between her fingers. Smoothing out her shocked expression, she settled back as if nothing had happened.

With a confident smile, Dreamy turned her attention to Gordon. "I'm sorry if I interrupted the presentation. You called my name?" she asked.

"Actually, *I* was the one who called your name," Karter admitted.

"And then you started moaning and groaning. Are you feeling all right?" Gordon asked, his bushy brows furrowed and concern showing in his eyes.

His question only made the two other women in the room snicker louder. It was as if they knew what she'd been thinking about.

Carl, oblivious to the entire interaction, was busy typing away on his computer, lost in trying to figure out the software problem.

"Uh, ye . . . yes. I—I feel fine," Dreamy said, placing her hand on the front of her neck. "Sorry if I interrupted the meeting. I just had something in my throat."

Samantha lost it. Laughing so hard, she snorted, then jumped out of her seat. "Excuse me. I'll be right back." She practically ran out of the room.

Fiona, on the other hand, didn't mask her laughter as she wiped tears from her eyes.

"Did I miss something?" Gordon asked quietly, still looking baffled.

"All right, you guys. I think we're all set," Carl said, unaware that he had lost his audience. "I'm not sure what happened with the software. Must've been a glitch."

Karter burst out laughing. If nothing else came out of this meeting, Karter could say he had a good laugh, and it all started with the beauty sitting across from him. He didn't know Dreamy well, but he sensed that there was never a dull moment when she was around.

ONCE THE MEETING WAS OVER, EVERYONE EXCEPT KARTER AND Gordon filed out of the conference room. Dreamy couldn't get back to her desk fast enough. She bent down and quickly unlocked the bottom drawer of her desk, hell-bent on getting out of the office. It would be a shame to leave without saying goodbye and thanking Karter for giving them another chance, but no way was she going to risk embarrassing herself more.

Yep, I definitely need to get out of here, she thought as she pulled her handbag from the drawer.

"Okay, you were right."

Dreamy's heart slammed against her chest, and she jerked her head up, surprised to see Karter standing in front of the desk. How the heck had he snuck up on her?

She pasted on her most confident smile, hoping he hadn't noticed that she was trying to run away. "Right about what?" she asked, standing to her full height and looping the purse strap onto her shoulder.

He folded his thick arms across his broad chest, and her gaze couldn't help but follow the move. Her mind took her back to what she had imagined him looking like under all of the expensive clothing.

Damn it. Stop, stop, stop, she chastised herself and then gave him her full attention.

"That is an impressive and funny team that's heading up the project."

The comment pulled Dreamy back to reality, and a grin spread across her mouth. "I told you! I'm glad you had a chance to meet them. Thanks for giving them an opportunity to present the project to you."

"I was already impressed by the idea, but now that I've met them and have a better understanding of how the mechanism will work, I'm even more interested. Carl is masterful at explaining complex algorithms."

Dreamy smiled harder and clapped her hands, but stopped short of doing one of her silly happy dances. "That's great to hear!"

Karter lifted his hands. "Don't get too excited yet. I still have to do some research and confer with my own team."

Dreamy nodded. "Okay, but you haven't said no."

Karter eyed her in that way that he'd done more than once. What was going through his mind? This time she wasn't as nervous under his perusal but, God, she hoped he didn't say anything about what happened in the conference room. Nor did she want to discuss whatever weird vibe was going on between them.

"You look . . . nice," he said, but Dreamy didn't miss the hesitation in his voice.

"Thanks. I wanted to dress a little more professional so that I could fit in with the group."

Why'd I say that out loud?

Jordyn was always fussing at her about saying everything that came to mind. One day Dreamy would listen. Clearly, it wasn't today.

"So . . . this isn't how you usually dress?"

Karter's question caught her off guard. "Um . . . honestly, no. I like bright colors and quirky combinations, but I didn't make a good first impression on you and—"

"What makes you think you didn't make a good first impression?"

"Because I looked like a tray of cotton candy at the carnival that day. Every color and every flavor."

Karter laughed. "I wouldn't go that far, but you were fairly colorful. I realized within minutes, though, that your style of dress mirrors your personality."

He had noticed her. That made Dreamy's attraction to him mount.

"I dress to match my mood," she said.

"And what was your mood the other day? Unlimited sunshine with a side of rainbows?" he asked with a straight face, but she didn't miss the humor in his eyes.

"Ah, I see you have a sense of humor, and for the record, that was exactly the mood I was going for."

Smiling, Karter nodded. "Yeah, I figured as much."

Silence fell between them as they stared at each other. It wasn't an uncomfortable silence. On the contrary. Instead, it was a moment that said, *I like you even if we come from two different worlds.*

"And for the record," he continued, "I think you should dress any way you desire and be who you are. As long as your company's dress code allows, if you want to look like flowers or cotton candy, you should. You're different, Dreamy. Unique, even. No harm in letting it show."

Now Dreamy was the one nodding. Her admiration of him leaped to a thousand on the *I think you're frickin' hot and I might love you* scale. She didn't even know this man, and he totally got her. *He sees me.*

"Are you heading out?" he asked.

"Yes, I need to grab some lunch before my break is over."

"I'll walk out with you."

"Okay, and thanks again for agreeing to meet with everyone," Dreamy said as she started around her desk. "You don't—"

Her foot caught on a loose thread of the thick carpet and her body propelled forward.

"Aaah!" She fell headfirst in what felt like slow motion, and her arms twirled like propellers as she tried catching her balance. But the floor rushed up to meet her. She closed her eyes, braced herself for the impact that never came.

"Whoa." Karter's arm tightened around her, and he pulled her close to his body. "Are you okay?"

All of Dreamy's senses went on high alert as she became more than aware of everything about him. Like how his large hand was splayed on her stomach. The way the front of his body hugged the back of hers. And damn if his intoxicating scent, something woodsy with a hint of citrus, wasn't making her weak in the knees.

Of course she wasn't all right! His closeness was making her crazy.

"You don't have to fall at my feet to get my attention," Karter said on a chuckle. "You had me the other day with your lubricated shoes."

Dreamy released a choked laugh, appreciating his humor as she tried freeing her foot from the heel-eating carpet, but she was still caught. "I'm never going to live that day down, am I?"

"Nope."

Turning slightly, she accidentally placed her hand on Karter's pecs.

Big mistake.

His rock-hard muscles contracted under her touch, and a sweet thrill galloped through her body. What the actual hell?

Dreamy lifted her eyes to his, and his smoldering gaze wrapped around her like a warm blanket on the coldest night of the year. For one second, her heart beat a little faster and everything around her ceased to exist as she got lost in the intensity of his stare.

It wasn't until the desk phone rang that she snapped out of the trance.

Oh, for goodness' sake.

What the hell was wrong with her, acting like some lovesick teen? This was ridiculous. He was just a man. A big, strong, virile man who had her thinking crazy thoughts and acting like an imbecile.

Realizing her hands were still on his chest, Dreamy quickly lifted them. "Uh, sorry."

The phone was still ringing, but technically she was on break and knew the voicemail would pick up at any moment.

Karter cleared his throat. "Let me see if I can help you get loose." With a hand on her waist, he kept her from tipping over. Dreamy stood frozen, loving the feel of his large hand on her body as he bent down to unhook the carpet thread. "There, you're free. It looks like something's wrong with your heel, though."

"Frickin' hell," Dreamy mumbled under her breath and eased away from him. She placed a hand on the desk for support and lifted her foot to examine the expensive footwear. For what she paid for the shoes, they should've come with five replacement heels.

Relief spread through her veins once she realized there wasn't anything wrong with the heel, except for a millimeter of a gap between the heel and the heel cap. Nothing that a little walking wouldn't fix.

Karter held out his hand. "Give it to me. I can fix it."

Dreamy looked at him suspiciously, but slipped off the shoe and handed it over.

He examined it, then scared her to death when he whacked the heel of the shoe against the desk three or four times.

Her mouth dropped open. "I cannot believe you just did that." That was something she would've done had he not been standing there. But to witness this multimillionaire doing something so inelegant pushed his likability even further up the scale.

Karter flashed her a sexy grin and handed over the shoe. "It should be fine now."

Dreamy nodded, thinking the day couldn't get much stranger.

"Thanks for your help. We'd better . . . I'd better . . . Uh, let's just go."

He extended his arm toward the door for her to precede him, and then fell in step as they headed to the elevators. They didn't have to wait long. As soon as the doors opened, they stepped on, and Dreamy pushed the button for the ground floor.

"Are you free for dinner?" Karter asked.

Shock pulsed through Dreamy's veins as she gaped at him. *Dinner? With him?*

Yes. No. Her mind volleyed responses back and forth as she mentally listed the pros and cons of going or not going. Thankfully, the elevator stopped two floors down, allowing her time to come up with an answer.

She took a step back, giving the five people who had just crowded into the small space more room. Accidentally bumping into Karter, Dreamy practically leaped out of her skin when his hand touched her hip for a second.

"Relax," he said close to her ear, as if his nearness hadn't awakened parts of her body that hadn't been touched by a man in a long time. First upstairs. Now here.

This is not good.

Sharing the same space with the guy had her senses reeling. His touch. His scent. His strong hand grazing her hip. Everything about the man messed with her sanity. And he wanted her to go to dinner with him? *Hell no.* She could barely handle sitting across from him in the conference room without drooling.

Nope. Can't do it.

There was no way they could have dinner together. Besides, she was done with men. Why couldn't she remember that? This shouldn't even be a discussion in her head. Her answer should've immediately been an easy *no*.

As the elevator glided down to the ground level, Dreamy debated how to turn him down gently. She didn't want to say anything that would keep him from investing in their company, but she also didn't want to lead him on. None of this should even be happening. He was champagne and caviar, while she was Kool-Aid and frickin' Kit Kats.

And what the heck did he want with her? Surely, he had his choice of supermodels or heiresses.

Once the elevator doors opened, everyone filed out, and Dreamy practically ran out of the metal box.

"Hey," Karter said when he caught up. With a loose grip on her elbow, he guided her off to the side to a quiet corner. "What's wrong?"

Seriously? This man clearly had no clue of the type of torture he was inflicting on her peace of mind. She sucked in a long breath and released it slowly.

"Nothing's wrong," she finally said with a calm that was opposite of the disarray battling inside of her. She wanted to say more, but the words wouldn't form.

Karter studied her for a moment as if waiting for a yea or nay regarding dinner. When she still didn't respond, he said, "Listen, if—"

"I hope you don't change your mind about investing in the company with what I have to say," Dreamy blurted. "I can't go out with you. You seem like a nice enough guy, but I'm taking a break from dating."

After a long hesitation, he said, "I see."

He rubbed the back of his neck, something Dreamy had seen him do a couple of times since arriving, and then returned his attention to her.

"Just so you know, whatever I decide about this company, my verdict won't have anything to do with you, Dreamy. It'll be a business decision either way," Karter said, still massaging the back of his neck. "I asked you out because I'd like to get to know you better. Sure, we just met and the invitation was a little forward, but you're easy to talk to, and I'm attracted to you. I'm pretty sure you feel it too."

She sure as hell did. It was too intense to ignore. Yet she had no intention of telling him that. "It was nice seeing you again, Karter. Thanks for the invitation, but my answer is still the same."

He nodded, disappointment marring his handsome face. *No* probably wasn't a word he heard often.

"I understand." Digging into the front pocket of his pants, he pulled out a thin, platinum compact and removed a business card. From the inside pocket of his jacket, he produced a pen and scribbled something on the back of the card. He held it up between two fingers and moved closer.

Dreamy's heart thumped a little faster, and a burst of need roared through her body, tempting her to change that no to a yes. What was it about him that made her want to throw caution to the wind and accept anything he offered?

She gave herself a mental slap. It was everything about him. Any woman would fall all over herself, and many probably had, to be with him. Here she was, turning down dinner. No doubt she'd be calling herself all kinds of fool on the way home.

Tempted to tell him that she changed her mind, that she'd go anywhere with him, she pursed her lips to keep from speaking. Her heart pounded even harder when Karter lowered his head, bringing his mouth inches from hers. Surely he wasn't about to kiss her. Was he?

As if sensing her nervousness, he put a little space between them. "If you change your mind about dinner or need anything, like a new pair of shoes, call me." His lips twitched before a fullblown smile appeared. "This card has all of my contact information. Don't hesitate to use it."

He handed Dreamy the card, then walked off. She watched as his confident stride took him to the main entrance. Once there, he slowed, glanced over his shoulder, and nodded before disappearing out the door.

Dreamy released the breath that had lodged in her throat, and glanced at the card with gold script lettering.

Karter A. Redford
Venture Capitalist

It included not only his email address, but also his work and cell phone numbers.

A smile spread across her lips and then turned into a laugh as she thought about his crack regarding new shoes. Dreamy liked his sense of humor, but considering how her dogs were barking, she should call and take him up on his offer.

Maybe another day.

She shimmied her way to the door that led to the parking garage. It wasn't every day that a multimillionaire asked her out to dinner. But as she walked out of the building, another thought came to mind and her smile slipped.

I just turned down dinner with a multimillionaire.

What an idiot.

Chapter Eleven

LATER THAT EVENING, KARTER DID SOMETHING HE RARELY DID— he sat on his back deck and stared out over the city. His Hollywood Hills home had a decent-size backyard, swimming pool, and killer views that he didn't take advantage of nearly enough. Which was one of many areas in his life that he planned on changing. He was quickly learning that no matter how many hours he put into working, there were still more hours needed.

A vibrant array of orange, red, and violet streaks painted the sky in the distance as the sun slowly descended into the horizon. The sight was incredible. On occasion, he stayed at his penthouse in the city, but most evenings, he could be found at home. He considered this property home because of Nana, his live-in housekeeper. More like a mother to him growing up than his socialite mother had ever been, Nana made the seven-thousand-square-foot space feel warm and cozy with music, decor, and even fresh baked goods whose scents wafted through the air. He had actually purchased the home with her in mind.

Karter picked up the beer that he'd been nursing for the last twenty minutes and took a generous gulp. What a day. He'd had back-to-back meetings, but there was only one that still took up space in his mind. Actually, it wasn't the meeting that weighed heavy on him. It was Dreamy.

I can't believe she said no.

He vowed to keep her out of his thoughts, to move on and forget that he'd made the colossal mistake of asking her to dinner. Yet here he was, still unable to believe she had turned him down. Karter didn't know what bothered him more. Almost breaking his strict rule about not mixing business with pleasure, or that she'd said no.

Okay, maybe that bothered him the most. His ego took a hit for a minute, but her rejection only made him more curious about the woman. It wasn't every day that someone said *no* to him. As a matter of fact, it was probably a first. That alone made her somewhat of a unicorn in his book.

I like bright colors and quirky combinations, but I didn't make a good first impression on you.

Her words from earlier ran through his head. It touched him that she'd wanted to make a good impression on him, but he wasn't sure if it was because of business and the possibility of his investment or something more. He was leaning toward the something more. The sexual tension pulsing between them had been hard to miss. Which was probably why he had been so impulsive—another first. Normally, he planned everything to the point of overthinking. Yet he'd asked her out without a second or third thought.

Melvin's barking nearby caught Karter's attention. He really should've brought the puppy outside with him, but just for a few minutes, he'd wanted to be alone with his thoughts.

The patio door slid open, and the dog darted out of the house like the place was on fire and flames were licking at his tail. He ran around the yard as if he hadn't been outdoors in years instead of an hour or two ago.

"I thought you were volunteering at the community center to-night," Morgan said when she strolled out of the house wearing an oversize T-shirt and baggy gray sweatpants. She curled up on a nearby lounger.

"I switched days with Melody. Now I volunteer on Wednesday evenings."

When he first started volunteering there, it was once a month, but wanting to make a bigger difference, he'd changed it to weekly. Meeting entrepreneurs who were trying to take their businesses to the next level, or those still trying to decide on a business, brought back memories of when he first started his company. The one difference, though, was that he'd had a safety net. Most of the people he met at the center invested their life savings and any other funds they could get their hands on. The hardest part was not offering loans to everyone he spoke to. On occasion, when he fell in love with one of their business ideas, he'd refer them to one of his associates.

Melvin caught Karter's attention as he ran around the perimeter of the yard, enclosed with clear acrylic fence panels, as if racing on a track. Just when Karter thought the dog would jump into the kidney-shaped pool, he changed directions and didn't stop running.

"Man, he has a lot of energy."

"Yeah, he does, which was one reason I thought he'd be great for you. You need a little excitement in your life."

"I have enough excitement," he countered, knowing he was lying.

"Yeah, tell it to someone who doesn't know you." Leaning forward, Morgan pulled a rubber band from around her wrist and gathered her long microbraids. "Face it, Karter. You need Melvin."

"What's wrong with him? He's running back and forth like something's chasing him."

"What do you mean? He's a dog. He's supposed to run around and enjoy the outdoors. He's always like that. You'd know that if you spent time with him. How are you going to have a dog and never take him for a walk or run?"

Karter turned and gaped at her. "Are you serious right now? You do realize that you gave me a dog without asking if I wanted one, right? Morgan, I don't have time for a pet, especially one who has more energy than the Energizer Bunny."

"But you need a pet, big brother. More specifically, you need Melvin. If you saw yourself the way I've been seeing you for the last few weeks, you'd know that I'm right. You haven't been yourself."

Karter gave a shrug. "I don't know what you're talking about. I feel fine. I'm the same as usual."

"No, you're not. Ever since Delton died, it's like you've lost a little of bit of yourself. Don't get me wrong," she said quickly when he started to speak, "I'm sure it's not easy losing a friend, someone who was as close as a brother. Still, there's something else going on, and actually, it started even before Delton passed away.

"When was the last time you worked out?" she asked. "You used to be up at the butt crack of dawn running at least four mornings a week. Or you'd be downstairs pumping iron. Now, most mornings, you slog into the kitchen looking as if you've been dragged behind a car on a bumpy road. You barely make time for a cup of coffee before leaving for work, when you used to sit down for one of Nana's famous breakfasts."

He could admit to missing Nana's breakfast enchiladas and her Oreo pancakes.

"Maybe I just don't feel like running the way I used to," he defended weakly. Because of his sleepless nights, he didn't have the energy to run his usual five miles most mornings. He just hadn't realized anyone noticed.

"You're also not making decisions as fast as usual."

He gave a startled laugh. "What? That's ridiculous. I spend the whole damn day making decisions. By the time I get home, I don't even want to think."

"I get that you might be tired by the time you get here, but in the past, when I came to you for advice, you always had some. Actually, you'd give me advice whether I wanted it or not. But when I moved in here, you didn't give me a hard time. When I admitted to still not knowing what I wanted to do with myself, you didn't say anything. There were no pedagogical speeches about this and that."

That was true. Mainly, he hadn't bothered with a speech because she'd heard it all before. But if he were honest with himself, he didn't have the energy to lecture her on adulting. Besides, how could he instruct anyone on what they should do with their lives when he was at a crossroads himself?

"Normally, you would've read me the riot act, telling me that I'm getting too old to be goofing off."

Karter smiled at that. How many times had he given her that speech? Each time, she sat there and listened without whining, usually only saying that she was going to make him proud of her. He had no doubt of that.

He looked at her, and his heart squeezed at the love he had for his little sister. With microbraids piled on top of her head, and her freshly scrubbed baby face, she appeared much younger than her twenty-nine years. At some point, though, she was going to have to grow up and become a productive part of society. Like Randy, she was more of a creative, but unlike Randy, she didn't have that same drive to accomplish anything specific. Because she was still trying to *find* herself.

"And Nana said you haven't been eating," Morgan continued. "I bet if I asked Gloria, she'd probably say that she's noticed some changes in you, too, and not for the better. I said all of that to say that's why I gave you Melvin."

As if he'd heard her, the dog trotted over with a tennis ball in his mouth. Who knew where he'd found it? Karter hadn't seen it before.

Melvin looked at him with his head cocked, then moved past Karter and dropped the ball in front of Morgan. She tossed it into the yard, and the dog went after it and brought it back to her. That happened several times before Melvin stopped and settled down near Morgan's feet.

"So, are you ready to tell me what's going on with you? And why are you back so early? I can't remember the last time you came home before nine."

"Would you believe me if I said that I came home to get some peace and quiet?"

"Nope, because you knew I'd be here and that was never going to happen."

Karter shook his head and smiled. He actually enjoyed having Morgan back in the States. She always made life interesting, but he wasn't sure what to tell her. It was rare for him to leave the office before nine, always seeming to have one more thing to do. Even Najee had been surprised when Karter told him that he was heading home.

"Is it woman trouble?" Morgan asked, sounding excited. "If it is, I'm a good listener. Unless of course it's about Angelica. I heard that you two were dating while I was out of the country. I always thought you were a better judge of character."

Karter grunted and took another swig of his beer. "Apparently not. Between her and Valerie, I'm clearly off my game in the woman department."

"I found you the perfect dog. Maybe I should find you the perfect woman. I'm pretty sure I know what your type is."

Karter laughed. "No, thank you. The day I start letting my little sister pick my dates is the day I stop dating."

"Oh, please. You can do a lot worse than who I would choose

for you. Oh, wait. You have!" She burst out laughing as if Tiffany Haddish had just told the funniest joke.

Karter ignored her, but wondered what she'd think of Dreamy. They were around the same age and would probably have more in common with each other than Karter had with her. Too bad he'd never know.

"Aha! So it is a woman."

Karter's gaze snapped to Morgan, who was looking at him with an amused expression on her face.

She sat upright and wrapped the blanket around her tighter. "Who is she?"

"I never said it was a woman."

"You never said it wasn't either. Who is she? And please don't tell me it's someone Mom picked for you. You have to be smarter than that to go out with another Angelica."

"Trust me. I've learned my lesson on that front. Now, this conversation is over."

"Ah, come on, big brother. Let me help you with your woman problems. What better way to figure out this woman than to ask another one?"

"You're not a woman. You're my little sister. This conversation is already weird."

"Like we've never had weird conversations before. Start talking. Dr. Morgan Redford, relationship guru, is at your service."

Karter shook his head. "I'm going to need something a lot stronger than beer to spill my guts to you."

As if on cue, Nana stepped out onto the patio wearing one of her usual floral dresses and a red apron. In her hands was a tray with a pitcher of margaritas and a large mug with steam billowing above it.

Melvin leaped up from where he was lying, and darted across the patio to meet her. He pranced around her legs, his tail wagging a mile a minute as he vibrated with excitement.

"Calm down, little man. I have something for you inside," she said to the dog.

Still brimming with eagerness, Melvin alternated between sitting and jumping up and down. Nana moved around him and over to where Karter and Morgan were sitting.

"I thought you two could use a drink before dinner."

She handed Karter one of the tall margarita glasses and poured some of the mixed cocktail into it.

"Nana, you're the best."

"I know," she said with a wink. "See what you be missing when you don't come home at a decent hour?"

"And this is one of many reasons why I always come home before dinner." Morgan grinned as she accepted the huge mug. "No one makes hot chocolate like you, Nana."

Their housekeeper kissed the top of Morgan's head. "Make sure you both are washed up and ready for dinner in forty minutes."

"Yes, ma'am," Karter and Morgan said in unison before Nana and Melvin strolled back into the house.

Karter sipped his margarita and sighed. "Her name is Dreamy Daniels," he said. "She's Gordon's assistant."

"Is Dreamy her real name? Sounds like a stripper. Not that I'd know anything about that."

The fact that she added the last part had Karter wondering if she'd ever given stripping a try. Then again, he didn't want to know. There wasn't much his sister hadn't tried, at least once, including starting a professional cuddling business. Someone who'd venture into that line of work might not mind trying her hand at stripping. He grimaced at the thought.

"I asked Dreamy out to dinner, and she turned me down."

When Morgan didn't respond, he glanced at her. Her mug was inches from her mouth and the whites of her eyes had doubled as she gawked at him.

"Does she know who you are?" she asked indignantly, and Karter smiled. Growing up, his sister was his biggest fan, thinking he could do no wrong.

"Yeah, she knows, but it's probably good she turned me down."

"Why? You're a great guy, and some women might even call you handsome." Her serious expression had him outright laughing now.

"Gee, thanks." He took another sip of his drink. "I *never* mix business with pleasure. That's a rule that I never break, and I'm not going to start now. So I'm glad she said no. I shouldn't have asked in the first place—it was unprofessional. Besides, she says she's taking a break from men."

"Hmm, that's code for *I had a bad breakup and men are the lowest form of human life.*"

Karter gave a slow nod. He'd figured as much, but he had a feeling it was more than that.

"It's for the best," he said. "We come from two very different worlds. I doubt we'd have anything in common, especially since she's your age. Way too young for me."

"That's bullshit, and you know it." Morgan set her mug on the table between them. "Apparently, there was something about her that enticed you enough to ask her out. You knew where she worked, her age, and probably other things about her. Yet you asked her out anyway. So don't sit there and act like you guys didn't have a connection. Besides, since when did you let a little *no* stop you from going after what you want?"

"Since I remembered I don't mix business with pleasure."

She waved him off. "That's a stupid rule in this case. One, if your company does business with Mathison, you'll probably hand them off to one of your managers. Two, your business is with Mathison, not her."

Considering he hadn't been able to think of much else after leaving Dreamy, he hadn't thought about any of the points that his sister made. What if he made an exception to the rule this one time? Would it come back to bite him in the ass?

"I believe in fate and stars aligning. What if you two are meant to be?"

Karter shook his head. "You read too many of those romance novels. I've seen her twice, in a business setting. I don't think fate had anything to do with it."

"You say that now, but I wouldn't be surprised if you saw her again."

Karter doubted that would happen. It was safe to assume that they didn't travel in the same circles. And he had no reason to go back to the tech company. Any more interaction with them could be done remotely or at his office.

"You like her, and that's saying a lot," Morgan continued.

Karter already knew if he told her to drop it, he'd be wasting his time.

"I know you goofed with Valerie and Angelica, but maybe the third time's the charm. I think you should call her and ask her again. Once reality sets in, and she realizes she turned down one of Los Angeles's most eligible bachelors, she's going to be kicking herself.

"Oh, wait. Maybe she's playing hard to get. Either way, call her."

Karter nodded as he thought about what his sister was saying. There was nothing he liked more than a worthy challenge, and he suspected the eccentric secretary would be worth the effort.

"Oh, and if you decide to invest in the tech company *and* get the girl, man, you're going to owe me big-time!"

"Yeah, we'll see."

Chapter Twelve

DREAMY TORE INTO THE COMMUNITY CENTER'S PARKING LOT, then slowed as she searched for a place to park. Construction equipment took up more than a few spaces in a lot that wasn't overly large. With less than an hour before the center closed, she hoped a few business owners were still on site and someone could help her with the business plan. If only her economics night class hadn't gone overtime. Otherwise, she would've been there thirty minutes ago.

After parking a distance from the main door, Dreamy pulled the visor down and touched up her lipstick and made sure her wig was on straight. Today she had opted for the reddish curly Afro and channeled her inner Pam Grier as Foxy Brown. The extra confidence boost it gave her had come in handy with the economics test that she'd had earlier. She always felt like a total badass, able to handle anything, whenever she wore an Afro wig. Add that to the fitted black tank top that made her breasts look like D cups instead of Bs, and the skinny black jeans paired with tall ankle boots, and she could be Foxy Brown reincarnated.

Dreamy grabbed her backpack from the passenger seat, as well as her short leather jacket, which she probably wouldn't need. The strong Santa Ana winds brought with them eighty-degree temperatures, but it was probably freezing inside the building.

Keeping a hand on the back of her wig, she darted across the lot, squinting against the dust and debris that was being kicked up by the winds. Dodging between parked cars, she finally made it to the front door.

"Good evening. It looks like it's getting windier out there," the woman at the registration desk said. "Is it still hot out?"

"Yes, unfortunately," Dreamy said, picking her Afro with her fingers, hoping the strands weren't sticking out all over the place. "It definitely doesn't feel like October. I am so ready for some seventy-degree weather."

"I hear you." The receptionist slid over a clipboard with a sign-in sheet attached to it. "You're not here for a class, are you? If so, the only one still going on is the house-buying seminar. The others ended about thirty minutes ago."

"No, actually, I'm hoping that some of the volunteer business owners are still here."

The woman glanced at a sheet of paper on her desk. "Yes, there should be one or two mentors still here. Check the small meeting rooms down the hall, and they are the last two doors on the right."

"Great, thank you. And the center is open until nine, correct?"

"That's correct. So you have about an hour."

Dreamy thanked her and hustled down the hall. Disappointed that no one was in the first room, she checked the second one, praying that she wasn't too late.

Arriving in the doorway of the last room, relief flooded through her body when she spotted a guy at one of the tables, looking down at his cell phone.

"Excuse me. Are you still offering help with business—"

The man glanced up, and Dreamy's breath caught when familiar light brown eyes met hers.

"Karter? What are you doing here?" she asked from the doorway.

His eyebrows dipped into a V, and he blinked several times as if he couldn't believe what he was seeing. Seconds ticked by as his gaze crawled down her body and slowly made its way back up to her face. Still, he said nothing.

Dreamy stepped into the small room, and that seemed to snap him out of whatever trance he had fallen into.

The confusion on his face morphed into recognition, and a slow smile spread across his lips. His tempting, juicy lips. Lips that she had imagined tasting and feeling everywhere on her body.

She hadn't seen Karter since the meeting six days ago, and today was the first day that her mind hadn't conjured him up.

Just when I thought he was out of my system, he appears.

Gordon had received word the day before that KR Ventures, Karter's firm, would be funding the new project. Her boss had been more excited than Dreamy had ever seen him and had acted totally out of character when he'd had lunch delivered to the project team. If that hadn't been shocking enough, he'd personally thanked Dreamy for all that she did to make the deal happen.

"Well, this is a pleasant surprise," Karter finally said, standing when she reached the table.

"Yes, it is. You're the last person I expected to see. How is it that a busy man like yourself has time to do volunteer work?" she asked.

He gestured for her to take the chair next to him, and she did.

Dreamy hadn't been to the community center in a few years, and even then, she had never seen Karter there. His was a face that she would've definitely remembered.

"I've been volunteering here for over a year," he said, reclaiming his seat. "Normally, I'm here most Friday evenings, but I agreed to switch days with someone else for the next couple of months. Now I'm glad I did."

"Yeah, it's good seeing you again," Dreamy said honestly.

After turning down his invitation to dinner, she hadn't expected to ever see or hear from him again. And like she had anticipated, she questioned whether or not it had been wise to say no that day when deep down she'd wanted to say yes.

But after the breakup with her ex, Dreamy didn't trust her judgment when it came to men. Especially prestigious, wealthy men. How had she not known sooner what Brandon really thought of her?

Not cultured.

Not sophisticated.

Not educated enough.

In the end, turning down Karter's invite had been a good decision. It was time to focus on herself and her goals. Not get involved with yet another man who was out of her league. Still, Dreamy wondered what it would've been like to spend time with Karter.

"By the way, I heard that your firm will be working with Mathison Technology," she said, placing her backpack in the chair on the other side of her.

"That's true." Karter explained that once the contracts were signed, one of his managers would take over from there.

Dreamy hadn't been sure of next steps with the somewhat partnership, but listening to Karter tell her how he and his company operated reminded her of the television show *Shark Tank*. Not only would KR Ventures fund the project, but they also would offer assistance with budgeting, marketing, and a host of other business-related items.

"Well, it sounds like you might be the perfect person to help me then," Dreamy said, and pulled a couple of folders out of her bag. She slid her draft business proposal over to him.

"What's all of this?" he asked before picking up the document.

While he skimmed the information and sifted through the pages, she soaked him in. He always smelled so good, but unlike the other times Dreamy had seen Karter, he was dressed down. The white Polo shirt he wore showed off muscular biceps and thick forearms. On his left wrist was an expensive-looking watch, but it was more casual than the platinum one he'd had on the other day. She had noticed his dark-wash jeans before she sat down, but she hadn't taken the time to really check him out in them.

Karter glanced up from the document. "You pulled all of this together by yourself?"

"Yes, with some help from the resources that my professor handed out in class." She explained how the business plan was not only one of the assignments, but also what she intended to use to start her nonprofit. "As you can see, there are some blank sections."

"So you're still in school," he said, glancing up at her.

"Yes. I went back a couple of years ago to finish my degree in public administration. This is my last year."

Karter set the papers down and listened intently as she told him about how she'd had to drop out of school years ago. Hearing herself discuss the last few years reminded her of how far she'd come.

"When Gramps was dealing with one health issue after another, I had to go to practically every doctor's appointment with him. There were so many tests, medications, and forms to fill out. There was no way he could've done all of that on his own. And with technology constantly advancing, so much of the paperwork has to be done online. People like my grandfather, who aren't computer literate and aren't interested in learning how to use one, are out of luck.

"When appointments have to be made online, I have to do it. When he has to find the telephone number for a company or a store, he doesn't know how to use a search engine. Or he doesn't want to."

Karter nodded. "Meaning that there are probably plenty of other elderly people in the same boat."

"Exactly. I thought about creating an organization that employed people who would go into homes and help the elderly with things like that. Or go to a doctor's appointment with them to be a second set of ears. I can't tell you how many times Gramps had an appointment, and then after it, couldn't tell me what the doctor said. Anyway, that was my original idea—an advocacy program for seniors. Which is something I still wouldn't mind doing down the road. But this past year, I've been longing to start a nonprofit."

"What type?" Karter asked, appearing genuinely interested.

"My ideas changed every few months. Everything from a temporary help company that matches support staff to executives, to dog grooming. You name it, I've considered it."

"You sound like my sister. She's been going through the same process of trying to decide her next steps, career-wise, for the last few years. She wants to be a business owner but hasn't nailed down what type of business."

"Exactly! I figured, if I'm going through that, others are too. And what happens once we do figure out what we want to do? Where do we start? That's when I thought, Hey, it would be great if there was some type of incubator for women entrepreneurs, or those looking to become self-employed. A place where women can go for help with business plans, start-up money, and even just a support system."

Karter nodded. "I can tell you're very passionate about this idea. Are there other organizations like your proposed one that already exist, that offer the same services?"

"Yes. Sort of." Dreamy leaned closer and reached for the business plan, then turned to the page with the Competition section. "There are organizations, but not many. They offer a place for women to get resources, and maybe even network. That's it. I want to offer more."

For the next few minutes, they went through her business plan. Karter asked questions, and she answered them to the best of her ability. During the conversation, she realized there were so many variables she still had to decide upon. Like location, type of staff needed, and funding, to name a few. She was also impressed with the way Karter really seemed to listen and ask thought-provoking questions. Even when she told him that she didn't have money yet to start the nonprofit, he offered a few ideas. Considering his experience and success, she felt lucky to be able to discuss her business idea with him.

"One of my concerns is I don't actually have experience running a business," she said. "At least not one that's not direct selling or a network marketing business." She'd tried a few of those, and though she made a few dollars, she didn't have a passion for them and soon got bored. "I'm great at managing an office, but once I start the nonprofit, I'm not sure people or potential clients will take me seriously."

"I think that's a valid concern, but all business owners have to start somewhere. I've already witnessed that you're amazing with people. Though some can learn that ability on the job, you're a natural. So even if you can't explain to someone about profit and loss or ROI, which is return on investment, you can always hire experts to handle those areas. They'll be a part of your team, and at the same time, you decide what role you want to play in the organization. Then do like other nonprofits often do—recruit from the corporate world or find individuals with nonprofit experience."

Dreamy had already been excited about her idea, but as she listened to Karter share his knowledge and give her helpful advice, her excitement grew.

Who would've thought their paths would cross outside of Mathison Technology? She sure hadn't.

Chapter Thirteen

KARTER HAD NEVER BEEN SO DISTRACTED IN ALL OF HIS LIFE. TO say he'd been shocked when Dreamy first showed up would be an understatement. At first, he feared he might've been hallucinating as she stood in the doorway, but each time he blinked, the vision didn't change.

He wasn't sure how long he sat there, taking in the sexy black outfit wrapped around her curvy figure, and those sexy-as-hell leopard-print ankle boots fit her style perfectly. But it was the red Afro that made the whole outfit. He would've thought it was her real hair had it not been for the fact that she had a different hairstyle every time he saw her.

Her style tonight was a far cry from the colorful attire she wore the first time they met, and he could honestly say she was making one hell of an impression on him. It wasn't even just the way she looked, but the positive energy oozing from the woman was palpable. He could feel it to the depths of his soul, and suddenly, the exhaustion from earlier in the day had drifted away.

"Question for you," Karter said. "Is your name really Dreamy Daniels?"

She stared down at the folder in front of her and fingered the edge of it without responding. Her gaze eventually met his, but she looked away again and went back to fiddling with the folder. One would've thought he had asked her a hard question.

"It's fine if it's too personal to discuss. I was just wondering . . ."

Before Karter could change his mind, he took a chance and reached for her hand. A prickle of awareness shot up his arm when he touched her, and an overwhelming desire to bring her fingers to his lips was almost his undoing.

The attraction that seemed to grow each time he'd been in her presence was stronger than ever. How was it possible to fall for this woman without even really knowing her? Karter wasn't a man who believed in love at first sight, and he was sure that the strong feeling he was experiencing wasn't love, but something was happening between them.

Clearly, she had put some type of spell on him.

They had only a few more minutes before the center closed, and they probably should be spending that time on her assignment. Yet that was the last thing he wanted to do. He had learned more about her in the last few minutes than he expected to ever learn, and what he knew for sure? He definitely wanted to know her better.

"Dreamy," he said, prompting her to talk to him.

"My birth name is Dremetrious Daniels," she said, and sighed as if she was carrying the weight of the world on her shoulders. "I had it changed to Dreamy years ago."

Interesting. That wasn't what he expected.

"Dremetrious is very unique. Does it have a meaning?"

"It means my flighty mother isn't very good at picking names. Or she has a sick sense of humor." All humor left her voice, and sadness shimmered in her eyes. "Can you imagine all the teasing I had to endure as a kid? An unusual name that no one could pronounce or spell. A mother who didn't give a damn about me and left me on my grandparents' doorstep. Having to wear used clothes because my grandparents couldn't afford to buy new ones. I always felt like I had a target on my back. Fair game for every bully within a mile radius. It was awful."

Karter squeezed her hand and rubbed the pad of his thumb over her soft skin. Though Dreamy's left eyebrow lifted as she glanced at their joined hands, if she thought the gesture inappropriate, she didn't say so. He could tell the conversation was upsetting her, but he had no clue what to say or do to make her feel better.

As for how she grew up, there was definitely some serious backstory in all that she said. Now wasn't the time or place to dig into what that was.

Instead of questioning her about her childhood and her mother, he said, "I can't even imagine how tough all of that had to be on you. It just proves what I already know. You're a fighter. Tough. Resilient. You didn't let those experiences hold you back, and I'm sure you're stronger for it. Which means you're going to be a kick-ass boss lady."

Dreamy didn't comment immediately, only stared at him. Some of the sadness left her eyes, but the joy and fun-loving persona she usually displayed had mellowed.

"Thank you," she said just above a whisper. "As you can probably tell, my mother is a sore subject for me."

"Is she still in your life?"

"Depends on what you mean by still in my life. She's still alive. She calls and tries to play 'mom' by offering her opinion about my life even though I don't want anything to do with her. I don't see her often. She lives in New York, and I'm glad we're on different ends of the country."

Karter nodded, wondering what type of woman would abandon such an amazing person like Dreamy. She was so full of life and compassion, he couldn't imagine anyone not wanting to be in her presence.

"I chose to change my name to Dreamy right after I graduated from high school. It suits me, and it's a good conversation piece. Granted, the name might seem silly to some, but it fits me."

"I agree. It fits you perfectly."

Her gaze lowered to their joined hands again. He hoped his touch provided her a little comfort. Interesting how they'd met just over a week ago, yet holding her hand felt natural. Like something he did all the time. He wanted nothing more than to keep touching her, but they needed to get back to work. Giving her hand another little squeeze, he reluctantly released her.

"You mentioned not having money to invest in the nonprofit. How do you plan to fund this venture? Because that's going to be needed for the business plan."

"I'm going to win the lottery."

Karter leaned in closer, sure that he hadn't heard her correctly. "Excuse me?"

She pulled something from the side pocket of her small purse and held up a lottery ticket. "I said I'm going to win the lottery. These six numbers are going to help me become a multimillionaire."

There was no smile on her tempting mouth, no humor in her voice, and the sincerity in her eyes had him wondering if something was mentally wrong with her.

"You're serious?" His words came out as part question and part statement. He'd heard a lot of nonsense over the years, especially where money was involved, but this was the craziest yet.

"I'm dead serious. These are winning numbers. I've been playing them for years, and it's only a matter of time before they hit.

And when that happens, I'm using half of my winnings to start up the nonprofit."

Dreamy opened the folder, pulled out a slip of lined paper, and turned it so that Karter could see what was written. An incomplete budget was scribbled on it. "I'm thinking the rest of the money will come from fundraising and maybe angel investors. As you can see, the financial section still needs work."

Karter sat back in his seat and tapped his pen against the yellow legal pad in front of him. He never wanted to say or do anything that could discourage a person from going after their dreams. Though he respected her desire to help others, the fact that she was counting on a lottery win to fund her business was just really . . . something.

"You do realize that the chances of winning a lottery are like one in three hundred million, right?"

She gave a nonchalant shrug. "Well, I guess I'll be that one in three hundred million. It's going to happen. I feel it," she said, patting the spot over her heart. The move pulled his attention to her perky breasts, the one area of her body he was trying to keep from staring at. The low-cut tank top, and what had to be a hell of a push-up bra, had them standing proud and demanding attention.

Karter fidgeted in his seat and promptly took his gaze back up to her lovely face. He'd had his share of beautiful women, but he couldn't remember the last time one affected him as much as Dreamy did. Hell, even her name was a turn-on.

He shook the thoughts free and ran his hand over his mouth as he glanced at her file folders. If nothing else, she was organized. They were all marked with typed labels that covered several sections of a business plan. Everything from budget to market analysis was represented on the files.

Most people these days did everything on a laptop, but it appeared that this was another area in which Dreamy was unique.

"Well, if that's your winning ticket, you should probably go ahead and sign the back of it."

"I will."

"Now when do you have to have this project done for class?" Karter asked, struggling to take the lottery part of her business idea seriously.

"I have a few weeks. Why?"

"Because if you're serious about creating a usable business plan, it's going to take us more time to get it done. But, Dreamy, I think it's unrealistic to—"

"Karter, I know you think I'm nuts and mentally living in la-la land, but I plan to win the lottery to fund the nonprofit. I honestly believe that I'll win, but in the meantime, I will come up with plausible ways to raise money to get the business off the ground."

He nodded, glad to know that she wasn't totally crazy.

"Excuse me, you two," one of the workers said from the doorway. "We're closing in fifteen minutes."

Karter glanced at his watch again, surprised to see that it was almost nine o'clock. "Okay, we'll be heading out shortly."

Dreamy started putting some of the folders back into her bag. "That time went too fast. I can revise the overview based on your suggestions, but I was hoping you could help me work on the budget and capital structure. Since the business hasn't kicked off yet, I'm not sure what those numbers will be."

"That doesn't mean you can't forecast an initial budget. That's where research comes in. We'll brainstorm initial set-up costs, what some of your fixed costs will be, and estimate variable costs. That's going to be a little tricky with this type of business, but I'm sure we can get it done."

Karter stood and slung his laptop bag onto his shoulder. "Have you thought about where you want to operate the nonprofit? Do you want to rent a space or buy a space? Do you know how many people you'll need on staff to start with? You mentioned wanting to be in a position to give small loans or grants to those who might need financial help starting off. Those are only a few line items that will need to go into your budget."

Dreamy huffed out a breath. "I guess I have a lot to think about," she said as they left the room. Except for one or two voices sounding in the distance, the building was quiet.

Karter wished they had more time tonight. The more he learned about Dreamy and what she was trying to do, the more he wanted to know.

"I like your business idea," he said as they strolled side by side. "KR Ventures has a community development arm specifically for offering grants to nonprofits. Once you're ready to start up, I'd encourage you to submit a grant proposal. I'd also be interested in investing in the nonprofit."

He really did like her ideas. Actually, he liked both ideas, the business incubator and the elderly advocacy. Both were projects he could get behind. And investing, instead of straight charity, could yield him a return on his investment.

Dreamy shook her head. "I don't want your money. I already told you that I was going to fund it with my lottery winnings."

Karter slowed, again trying to determine whether she was serious. She was an intelligent woman with good business sense, but when she said stuff like that, he didn't know how to take it. Yet she said it with such conviction that if he didn't know better, he'd believe her.

"Dreamy, I think it's fine to hope for something so strongly, like winning the lottery. Just don't bank your business plan on it. For the best chance of success, I'd suggest thinking of other ways to raise the money for the nonprofit. If you don't want my money . . . Wait. Why don't you want my money?"

He could respect her decision to fund the venture without his financial investment, but he didn't know why she was so adamant about it—lottery winnings aside.

"I appreciate you even considering investing in me and my business. It would just be too weird to take money from you."

He slowed when they reached the foyer, hating that their time together was up. "Why would it be weird? It wouldn't be like I was giving it to you for no reason. It would be business. Or what if it was a loan? Would that make a difference?"

Her perfectly arched eyebrows dipped into a frown as she twisted her bottom lip between her teeth. She glanced at the floor, pondering his question.

"I guess . . . I'm not really sure," she finally said when she returned her attention to him. "I have a rule. I never borrow or even ask people I know for money. I watched my grandparents struggle financially, but the one thing they refused to do was borrow money, except to buy the house that I live in with my grandfather and cousin. It wasn't that they were too proud; they instilled in us that being a borrower, especially from friends or family, could ruin relationships."

"So you're saying we're friends," Karter said, unable to hide his smile when her eyebrows shot up.

"Um . . . I don't recall saying that. I barely know you."

"Well, we can change that. Have dinner with me."

Over the weekend, he had talked himself out of pursuing Dreamy. Actually, he went back and forth on the idea, weighing the pros and cons. But after tonight, spending time with her made him want more. Morgan might've been right. It could be fate or maybe the stars really were aligning or some shit. Either way, he wanted Dreamy.

"I can't," she blurted.

"Why not?"

"It would be like accepting money from you. It would be too weird. Besides, I don't mix business with pleasure."

He thought the same thing—at first. "If you're not taking money from me, then we won't be doing business together. It would be just pleasure."

A grin spread across her red lips before she fell into a full belly laugh. "You're funnier than I imagined, but you and me?" She pointed her finger back and forth between them. "Not a good idea, especially since you're working with Mathison Technology. I don't trust myself not to say or do something that would jeopardize your working relationship with Gordon. It would be too risky."

Says the woman who plans to fund a nonprofit from her lottery winnings . . . a lottery she hasn't won and has no chance of winning, Karter mused, but kept the thought to himself.

"Okay, I won't push, but know this. Taking risks is part of who I am, and I always go after what I want. So, expect me to ask you out again. Eventually, I think you'll say yes."

"Why me?" she asked when they reached the exit, genuinely curious. "I'm sure lots of other women are dying to go out with you."

"Why not you? You're fun, smart, business minded, compassionate, and that's just based on the little that I know. I'm interested in getting to know you better."

Dreamy released a shaky sigh. "I don't know, Karter."

"What's keeping you from saying yes?"

He glanced out the door window and saw Najee pulling up to the building.

"It's because you're . . . you." She waved her hand up and down in front of him. Then moved a little closer, giving him a good whiff of her sweet-smelling perfume that had tortured him in the small space. "I'm a secretary who's still in school and trying to get my career together. Oh, and I currently live with my grandfather and cousin. I just don't think it would work out right now."

She pushed open the door before he had a chance to respond, and they stepped outside. A big gust of wind pushed her into him, and he caught her around the waist.

"Damn, it's getting worse out here," Dreamy said, righting herself.

Karter glanced over to Najee, who started to climb out of the vehicle, but Karter stopped him. "Give me a minute. I want to see Dreamy to her car." He handed his laptop back to the driver.

Najee gave a slight nod. "No problem."

"You didn't have to do that," Dreamy said as they started across the parking lot.

"It's not a problem. It's late, and you shouldn't be out here alone."

"Oh please, this is nothing new for me. Though I appreciate . . ." A gust of wind had them both swaying, and then Dreamy's Afro wig flew off.

"What the . . ." Karter's words trailed off, and his mouth gaped open while he stood in shock.

"Argh!" she shrieked, her hands going to her head, where she had two long French braids braided down the back.

He watched the red, hairy blob float through the air and between a few parked cars.

"Don't just stand there! Get. That. Wig!" Dreamy shouted and took off in a sprint. She tore across the parking lot like she was being chased by Olympic track star Allyson Felix. And to run like that in heels was beyond impressive.

"Stop that wig!" she hollered.

Before he knew what he was doing, Karter took off running, ducking between cars as the wig flew through the air. When it dropped to the ground, he made a mad dash toward it, only to have the mop of hair take off again when he was within a foot of it. He picked up speed, chasing the curls around the parking lot until he was able to get close enough to snatch it out of the air.

Fisting it, he bent over with his hands on his knees as he struggled to catch his breath.

"Oh my goodness. Thank you. Thank you," Dreamy panted, her posture similar to his when she stopped next to him.

"I think this belongs to you." Karter held up the wig and started laughing uncontrollably. "I can honestly say that I have never in my life had to chase down a *wig*."

Dreamy grinned and accepted the hair from him. "Hang around me long enough, and you'll have a lot of firsts."

Humor laced her voice, but Karter had no doubt that hanging out with her would definitely be an adventure.

She put the curly Afro back on her head as if it were the most natural thing to do, then tucked her long braids underneath it. Karter always assumed women wore wigs when they had hair issues, or as part of a costume. But Dreamy had a head full of hair. It didn't seem appropriate to question her about it. Maybe one day.

"So, how about Saturday night then?" she asked once she was all pulled together and her confidence was fully intact. She didn't seem at all fazed by the wig-chasing incident.

It took him a second to realize what she was talking about. Surprised she had changed her mind about dinner, Karter said, "Saturday would be perfect." Even if he already had plans, he'd reschedule them for a chance to spend time with Dreamy. "Seven o'clock work for you?"

"Yep." She gave him her address, and he typed it into his cell phone.

"Now, how about we try to get to your car before something else blows away?"

"Sounds good, but first"—Dreamy gently gripped his forearm and leaned into him—"I just want to say thank you." She placed a lingering kiss on his cheek that sent a surge of excitement pulsing through him. It was a simple, chaste kiss that felt more intimate than it probably should.

"Now we can go," she said, and hooked her arm through his as they strolled across the lot as if nothing happened.

Once she was safely inside her car, Karter headed to his SUV, where Najee held the back door open. He had no doubt that the conversation during the ride home was going to be a lively one.

Najee nodded as Karter climbed into the back seat. It wasn't until his driver was in the driver's seat that he spoke.

"I guess you probably don't need to go on your evening run, huh?" Najee said with a straight face, then crumpled into a fit of laughter.

Karter couldn't help but join in. For the next few minutes, they laughed, recapped what happened, and laughed all over again. He dabbed the corners of his eyes with the back of his hand.

"I can't remember the last time I laughed or ran that hard. I will never in my life forget this moment."

"Well, if you do"—Najee held up his cell phone—"I'll be glad to share the video with you."

"You didn't . . ."

"*Oh*, but I did. I figured I might need this footage as a bargaining chip the next time I ask for a raise."

"Is it crazy that I can't wait to see her again?"

"As hard as you work, you need a little crazy in your life. And if what I just witnessed is any indication, you're in for a wild ride."

Karter hoped so. He needed to shake up his life a little, and Dreamy was just what he needed to make that happen. He just hoped he didn't get himself killed in the process.

"I promise I won't share the video. I only recorded it because I couldn't resist. Check it out."

He handed Karter the phone and they laughed all over again.

What a way to end a long day.

He couldn't wait for Saturday to roll around.

Chapter Fourteen

DREAMY STOOD AT THE FOOT OF HER BED AND STARED DOWN AT the dressiest outfits she owned. Nothing seemed to be good enough. Nothing she had was good enough to wear for a night out with Karter.

What was I thinking saying yes?

He was Karter frickin' Redford, son of a famous movie star. What was she doing? She couldn't go out to dinner with a multimillionaire looking any old kind of way. Dreamy had thought of little else over the last few days. One minute she was excited about the prospect of seeing Karter again. The next, she felt as if she would throw up from nervousness. She tried telling herself that even though they came from two different worlds, it wouldn't matter. They could still have a good time hanging out.

But honestly, those were just lies. Karter was accustomed to having dinner with women who knew the proper fork to use with their salads. Women who knew how to carry themselves around the rich and famous. And women who knew what to wear to the most exclusive five-star restaurant in Los Angeles.

"Who am I kidding? I'm not that person," Dreamy mumbled under her breath. "I can't do this."

"You can, and you will," Jordyn said, appearing in the doorway. "I already know what you're thinking."

Her hands were on her hips, and the scowl, or what Dreamy referred to as her stink face, was on full display. It was the face Jordyn made when they were kids and she was practicing how to cross-examine a witness. Even back then her cousin knew she wanted to be a lawyer.

"Don't start doubting and comparing Karter with your ex-boyfriend. I should personally hunt Brandon down and beat his ass for screwing up. Your self-esteem was securely in place before his trifling butt came onto the scene. You've been doubting yourself ever since his stupid speech about you not being good enough."

"Maybe, but right now I'm thinking I should've stuck with my no-dating vow. It's too soon for me to get back out there. I was supposed to be spending this time on improving myself."

"There's nothing wrong with you."

Dreamy walked over to the full-length mirror, taking in her frumpy pink robe and big, fluffy house slippers. "I'm supposed to be focusing on my goals and starting my career. I have no business going—"

"You're going." Her cousin strolled farther into the room and stood next to her in front of the mirror. "You told me that Karter *sees* you. That he *gets* you. If that's the case, give him a chance to show you what his intentions are. Give him a chance to treat you like the queen you are."

"What if he ends up humiliating me the way Brandon did?"

"Then you'll kick his ass."

Dreamy stamped her feet, which were soundless on the carpet. "I'm being serious, Jordyn!"

"So am I. Brandon caught you off guard and made you start

questioning who you are. You know who you are. You've always known your worth and didn't start having self-esteem issues until he got into your head."

Dreamy listened as her cousin went on and on with her pep talk. The truth was, there were times, especially while she was growing up, that Dreamy had suffered from lack of self-esteem. It had started when her mother, Tarrah, left her in Los Angeles to chase after a man.

For years, Dreamy assumed that she was unlovable and unworthy to have a mother who cared enough to stick around. Why else would her mother have left? Her grandmother, God rest her soul, had been great about instilling positive affirmations into Dreamy. Still, deep down, she questioned her worth.

As she got older, her self-confidence improved and she thrived in everything she set out to do . . . until Brandon came along. He reminded her of all that she didn't have, but desired.

"Truth is, Brandon was the problem," Jordyn was saying when Dreamy tuned back in. "He was the one with the insecurities, and needed to make himself look like the big man because he wasn't good enough for you. Get him out of your head."

"I thought I had, but—"

"But nothing. It's time for you to move on, and I think you're ready for someone like Karter. I mean, come on. Any man who will chase down a flying red wig for you in a three-piece suit is definitely a keeper. I'm just sayin'."

Dreamy couldn't stop the smile from pushing up the corners of her lips. "Well, he wasn't wearing a suit at the time, but you're right. I don't know if he's a keeper yet, but there's definitely more to him than I expected. I guess I'm just . . . I'm second-guessing myself, because I don't trust my judgment when it comes to choosing the right guy."

"Well, technically, Karter chose you. And before you change

your mind about giving him a chance, let me check him out. When he gets here, if I'm getting any loser vibes from him, I'll let you know. I'll also ask him a few questions to make sure he's on the up-and-up."

"Okay, but if you ask him if those are his real teeth or if he grew up with an invisible friend, I'm putting a stop to the questioning."

Jordyn waved her hand dismissively. "Fine. I guess this means the date is still on, which is good. I heard that restaurant serves a Hawaiian rib eye that melts in your mouth."

Suddenly feeling a little more encouraged about the evening with Karter, Dreamy returned to the clothes on the bed. All she had to do was decide which one to wear. Most of her attire was made up of separates that she'd mix and match. Tonight required a special ensemble.

Jordyn stared down at the three outfits. "These are your only choices? You should've gone shopping."

"Yeah, but money is a little tight this month. It was either buy a new outfit or get my hair done."

She had chosen the latter. Tonight, she had opted to wear her natural hair. The stylist had shampooed, conditioned, and then straightened her hair before adding big curls that brushed her shoulders. She loved getting her hair done but was too lazy for the upkeep. Most days, it was just easier to grab a wig, but not tonight. Tonight, she didn't want to risk having hair flying around the parking lot—again.

Dreamy grunted under her breath. She couldn't believe her wig had flown off. That had been a first. Seemed she'd had a number of firsts with Karter already, and they had only known each other for almost two weeks. Hopefully, their night would be fun, relaxing, but uneventful.

"Okay, I need to make some decisions," she said, studying the mustard-colored dress, a color that looked great against her dark skin. "I want to wear something cute, but this might be a little too cutesy." It had a jewel neckline and a flirty ruffle hem. It fit the cute criteria, but seemed a little too juvenile for a night out with Karter.

After returning the dress to the closet, Dreamy went back to the bed and picked up the red outfit. She'd worn it only a couple of times, but not recently. It hugged every one of her curves and didn't leave much to the imagination.

"This might be too much. I want to look cute and sexy, but this might be a little too ho-ish."

Jordyn plopped down on the bed. "I would say so. I remember the little strip of material you're referring to as a dress had barely covered your butt cheeks. You should consider giving that to Goodwill. Or you can always use it as a headband."

Dreamy laughed, but her cousin wasn't wrong. The jersey material probably would be better suited for a head wrap.

"When I win the lottery tonight, I'm going to hire a fashion stylist so that I don't—"

"Oh, good Lord. Please don't start with that lottery crap, and whatever you do, don't mention it tonight over dinner. Karter probably already thinks you're a nutcase. No need to prove him right."

For the next few minutes, they went through Dreamy's closet trying to pull a presentable outfit together. One thing was for sure, she had wigs and shoes for every occasion, but her wardrobe was deficient.

"I need something sophisticated without being stuffy. Something tasteful while also alluring." Dreamy snapped her fingers and whirled around to face her cousin. "Oh my, God. I know the perfect outfit! Can I wear your new black dress?"

Jordyn reared back with her eyebrows dipped into a severe V. "You mean the one I paid an arm and a kidney for? The one I'm planning to wear to the reception at the governor's mansion next weekend? The one that still has the price tag on it because I haven't worn it yet?"

Dreamy nodded. "Yeah, that one." Jordyn stood and started shaking her head before Dreamy could barely finish the sentence. "Come on, cuz. Don't you want me to look nice and make a good impression? Please, can I borrow it?"

Jordyn huffed out a breath and headed to the door. "Fine, you can borrow it, but if anything happens to my dress, I will kill you!"

Dreamy grinned. "Fair enough."

Thirty minutes later she stood in front of the full-length mirror, admiring how perfectly the ultra-chic black dress molded to her figure and stopped just above her knees. Though she loved colorful attire, black always made her feel sophisticated, dressy, and, at times, like a badass.

The outfit was tight enough to show off her curves, but not too tight. Rarely did she go without a bra, but she couldn't wear one with this dress because of the seductive cutouts across the chest and near the sides of her breasts. The shoulders were bare, though the outfit had long sleeves.

But it was the double-wide sash, accentuating her thin waist, that totally made the dress. Though it was tied, the end of it hung down the front of her right leg, practically touching the floor. Each time she took a step, her leg peeked out from behind the material, and that alone made the short dress extremely sexy.

Her gaze dropped to the tall, red heels that had a bejeweled strap around the ankles and accentuated her legs, and Dreamy smiled. Her shoe game was definitely on point, and no doubt she would turn heads tonight.

"I have to admit, the dress looks *hot* on you. Not as good as it'll look on me, but you're wearing the hell out of it," Jordyn said, smiling as she made a slow circle around Dreamy and inspected the garment. "Girrrl, Karter is going to swallow his tongue when he sees you in this outfit."

Dreamy smoothed a hand down her hips. "Well, I don't want that to happen, but I'd be totally fine with his eyes bugging out."

They shared a laugh, and Dreamy grabbed her small red clutch off the dresser. The doorbell rang just as she walked out of her bedroom.

"Okay, so he gets points for being on time *and* coming to the door," Jordyn said as she leaned against a nearby wall.

That comment had been a dig at Brandon, who'd failed to do the gentlemanly thing when he picked her up on their first date. Her grandfather had stomped out to the car, cursed him out for disturbing the peace with his horn, and then proceeded to ream him out for proving that chivalry was indeed dead.

Whatever else her grandfather had said to him that night had worked. From that point on, Brandon was quick to ring the doorbell whenever he picked her up, and he'd been a gentleman . . . for the most part.

Dreamy blew out a cleansing breath, then opened the door. But her next breath stalled in her throat at the sight of the man she hadn't been able to stop thinking about.

"Wow," they said in unison.

"You look great."

"You clean up well."

They spoke at the same time and then laughed like two nervous teenagers. Dreamy wasn't sure how long she stood there perusing everything about the man before Jordyn cleared her throat.

"Oh, shoot. I'm sorry. Come in." Dreamy ushered him into the house and closed the door.

Karter held out a beautiful bouquet of daffodils arranged in a large crystal vase. "These are for you," he said, handing them over.

Dreamy accepted the gorgeous bouquet but noticed a bead of sweat popping out at his hairline. "Are you okay?"

He gave a slight shrug. "Yeah, I'm great . . . and you're stunning."

She glanced down at the flowers, and her heart thumped a little faster. He remembered. During one of their conversations, she'd mentioned that daffodils were her favorite flower. She reached up on tiptoe and placed a light kiss on his cheek.

"Thank you. These are beautiful. I'm surprised you remembered."

"I remember everything you've told me."

They stared into each other's eyes, and it was as if everything around them disappeared.

"Oh, for Christ's sake. You two are nauseating," Jordyn said.

So caught up in Karter, Dreamy had completely forgotten about her cousin.

"I'm sorry. Karter, this is my cousin, Jordyn. The future badass defense attorney that I told you about."

Karter gave a slight smile and extended his hand. "It's a pleasure to meet you."

"Same here," Jordyn said, shaking his hand. "I've heard a lot of good things about you. I like all that you're doing with the community center. I hear that your firm is working with mine on a project that will build up around that area."

"Really? You're with Hawlsey and Meyer?"

"I am. I—"

"Wait. You didn't tell me you knew Karter like that," Dreamy said, setting the vase of flowers in the center of the coffee table.

"I don't know him. I just know some of the projects he's invested in around the state."

"I see you've done your homework."

She gave a nonchalant shrug. "All part of the job. Now don't you have a reservation to get to?"

"Yes, actually we should get going." Karter opened the door.
"Not so fast."

Dreamy groaned when she heard her grandfather's voice. She
thought he'd already gone to bed. Almost afraid to turn around for
fear of what he'd have on, she snuck a glance over her shoulder and
almost choked.

She whirled around so fast, she lost her balance and slammed
into Karter. He wrapped his strong arms around her, and she
wanted to stay in the comfort of them, but she was too shocked to
stand still.

"Gramps, where are you going all dressed up?"

The three-piece suit looked good except for the way the buttons
on the vest seemed like they were about to pop off. The outfit had
to be at least ten years old, and Dreamy had seen him wear it only
a few times, one being at her grandmother's funeral.

"You're not the only one who has a date," he said. "I have
one too."

"Like hell you do," Jordyn piped up. "You can't drive."

His gray bushy brows lifted. "Who said I was driving?" He
turned to Karter. "Who are you?"

"Karter Redford, sir. You must be Dreamy's grandfather."

"Lester Daniels, but my friends call me Slick Lester. You can
call me Slick."

Karter laughed, and Dreamy rolled her eyes as the two men
shook hands.

"You running off already?" her grandfather asked. Funny how
he looked ten years younger and seemed a bit taller while talking
to Karter. "I was just getting ready to go outside for a smoke.
Wanna join me?"

He held up a joint, and Dreamy gasped.

"Gramps!" Dreamy and Jordyn yelled at once.

"What? It's medicinal." Their grandfather frowned and shook

his head. "See what I have to go through. So, whadaya say?" he asked Karter, who was doing a horrible job trying to hold back a laugh.

Karter placed his hand at the small of Dreamy's back, sending an electric current racing through her body and nipping at every nerve on the way. She'd been close to him before, but tonight, her body was even more aware of him than usual. Maybe it was the fact that they were both dressed up. Or maybe it had to do with their being in close quarters with her family staring on. Then again, maybe it had everything to do with their undeniable attraction to each other.

Either way, she loved being near him and enjoyed having his hand on her body even more.

"Unfortunately, I'll have to take a rain check. Dreamy and I have reservations. We should probably get going."

"Well, shame you're going to pass up on some good ganja. But I guess that means there's more for me," Gramps said, and turned to leave the room. "Have fun, Dreamboat."

"Don't worry, I'll handle this," Jordyn said to Dreamy, and followed their grandfather down the hall. "Gramps, you're not smoking that crap, and you're not leaving this house. I mean it."

Dreamy sighed. "Welcome to my world. You've now met my slick-talking cousin, who will hunt you down and curse you out if you get out of line. As well as my weed-smoking grandfather, who might show up at the restaurant in an orange Studebaker, insisting that it'll turn into a pumpkin at midnight."

Karter chuckled and guided her out the door. "Your family sounds like people I'd like to get to know better. But first, let's go and get something to eat."

Her family was special in so many ways, and Dreamy's heart swelled knowing that Karter didn't have a problem with that.

He just might be a keeper.

Chapter Fifteen

"MR. REDFORD, THANK YOU AND YOUR GUEST FOR JOINING US this evening. I'm Candace and this is Gregory"—the woman pointed to a man beside her—"and we'll be your servers this evening."

Two servers? Dreamy thought.

She was even more surprised when Karter requested wine and a sommelier showed up at the table within seconds. Dreamy listened as a guy, who was no older than she was, showed off his knowledge of wines, spouting off everything from grape types to vineyards.

Dreamy knew red wines from white ones for the obvious reason, but she didn't know Cabernet Sauvignon from Boone's Farm Strawberry Hill. If she were Karter, she'd shut their wine connoisseur up and insist he just tell them what tasted good. But her handsome date for the evening listened with rapt attention before finally deciding on something from 2007.

Dreamy glanced around the dimly lit restaurant. Decorative cylinder light fixtures, like nothing she had ever seen before, hung from the ceiling. The effect was like eating under the night sky with stars sparkling in the distance. They added to the ambiance of the candlelit tables, soft jazz playing in the background, and the aura of love and romance filled the space.

Some of the tables were a little closer together than she would've thought for such an exclusive restaurant. Yet there was just enough space between them that she really couldn't hear anyone's conversation.

When the sommelier returned with a bottle of wine, Dreamy watched as Karter went through the process of swirling the dark red liquid before sniffing it. She never understood the ritual, but she wasn't a big drinker anyway, so it didn't really matter. Then again, once she won the lottery, would she dine at places like this and need to know all these things? Maybe.

Tonight was another Powerball drawing, and she felt deep down inside that she and her grandfather were going to win. If not tonight, it would happen soon. Dreamy just knew it, though she couldn't explain the powerful gut feeling that it was going to happen any day now.

After Karter nodded his approval, the server filled Dreamy's glass first, then Karter's before leaving the bottle on the table.

Dreamy brought the wineglass to her lips and took a small sip, then another. She had to admit that it was delicious.

"Great choice," she said. "Do people know you by name everywhere you go?"

The restaurant staff had been addressing him by Mr. Redford from the moment they arrived. Then again, it could be that they just made it a point to know their guests based on the reservation.

"Not everywhere. Some restaurants and certain events, yes. A few stores, maybe. But outside of that, I'm just an ordinary guy."

Dreamy snorted, but quickly covered her mouth. "Sorry, but I doubt if you've ever been ordinary." She smiled as a tinge of red painted his light brown cheeks.

Was he blushing?

From what she'd seen of Karter, he was the most confident and composed person she'd ever met. But now that she thought about it, he'd seemed a little on edge since picking her up from home.

"Are you feeling okay?" she asked, genuinely concerned. "You seem a bit anxious. Is something wrong?"

He gave an uneasy chuckle and rubbed a hand over his mouth and beard. "I don't know what's going on, but you make me nervous." He reached for his wine, but the back of his hand bumped his water glass, sending it crashing to the table. "Damn."

He leaped out of his chair, which immediately slammed into a server behind him who was holding two large, steaming plates.

Dreamy gasped when the dishes and the food went flying. Some landed on the floor, most landing on the next table as well as the customers.

Oh no. Dreamy slid out of her seat, prepared to help with the cleanup, but bumped into another waiter. He barely held on to the silver pitcher in his hands but couldn't stop water from splashing all over himself.

"Oh my God! I'm so sorry."

She turned her horrified gaze to Karter, who was hurrying to help clean up the shattered dishes on the floor. While bent down, he insisted that he'd pay for all of the damage and the customers' meals, as well as their dry cleaning.

Dreamy glanced around that section of the restaurant, and heat rushed to her face. All eyes were on them as a flurry of activity took place around them. It seemed that every employee had jumped in to clean up her and Karter's mess.

"Oh, Mr. Redford, you don't have to do that," the manager said. "Our staff will take care of everything quickly. Please take your seats and your server will be right with you."

Aware of the attention they were getting, Dreamy kept her head lowered and hurried to sit down. Just once she'd like to spend time with Karter without there being an embarrassing moment. Clearly, that wouldn't be tonight.

When they were finally seated, she and Karter made eye contact. They both struggled to not laugh at the situation, but the harder he tried to keep a straight face, the funnier the situation got.

Dreamy couldn't hold it in. She placed the cloth napkin over her mouth to stifle her laughter. It didn't help that they were practically sitting in the middle of the restaurant for all to see. Within minutes, they had turned a fine-dining experience into a circus. She felt awful about the people sitting near them, the ones who had mashed potatoes and gravy sliding down their arms, but it was too funny not to laugh.

Karter's low chuckle met her ears as he leaned forward. "You were right when you said I'd have lots of firsts with you," he whispered. "Because that was *definitely* a first."

Dreamy grinned and picked up her glass of wine. She lifted it in a mock toast. "Stick with me, and there will never be a dull moment."

Karter held up his wineglass to her and nodded. She didn't miss the amusement in his gorgeous eyes when he said, "Bring it. I'm looking forward to spending more time with you."

A short while later, their server returned with their meals.

"For you, madam, we have the Hawaiian rib eye with herbed rice and broccoli," she said, placing a steaming hot plate in front of Dreamy. "And for you, sir, we have the prime New York strip, mashed potatoes, and crispy brussels sprouts." She set the plate down and glanced back and forth between them. "Is there anything else I can get either of you at this time?"

Dreamy shook her head. "The meal looks fabulous." And the smell of the food had her mouth watering.

Considering the fanciness of the restaurant, she expected the plating to be super fancy with tiny portions. That wasn't the case. The steak took up much of the space on the large plate, and after skipping lunch, she planned to eat every single morsel.

"Let's play a game," Dreamy said as they ate.

Karter narrowed his eyes at her. "What type of game?"

"Perfect questions."

"Never heard of it. Is that like twenty questions?"

Dreamy gave a nonchalant shrug. "Yeah, but I changed the name just in case I want to ask more questions."

Amusement flickered in his eyes. "Okay, I'll play, but only if I get to ask questions too."

"Well, that's not included in the rules of *my* game, but I guess I'll allow it."

Karter laughed. "Gee thanks. I guess that means you'll want to go first."

"Correct. First question. Do you have a favorite spot or favorite place to visit in Los Angeles?"

At first Dreamy had planned to ask him why he wasn't married, but thought better of it. She would imagine a man like him got approached often by thirsty women trying to nab themselves a rich, good-looking guy. She didn't want him to think that she was one of them by asking the question.

"Hmm . . . that's a tough one. The first place that comes to mind is a spot at the Santa Monica Pier where my dad once took me fishing."

"Only once?"

Karter's expression turned serious. "Yeah. He worked and traveled so much when my siblings and I were younger that we didn't see him much. It was a big deal when he took me, mainly because it was just him and me. He'd said that we didn't spend enough time together, and he wanted to change that. But as his popularity grew and he picked up more roles, family time dwindled. We took vacations and sometimes visited some of the movie sets where he was filming on location, but we only went fishing that one time."

Dreamy nodded and appreciated her grandparents even more. They might not have had much money, but they always made time for her and Jordyn.

"Now I visit the pier occasionally to just think," Karter said between bites. "My turn. What's your biggest pet peeve?"

"Oh, that's easy. People who are mean to others. There's no excuse to be nasty for the hell of it, and it pisses me off whenever I hear someone belittling someone else." Dreamy reached for her glass of water. "I have another question. What do you do in your spare time?"

Karter paused to think and frowned. "I wish I had a better answer for this, but I rarely have spare time."

"Why is that? You're the boss. You should be able to take time off whenever you want."

Karter moved food around on his plate, seeming deep in thought. "That's a good question. I guess . . . I enjoy my work, and it keeps me busy, but I don't have a good excuse for why I don't take more time off."

"Well, you should work on changing that. Life is short. It's important to throw some fun in the mix as often as possible."

He cracked a smile. "Is that right?"

"Yep, it is. Okay, I have another question."

"Wait." Karter pointed his fork at her. "It's my turn."

"And it's my game," Dreamy countered, and rolled into her next question.

Once the usual first-date awkwardness passed, the rest of dinner was full of easy conversation and laughter. She marveled at how well they got along, despite their different backgrounds.

"I just thought of something. You never answered my original question about why you were nervous earlier," Dreamy said.

He set his fork down and wiped his mouth. "I think I was a little anxious to make this a nice experience for you."

"Was there any doubt?" After a long hesitation in answering, she wondered if he was going to respond. "Karter, if—"

"Not so much doubt, but more like concerned that my plans for the evening wouldn't be up to par." He must've seen the confusion on her face because he lifted his hands when she started to speak. "Dreamy, you are full of energy and probably the life of any party. You deserve to hang out with someone who's fun and brings the same vivacity. Instead, you have me. A stuffy old workaholic whose definition of excitement is taking a beautiful woman to a restaurant for a simple meal."

"Simple?" Dreamy said on a laugh, then leaned in, trying to keep her voice down. "Are you kidding me? This is the classiest restaurant I've ever been to, and there is nothing simple about this steak. Oh my God. It's *to die* for. And though I can't speak on your workaholism, you don't come across as stuffy at all."

She was surprised he saw himself that way. If anything, she'd refer to him as worldly. There might be an air of royalty about him in the way he carried himself, but his sincere smile and his sense of humor, which peeked out occasionally, made him approachable and, in some aspects, relatable. And that's what she told him.

Then she added, "If anyone should be nervous, it's me. I am so out of my element here. I thought for sure that I'd be the one slamming into servers and sending food flying across the restaurant."

They both laughed and lobbed compliments back and forth. Their date was turning out much better than she'd thought it would, and Dreamy hoped there would be a second one.

She speared another piece of steak and put it into her mouth. Her eyes drifted closed as she chewed and savored the tenderness of the beef.

"Everything is so good," she told Karter.

"I'm glad you enjoyed the meal. Do you cook?" he asked.

"Not like this, but I do all right."

Okay, maybe she was exaggerating, but Dreamy wanted to believe that she could cook just as well as the next person. She loved trying new recipes and adding her own personal touch. Granted, there were times when the meal didn't come out as planned, but at least she hadn't killed anyone with her culinary creations.

"Can you?" she asked. "I imagine you probably don't have to cook for yourself."

"I can make simple things like eggs and grilled cheese sandwiches," he admitted. "Outside of that, I'm pretty useless in the kitchen. And you're right, I usually don't have to cook for myself."

He told her about his housekeeper, who sounded more like a mother. The animated way he described the woman, sharing one entertaining story after another, revealed just how much he adored Nana.

"She's the sweetest person you'll ever meet, but she won't hesitate to put you in your place if you step out of line," he said on a laugh. "I'll never forget when I was in high school and missed curfew. I tried to sneak in, but she had planted herself in a chair just inside the door. She, and the bat she'd had in her hand, scared the crap out of me."

"Seriously? A bat? Where were your parents?"

"I don't know. Probably out of town or at some event. Nana was the constant in our lives. The bat was just for effect, but that night, I would've preferred a knock upside the head. Instead, I received a lecture from her about the importance of following rules, or at least calling when I was going to be late. Needless to say, she only had to give me the speech once. Unlike my sister who, as a child, pushed *every* limit."

Dreamy could listen to him talk about his Nana and siblings all night. The love he had for them made her wish that she had people in her life like them. Though she, her cousin, and their gramps got along great and had their share of fun stories, Dreamy had always wanted siblings.

"My brother, Randy, is the oldest, and what I would call the clown of the family. He used to always have some type of shenanigans going on. While my sister is the sweet and compassionate one, and maybe a little spoiled. She's around your age and recently returned from traveling around the world."

"Wow, that had to be exciting."

"She enjoyed herself. Is that something you'd want to do someday?"

Dreamy propped her elbow on the table and rested her chin in her hand as she pondered the question. "I can't say that I've ever thought about traveling the world. I'm pretty simple. I wouldn't mind maybe checking out Hawaii or even New York. Then again, maybe not the Big Apple. Wouldn't want to risk running into my mother. You probably figured from what I said back at the community center, but she and I don't have the best relationship. We might talk on occasion, but usually, five minutes into the conversation, and I'm ready to throw the phone across the room. She doesn't know me . . . I mean *really* know me. Yet, she has an opinion about how I choose to live my life. I'm sure my irritation with her centers around how she left me behind, and I can't seem to let it go. I know I shouldn't hold a grudge, but—"

Karter reached for her hand and squeezed it. "You don't have to explain it to me. I understand. I'm not as close to my parents as I could be, even though I see them regularly. Growing up, my father was on location a lot for his movies."

"Did you guys travel with him?"

"Occasionally, when we were little."

"Despite not seeing him all the time, it had to be amazing growing up with a famous father."

"It had its moments."

"Is your mother an actress too?"

"No. She's more of a professional socialite," he cracked. "She's . . . special."

He smiled when he said it, but there was an edge to his tone, Dreamy noticed. Maybe she was a piece of work like her mother, Tarrah.

"Well, your family sounds great," she said.

"Yeah, you know how family is. Gotta love 'em. Who knows, maybe you'll get to meet them someday."

Dreamy hadn't gone into the evening expecting another date would come out of it, but she wasn't totally opposed to it either. But meeting his family? Now that was something she couldn't imagine . . . yet.

The server, Candace, seemed to materialize out of nowhere the moment Dreamy finished eating. "How was your dinner?" she asked with a smile.

"Amazing. My compliments to the chef."

"I'll be sure to pass that along. May I take this for you?" she asked, pointing at Dreamy's empty plate.

"Yes, please."

Once the server cleared the table, she returned with the dessert menus. Dreamy scanned it, thinking she didn't have room for another bite of food. That was until she saw the list of choices.

"Oh, my goodness. You guys have Vesuvius cake?"

"Yes, and I can attest that it's the best that you'll ever have. Would you like a slice?"

Dreamy glanced across the table at Karter, who was looking at her instead of the menu. "Wanna share a slice?" she asked.

"I'm not much of a sweet eater, but for you? Sure, even though I have no idea what a Vesuvius cake is."

"Bring us a slice while I school him on the best cake that's ever been created," Dreamy said, handing Candace the dessert menu before she left the table. "So I was first introduced to the cake during my breakup party."

"A breakup party? Now that's something I haven't heard of before. What all's involved? Music? Dancing?"

"More like cake, tubs of ice scream, name-calling, and tears. *Lots* of tears," Dreamy said, remembering how devastated she'd been. "Jordyn called it a *kiss my ass, Brandon* breakup party. I think it was a first for both of us." Dreamy laughed, recalling how supportive Jordyn had been. "My cousin walks to her own beat and is very outspoken. I had to practically hold her down to keep her from hunting my ex."

"She sounds like the type of person we all should have in our corner."

"Yeah, she's the best, but don't get me wrong, she can be a pain in the you-know-what too. But that night, Jordyn knew just what to say and do. As for the cake, it's a decadent dessert that's like a chocolate explosion in your mouth."

Karter gave a mock shiver. "Sounds intense."

Dreamy laughed at his horrified expression. "It is, but don't worry. I won't force you to eat a lot of it. You just have to try a bite or two. Then you'll understand why it's the perfect cure for being dumped."

"I don't know what type of idiot would let you go, but he must have been a fool," Karter said with an edge to his tone. "If you were mine . . ." He reached for her hand, but his jacket sleeve made contact with the candle in the middle of the table.

Dreamy let out a little scream and jumped back when his sleeve went up in flames. "Karter!" She gasped and threw what was left in her water glass at him, totally missing his jacket sleeve.

He sputtered and let out a string of curses when the water hit his face, but he still managed to quickly put out the small fire. The waitstaff rushed to the table to offer assistance.

"Are you okay? Did it burn your skin?" Candace asked in a rush, while a waiter swiped the candle from the table, leaving the space even darker than it had been.

"No, no, I'm fine. Apparently, just . . . clumsy or maybe accident prone." Karter shook his head and grunted as he inspected the wrist of his singed jacket.

"Okay, if you're sure you're all right," Candace started, not looking convinced, "I'll bring your dessert shortly."

She hurried away, and Karter glanced at Dreamy, who still had her hand over her mouth.

"How do you feel about us taking the cake to go?" he asked. "I'm afraid if I stick around much longer, I might accidentally burn the place down."

Dreamy burst out laughing, not even embarrassed that she was drawing attention again. This was a first date that she would remember for the rest of her life.

"I think that's a good idea," she said, still giggling. "Let's make a run for it."

Chapter Sixteen

"THANKS FOR COMING OUT HERE WITH ME," KARTER SAID AS HE and Dreamy stared out over the Pacific Ocean.

"It's beautiful out here. I can see why you love this spot," Dreamy said, snuggling back against him. He had his hands on the railing on either side of her, cocooning her against him. Even with other people moving around them and hanging out at the nearby amusement park on the pier, it still seemed as if it were just him and Dreamy out there.

When she asked him about his favorite place, it reminded him that he hadn't been to the Santa Monica Pier in a long time. Karter hadn't even realized just how long it had been, at least not until tonight, and what a beautiful night it was. Stars twinkled in the distance while moonlight glinted off the water and a light breeze cooled his skin. It was a perfect moment to just be.

Karter couldn't stop thinking about their time at the restaurant. He had wanted to run out of there and pretend that they hadn't made complete fools of themselves. Actually, that title went to him alone. What the hell had been wrong with him tonight?

Sure, he'd been looking forward to taking Dreamy out and hoped to show her a good time, but his brain short-circuited the moment she opened the door to her house. That sexy-ass dress had completely floored him.

Stunning didn't begin to describe how incredible she looked tonight. From day one, he thought she was a beauty, but tonight? Dreamy was on a whole different level, and could rival any model that he'd ever dated. Confident. Poised. Witty. She had it going on, and his concerns from a week ago completely vanished. He no longer cared that they came from two different worlds. All that mattered in this moment was that he had every intention of spending more time with her. Assuming he hadn't completely blown his shot.

Still feeling the anxiety that had been ever present during dinner, he inhaled a cleansing breath and released it slowly. It felt good to finally breathe. For the last hour and a half, he'd been wound tighter than a pair of alligator shoes that were three sizes too small. It hadn't been until after the flying food fiasco that he started to relax.

Karter cringed just thinking about the mess he had caused. Food flying, glass breaking . . . the only thing that saved him from cutting their dinner short and getting the hell out of there was Dreamy. Her humor and easygoing persona were like a breath of fresh air. Now, had that been Angelica sitting on the other side of the table from him, she would've run out of the place screaming like a banshee. But not Dreamy. The woman was definitely one of a kind.

He bent slightly, his mouth close to her ear. "Listen, I'm sorry about what happened at the restaurant. I wanted this night to be perfect for you, and I hate that I blew it. I . . . I can honestly say that—all of that—was a first for me."

She turned in his arms, and a smile spread across her lips. "I think it's sweet that you were nervous. And *I* can honestly say I have never had that effect on a man before."

Karter slowly brushed the back of his hand down her soft cheek. "I find that hard to believe."

"Believe it."

"I hope you'll let me make tonight up to you?" Considering how bad the early part of their evening had gone, he shouldn't be asking for another chance to possibly make a fool of himself all over again.

"Hmm . . . what did you have in mind?" she asked saucily, a wicked gleam in her dark eyes.

His immediate thought was to invite her to his penthouse to make mad passionate love. Too bad suggesting that would probably get him slapped, or maybe kicked in his private parts.

Instead, he said, "Dinner . . . but not at that restaurant." There was no way he'd ever return after the chaos he had caused.

"I have a better idea," Dreamy countered. "How about I plan our next date? Or better yet, I'll cook for you."

Karter arched a brow. "So this means you're giving me another shot? You want to see me again?"

Her gentle laugh traveled on the night air. "Of course, silly, but only if I plan the date. Fancy places like that restaurant give me the heebie-jeebies. Before we arrived, all I kept thinking was that I was going to make a fool of myself. I was afraid I'd forget and lick my fingers, spill wine all over my dress, or throw up from nervousness."

"Well, I definitely couldn't tell you were nervous at all tonight. Then again, I was busy causing so much damage at the restaurant I wouldn't have noticed."

"Okay, true, but I'm talking about before you picked me up. I almost canceled on you."

Karter leaned back. "Really? Why?"

"Because you're . . . you. Karter, I'm so far out of my element when I'm around you. I'm still trying to pull my life together, but you? You've already been where I'm trying to go. Literally and figuratively."

Karter used to think he had his life all figured out, but lately, he didn't feel like it. What came next? A wife? Kids? More property? He didn't know. At the moment, he wasn't sure of anything. No. That wasn't true. He was sure that he wanted to kiss this beautiful woman who had finally agreed to have dinner with him.

"I don't need to be wined or dined at the most expensive restaurants," Dreamy continued. "Nor do I have to drive around in the shiniest or fastest cars. Give me a fat, juicy hamburger, a spectacular glass of grape Kool-Aid, and a car that goes faster than thirty miles an hour without overheating, and I'm good."

"Great. Now you tell me," Karter cracked, and he reveled in her laughter until he thought about what she'd just said. "Wait. Your car only goes thirty miles an hour?"

"Oh, please. If I can get it to go that fast without clunking out on me, it's a good day. A very good day."

Revelations like that reminded him just how different their lives were. Karter had picked her up in his Maserati, never thinking about the struggles she might have with her car that he'd seen the other day at the community center. It was old, but he'd assumed it ran perfectly fine. He prided himself on being in tune with those who weren't as fortunate as him, but other times, he was so far removed from their realities.

As Dreamy rambled on about cars in general, Karter's gaze drifted to her red lips, and all he wanted to do in that moment was smudge her lipstick with a kiss. He wanted to taste her. It was something he'd been thinking about each time he looked at her across the table. Which was probably why he'd been so distracted.

As if reading his mind, Dreamy lifted her hand and cupped his cheek. After that, Karter wasn't sure who moved in first. All he knew was that one minute they were staring into each other's eyes. The next, his mouth covered hers. Nothing else mattered. Her lips were as soft as he imagined them to be.

He slipped a hand behind her neck, his fingers sifting through her long hair as he pulled her closer. This was one time he was glad she hadn't worn a wig. Less chance of causing more chaos, like getting his fingers tangled in it and sending it flying around the pier.

Dreamy's arms went around his waist, and Karter took his time savoring her sweetness. As their tongues tangled and they passionately explored the inner recesses of each other's mouths, Dreamy moved closer. Her lush body molded into his, and all rational thought flew from his mind as his body tightened with need.

He'd kissed his share of women, but kissing Dreamy felt different. It felt right. It felt like . . . home. Their lip-lock was explosive, and Karter knew one kiss was never going to be enough. He wanted to explore every inch of this woman's body.

Slow down, man, the irritating voice of reason blared through his mind. He was pretty sure it wouldn't be the only time tonight that he heard it, and this was one time he should probably listen.

He couldn't. Instead, he cradled the back of her head and increased the pressure of his mouth over hers. As he devoured her, a rush of need plowed through his body, and a moan, similar to the one she had released in the meeting the other day, pierced the air.

Before now, he had never been into public displays of affection, but that was before he met the vibrant woman in his arms. And their soul-stirring kiss was getting more heated by the minute. If he didn't slow things down, he might be tempted to explore other parts of her body.

Karter reluctantly lifted his head and gazed into Dreamy's lust-filled eyes and knew they would share another kiss before the night was over.

"Wow, you're a good kisser," she breathed, and a small smile spread across her mouth. "I can honestly say this is the best first date I've ever had."

"I'm glad to hear that, and it's not even over yet."

Outside of planning dinner, Karter hadn't thought much past that, but he wasn't ready to take her home yet.

"How are you in those shoes? Are you up for walking back to the car?" It was becoming clear that she loved high heels, and apparently had a nice collection of shoes. So far he hadn't seen her in the same pair twice. "The shoes you have on are very sexy, but they don't look all that comfortable."

Dreamy glanced down and turned her foot to the side. "These are more like sitting shoes than walking shoes. But I should be able to trudge back to where you parked the car. Besides, what would be the alternative? You gon' carry me or something?"

"I would if you needed me to. Or I'd call an Uber to pick us up and take us to the car."

Dreamy tsked. "Now that would be a waste of money. I think I can handle a few blocks. Worst-case scenario, I can always slip them off and walk barefoot."

"I'll carry you before I let you do that. Let's get going before your sitting shoes give out on you."

A short while later, Karter helped Dreamy into the car and closed the door. He strolled around the back of his vehicle, trying to come up with someplace else they could go.

Just another sign that I need to get out more.

Ten minutes into their drive, he was still tossing ideas around. He considered taking her for a ride up the 101. That was something he hadn't done in years.

"Are you in a hurry to get home?" he asked.

"Nope. What did you have in mind?" Dreamy turned in her seat to face him, and a loud rip filled the quietness of the car.

She gasped, then shrieked. "Oh, no! My dress! Jordyn's going to kill me!"

"What?" Karter asked. He split his attention between her and the road, confused and concerned by her screaming. Each time she moved, there was more tearing. "Dreamy, calm down."

"Calm down?" she yelled, her eyes shooting daggers at him. "I can't calm down. My life as I know it is about to be over! You don't understand. Jordyn is going to *kill* me, and she doesn't make idle threats!"

Still not understanding, Karter glanced around for someplace safe to pull over. Bumper-to-bumper traffic on Santa Monica Boulevard was making that difficult, but moments later, he turned into a gas station and found a park. Shutting off the car, he faced Dreamy, surprised to see that her eyes were shimmering. Whatever was going on was serious.

"What happened?"

"My dress . . . no, Jordyn's dress. It must've gotten caught in the door." She fumbled around with the seat belt and finally unbuckled it before shoving open the door. "Oh, no, no, no. This is bad. This is really, really bad. Worse than I thought," she screeched. The pitch of her voice rose with each word.

Karter couldn't see the damage from where he sat but was glad he managed to park near an overhead light that was attached to the side of the building. When he climbed out of the vehicle and rushed to the other side of the car, his brain froze.

Legs. That's all he saw at first, and not just any legs but one in particular. His gaze raked over her hip, where a black string was showing from what he could only assume was a thong. His eyes kept moving along a beautifully toned thigh on down to a long, shapely leg, which was on full display. Add that to the sexiest red shoe he'd ever seen, and you had a sight that stole his breath.

Dreamy gripped the door of the car and stumbled out. Karter had just enough time to reach out and grab her hand before she fell to the ground.

"This is so bad," she repeated as she examined the side of the dress.

The belt or sash thing was practically ripped off, and Karter could see that the whole right side of the dress was open. Dreamy feverishly tried to pull it together, but it was no use. She couldn't close it up, and she was probably showing way more skin than she wanted to.

Karter's brain still wasn't working on all cylinders now that he had a better view of her legs and a glimpse of black lace between her thighs. His body responded, tightening to a point where if he didn't get his head on straight, Dreamy was going to know exactly how much she was turning him on. He was as bad as a middle school kid seeing a woman's sexy underwear for the first time.

What the hell, man? Pull yourself together. He had definitely gone too long without the company of a woman if his mind was conjuring up that type of craziness.

"I can't go anywhere like this!" she shrieked. Her voice was still about ten octaves higher than normal. "I can't even go home, because if I do, tonight will be the last time you see me. Hell, it'll be the last time anyone sees me, because I'm not kidding when I say Jordyn is going to kill me! You're going to see me on the cover of the *LA Times* with the headline 'Death by Dress' in big bold letters. What am I going to do?"

"Okay, first, let's calm down."

"Did you not hear me when I said my life is about to end? Jordyn hasn't even worn the dress yet, and . . . and I've ruined it. God, I can't believe I destroyed her dress. Why does crap like this always happen to me?"

She slumped against the car, and tears filled her eyes, but thankfully none fell. Karter didn't know a damn thing about dresses or fixing them, but he knew someone who did.

He cupped Dreamy's face, and the sadness in her eyes made his heart practically split in two. "This is my fault, and I'll fix it."

He'd been so thrown by their kiss at the pier that when he closed the car door, he hadn't been paying attention. Otherwise, he would've noticed that the dress was caught.

A rogue tear slipped down her cheek, and she quickly brushed it away.

"I promise you. We'll fix this, and if we don't, you can blame the mishap on me."

Dreamy sniffed and released a humorless laugh. "You don't know Jordyn. She's a law student who is planning to be a defense attorney. Do you have any idea how much she's looking forward to ripping people apart? It doesn't matter if it's with her words or her hands. She's going to be out for blood."

"I'll take my chances."

Dreamy flashed him a half-hearted smile before it slipped from her lips. "It's not just about ruining the dress. Karter, she trusted me. She planned to wear this to an event at the governor's mansion in a couple of weeks.

"For a person who rarely goes out on the town and favors jeans and T-shirts over anything dressy, it would've been nice to see her in this one. That's not going to happen now," she mumbled, and glanced down at the garment. "I've ruined it, and, knowing my cousin, it was probably also going to be the dress she wore to graduation. You have no idea how big of a deal it is that she's graduating with a law degree. It's huge for our family, and—"

"Sweetheart, I'll fix this. I'll fix everything," Karter promised again.

Unable to help himself, he lowered his head and pressed a gentle kiss against her lips. What was intended to be a light peck quickly turned into something more. He took what he wanted as their tongues tangled, and Dreamy kissed him with a passion he hadn't felt in forever.

She slid her hands up his torso and tightly gripped the lapels of his jacket. She pulled him closer and he deepened the kiss. Karter was vaguely aware of vehicles passing, car doors slamming, and people talking in the distance. Yet he couldn't let her go. A protectiveness that he hadn't felt for anyone in a long time gripped him. At that moment, there was nothing he wouldn't do for this woman, even face off with her bloodthirsty cousin.

Chapter Seventeen

DREAMY STARED OUT THE PASSENGER-SIDE WINDOW OF KAR-
ter's car, watching as the landscape went by in a blur. Neither of
them said much after leaving the gas station and, unlike her, Karter
apparently preferred driving without music. Normally, she blasted
her radio, which was the best working part on her car.

Sighing, she reflected on the night. It had evoked a mix of emotions, and at the moment, she wasn't sure what to feel. Part of her
wanted nothing more than to spend more time with Karter. While
the other part of her just wanted to get her cousin's dress repaired.

Dreamy glanced down at the outfit again, then tightened Karter's suit jacket around herself, grateful that it was big enough to
cover the damage. They didn't swap clothes often, mainly because
Jordyn didn't have much outside of business suits, T-shirts, and
jeans. The one beautiful dress she owned, Dreamy had just ruined.

*I should've been more careful. No, I shouldn't have worn it in the first
place.*

Right after they'd pulled away from the gas station, Jordyn had
texted her. She was just checking in to see how things were going.

It was as if her cousin already knew. Not accustomed to lying, Dreamy texted back saying everything was great.

Actually, that hadn't been a total lie. Dinner was fun despite the number of mishaps, but that kiss at the pier? Had been a total, but welcome, surprise. Who knew the man was so skillful with his tongue? She wondered what else he could do with it.

Wait. Don't go there.

They were going to his house to see if his sister, Morgan, could repair the dress, and that was it. There wouldn't be any rolling around in his bed, or sex against a bathroom wall. All they were going to do was see about getting the dress fixed. Then Karter would take Dreamy home, and maybe they'd plan that second date.

But her weak mind still went back to their tongue aerobics. She hadn't been lying when she told him he was a good kisser. Hell, Mr. Karter Redford was probably great at everything he did. He seemed like the type who wouldn't do anything half-assed, and tonight, she really appreciated that.

Dreamy wasn't sure what she had expected to come out of their date, but definitely not everything that had happened in the last few hours. Their connection had already been undeniable, but after the first kiss and then the last one, she wanted more.

And after the dress fiasco, he'd been so amazing. When he promised to fix the situation, she thought it impossible, but there was a part of her that knew he achieved whatever he set out to do.

Dreamy had hoped to one day meet his family, but not like this. Not when she was half-dressed and needed a huge favor.

Karter made a few turns before they started their incline up the hill. They entered the Oaks neighborhood, an affluent area where several celebrities lived, and apparently Karter too.

"This is a pretty area," Dreamy said after entering the gated community. Though there were a lot of lights on the streets, one huge home after another had large front yards with floodlights showcasing the homes.

"Yeah, it's nice, but you can't really see much now. The homes are unique and grand. I'll have to bring you here during the daylight."

He pulled his car onto a stamped concrete driveway that curved in front of a home that was at least twenty times larger than what she lived in.

"This is your house?" she asked, unable to keep the awe out of her voice. The two-story Spanish-inspired home with a clay roof, tons of windows, and a huge orange front door was absolutely stunning. "This is beautiful . . . and a lot."

Karter chuckled. "It can be a bit much sometimes, but after a grueling day, I can't think of a better place to regroup."

He pulled up to a four-car attached garage. There was another garage, a freestanding three-car one, a few feet away.

The overhead door on the far left lifted, and Karter pulled inside and parked. To Dreamy's right were three other vehicles. A Range Rover, some type of sports car, and a modest SUV.

Why one person needed so many vehicles was a mystery to her, but then she remembered that he wasn't the only one who lived in the home.

That thought brought a whole new wave of anxiousness. Again, she hated the idea of meeting his family under these conditions, especially his sister. She'd probably think that Dreamy planned this fiasco in order to get a peek at how Karter lived. Or that she was trying to get him into bed. Actually, that last thought wouldn't be all that bad an idea, but . . . not like this. Not on the first date, and definitely not while she was wearing a raggedy dress.

God, why me? Why do I always end up in messes like these?

Karter opened her car door and extended his hand to her. She grabbed hold, and with her free hand, clamped his jacket closed and walked with him to the door.

"One good thing that's come out of this evening," he said, and lifted the bag that was in his hand, "we still have cake."

Dreamy smiled, grateful for his good attitude. "If I forget to tell you, thanks for tonight. Despite some of our mishaps, I've had a wonderful time with you."

He wrapped his arm around her and pulled her close. "The night isn't over yet," he said just before kissing her.

Dreamy melted against him, reveling in how good his lips felt against hers. He made it so easy to forget everything else whenever their mouths connected.

A dog barking on the other side of the door snagged her attention when the kiss ended, and she perked up.

"I didn't know you have a dog." She had always wanted a pet, but when she was younger, her grandparents couldn't afford one. Now, with school and work, she didn't have the time to commit to one.

"Yeah, Morgan sprung him on me a few weeks ago. His name is Melvin."

"Aww, what a cute name. I can't wait to meet him."

"Well, brace yourself. He's a ball of energy."

Before Karter could unlock the door to the house, it swung open and the cutest puppy greeted Dreamy.

"Oh, my goodness." She bent down to rub the dog. "You have to be the cutest little guy I've ever seen. Hi, baby."

Dreamy hugged the overzealous puppy, whose tail wagged a mile a minute as he jumped up and tried licking her face. She giggled at his antics, and all of the stress of the day melted away.

"See now, Karter, *that's* how you greet a dog."

So caught up with Melvin, Dreamy had failed to speak to the woman who had opened the door. She gave the dog one more rub behind his ear before standing.

"You must be Dreamy," the woman, who had to be Karter's sister, said. Though her eyes were a dark brown, instead of light brown like Karter's, she had his same sepia-brown skin tone and slightly crooked grin.

"Yes, and I assume you're Morgan," Dreamy said. She started to extend her hand, but the woman lunged forward and pulled her into a tight hug.

"I should've warned you that she's a hugger," Karter murmured.

"It's so nice to meet you," Morgan said, as if her brother hadn't spoken. "Come on in. I heard you had a little mishap."

"I wish it was little." Dreamy followed her inside with Melvin walking alongside her, and Karter pulling up the rear.

They strolled through a mudroom that led to a kitchen that was a cook's paradise. Dreamy had to keep herself from gawking, since she wanted to act like she was accustomed to nice things, but the kitchen was massive and gorgeous. Like something right out of *House Beautiful* magazine.

She might not be much of a cook, but even she could appreciate having top-of-the-line stainless steel appliances, marble countertops, and white cabinets. The center island was the size of Punta Cana, and there was also a bar that had a least five bar stools.

She turned to Karter. "Your home is lovely." Then her attention went to the woman who was walking toward her in a multicolor caftan. "You must be Nana."

The woman, with smooth skin and a fair complexion, smiled. As she got closer, Dreamy also noticed a smattering of freckles around her nose and cheeks.

"And you must be Dreamy. It's a pleasure to meet you." Like Morgan, Nana greeted her with a warm hug. "Come in and make yourself at home."

"Actually, come with me so I can take a look at your dress," Morgan said, looping her arm with Dreamy's.

Dreamy glanced back at Karter, feeling a little weird going through his house without him. "Don't eat all of my cake," she said.

He smiled, amusement brimming in his eyes. "I won't, and holler if you need anything. I'll be either down here or in my office."

"Don't worry. She's in good hands," Morgan said over her shoulder and continued guiding Dreamy out of the room, with Melvin trotting behind them.

As Dreamy strolled through the first floor, every room got more impressive. The Spanish style that was the outside spilled a little indoors with wooden support beams on the super-high ceilings, stucco walls, and arches that led from one room to another. The contemporary furnishings were a nice contrast to the building itself.

"This place is huge," Dreamy said, no longer able to keep the awe out of her voice.

"Yeah, it's a little overkill in size, but considering I'm kinda squatting here, I can't complain."

After giving her a tour of the first-floor living space, as well as a sunroom that overlooked a massive deck and pool, Morgan led Dreamy down a different hallway. "We'll start in here so I can see what's going on." They strolled into an equally impressive bedroom with a huge four-poster bed.

Dreamy was tempted to jump on it and see if it was as comfortable as it looked.

Morgan stood in front of her with her hands on her narrow hips. "Okay, so let's see the damage."

Dreamy reluctantly shrugged out of Karter's suit jacket and laid it across an upholstered chair. Cool air hit her bare skin where the dress had ripped.

"Your brother mentioned that you have a background in fashion design."

"Yeah, that's what I went to school for. Well, before I dropped out, but don't worry. I'm sure I can fix whatever the problem is. Hmm . . ." she said as she examined the dress. "This is cute. It's a knockoff from Rihanna's fashion line."

"It is?" Dreamy asked in shock. She wondered if Jordyn knew, not that it would matter.

"Yeah, and whoever made this one did an okay job, but the way they attached the sash, it's always going to be problematic."

"But you can fix it, right?" All Dreamy wanted to do was get the outfit back to Jordyn just like it was before tonight.

"Yup, I can do it. Hopefully, you're not in a hurry. It's going to take a while. Oh, and by the way, I'm loving those shoes." Morgan fingered the gemstones covering Dreamy's ankle strap. "Remind me to show you my shoe collection before you leave."

"Oh, sounds like we have a love of shoes in common," Dreamy said.

"Girl, yes. I might not dress up a lot, but my shoe game is always on point. Now, take off your dress."

"Um, I don't have anything to cover up with." And except for her thong, Dreamy was naked underneath. She had already given Karter an eyeful in the car. She wasn't about to give his sister whom she just met a peek at all of her goodies.

"Oh, yeah. I guess walking around here in the nude could be a problem. I'll see if I have something for you to wear."

Dreamy looked at her with a raised eyebrow. "I doubt I'd be able to get a leg into anything you own." Morgan had some height on her, but considering how huge Karter was, his sister couldn't be bigger than a size 4. Whereas Dreamy wavered between an 8 and a 10.

"Good point. I have an idea." She grinned, and a wicked gleam radiated in her dark eyes.

Dreamy didn't know what she was up to, but she picked Melvin up and they followed Morgan out of the room and up the stairs.

Once they arrived on the second floor, they strolled down a long hallway to the last door at the end.

Dreamy knew the moment they stepped into the room that it was Karter's domain, and she pulled up short. Her gaze swept the space, taking in the wall-to-wall windows on the opposite side of the room and the recessed lighting that went around the gray-and-black tray ceiling. A sitting area with two comfortable-looking chairs and a small round table was positioned near the windows. The pale gray walls were adorned with colorful abstract art strategically positioned, and then there was the massive bed.

Not even a blind person could miss how huge the bed was. Dreamy didn't even want to think about how many women he'd probably shared it with. Yet, that's exactly where her mind went.

What he's done and with who is none of my business. At least that's what she told herself. They were just hanging out and getting to know each other. So what if she'd fallen hard for him? She had no real claim over him.

She shook all thoughts of Karter and his bed from her mind. "Are you sure it's okay to be in here?"

Morgan waved her off and strolled across the room as if she owned the place. She stopped in front of double doors and pulled them open with a flair.

"If you don't want to walk around in your panties, I suggest you get over here. Oh, but Karter will have a conniption if he finds out Melvin was in here."

As if understanding Morgan, Melvin started whining and wiggling in Dreamy's arms.

"Why can't he be in here? He's such a sweetheart," she said, snuggling him close.

"He and Karter don't really get along yet, especially after Melvin chewed on one of his expensive shoes."

"Ah, I see." Dreamy went back to the hallway and gave the

puppy a quick hug before setting him down. "Stay right here, and I'll be back for you."

He barked and whined, but she closed the door and walked over to where Morgan was still standing.

Dreamy gasped. "You gotta be frickin' kidding me. Who needs a closet this big?"

"Apparently your boyfriend, and this is not even the only one."

Boyfriend? She was about to correct Morgan and say they were just friends, but then she thought about the kisses they'd shared. Okay, maybe they were a little more than friends. Or maybe they were special friends.

"I think you have the wrong idea about me and your brother. We're just hanging out. Tonight was our first date."

"Girl, my brother doesn't date. All he does is work. If he took you out *and* brought you here, you're his girlfriend."

Dreamy didn't know what to say, though a ton of questions rattled inside of her head. One thing she hadn't asked Karter was whether he was seeing anyone. But the way he'd kissed her tonight, it was safe to say he wasn't. No way would he be with her if he were involved with someone else. That, she was sure of.

"Don't look so worried." Morgan looped her arm around Dreamy's shoulders. "Let me tell you about my brother. Karter is not a player. He's only lived here a couple of years, and I can count on one finger how many women he's brought here. Trust me. If he brought you home, then he's looking for your first date to turn into many more."

Butterflies took flight in Dreamy's stomach, and she tried not to get too excited about the prospect of dating Karter. Neither she nor he could deny their attraction for each other, but Dreamy didn't want to get her hopes up. She liked him a lot, and though she had sworn off men for a while, if she was going to break that vow, it would be with Karter.

"I think he's amazing. One of the nicest men I've ever met."

"Would you say he's boyfriend material?"

"I'd say I'm still getting to know him, but yes." She didn't bother telling Morgan that she thought Karter was way out of her league. Nor did she mention that he was older than she usually preferred.

"Now come on in and pick something. I would suggest something on the left side." Morgan pointed to the long row of dress shirts hanging in color-coordinated fashion. "I'll be right back."

Dreamy scanned the closet, taking in the shoe rack that held at least a hundred pairs of expensive footwear. Even his collection of ties and belts was impressive. She strolled along the right side of the closet, admiring what seemed to be fifty million suits hanging in perfect order. He didn't come across as a materialistic person, but seeing his closet made her wonder if he was.

A heaviness settled in the center of Dreamy's chest as she moved to where he hung his pants and jeans. The fancy cars, the house, and even the closet were yet another reminder of how different their lives were. Heck, this room alone was bigger than her house. What in the world did he want with someone like her? She hated that she kept feeling like she wasn't enough, but it was hard not to make comparisons between their lives.

Dreamy moved to the left side of the closet, where there were at least a thousand dress shirts in every possible color. Toward the end of the row were the shirts with patterns, and that's what she gravitated to. She quickly changed out of Jordyn's dress and slipped her arms through the sleeves of a green, purple, and yellow flowery shirt. The flowers were pale and the shirt was cute and soft against her skin, but she couldn't see Karter ever wearing it.

She glanced in the full-length mirror that hung on a nearby wall. The shirt covered all of her assets and stopped at her knees. If she had a wide belt, it would make a pretty dress.

Morgan strolled back into the closet, laughing and clapping her hands. "Oh, wow. My brother is going to love seeing you in one of his shirts, especially that one."

"Why especially this one?"

"Because it's his favorite. I have to say, I already think you and Karter are made for each other."

Dreamy had thought so, too, but now that she saw how he lived, she wasn't so sure.

Chapter Eighteen

KARTER SAT AT THE BREAKFAST BAR SIPPING HIS BRANDY, WON-dering what was taking Morgan and Dreamy so long. As far as he was concerned, he and Dreamy were still on a date, and he didn't want to waste another minute of it.

Nana strolled to the small built-in desk near the pantry and pulled a white envelope from the drawer. "This came for you to-day," she said.

Karter didn't have to open it to know what it was. His mother's perfect calligraphy was scribbled on the outside of the envelope. It was that time of the year, his parents' wedding anniversary. A time when his mother went all out inviting anybody who was anybody to an elaborate celebration.

"She also called this evening, twice, wanting to make sure you received the invitation. When you call to RSVP, she's expecting you to give her the name of your plus-one."

"I'm sure she is," Karter said dryly. "I'm surprised she didn't tell you that I was bringing Angelica."

Nana smirked. "Actually, she did, and she insisted that I call

Angelica to find out what color she's wearing. That way you can color coordinate and not clash with her."

Karter shook his head. "She's too much. I haven't even decided if I was attending this year. It's the same ol', same ol' with bourgie folks trying to outdress the next and bragging about their latest movie script or megamansion, or who donated the most money to a worthy charity. I'm over it."

"I get that, but if you don't show up, she'll probably call the president of the United States and insist he send the National Guard here to get you."

Karter laughed, mainly because she was right. His mother was a diva to the nth degree, and wouldn't stand for any of her children not showing up to her event. Who would she brag to if they didn't?

If, and that was a big if, he attended, he already knew whom he'd want as his plus-one. He just wasn't sure if he would extend the invitation. Not because he wouldn't want her there. No, it had everything to do with his mother, who was a world-class snob. He didn't trust her to treat Dreamy kindly. Then again, from what he knew of Dreamy, she could probably hold her own in any situation.

Karter glanced at the back staircase that led to the second floor from the kitchen.

"I'm sure she's fine," Nana said, smiling. "You could always go up there and check on her."

"I don't want to come across as overbearing." Which was true, but Karter felt a possessiveness that he hadn't felt in a long time. "I like her. A lot," he said, more to himself than to Nana, who was plating up the cake from the restaurant.

"I can tell, and I can see why. She's very pretty . . . and young."

"Yeah, I know. She's Morgan's age. That was one of the reasons I was hesitant to ask her out. But . . ."

Who am I kidding?

Karter lost all rational thought whenever Dreamy was around.

He couldn't explain it, except that he felt a little reckless when it came to her. So what if they were from two different worlds? All that mattered was that they got along great and had a good time together.

They'd known each other only a short time. Yet he felt as if he'd known her forever. Funny. Sweet. Intelligent. Engaging. There was so much to like about her. If only he could stop worrying about their age difference. Granted they were only ten years and a few months apart, but still. Knowing she and Morgan were the same age made him feel like an old dude going through a midlife crisis and searching for a younger woman.

Nana set a small cheese-and-cracker plate along with grapes and Dreamy's cake on a tray in front of him. Karter's left brow lifted skyward.

"What's all of this?"

"In case you wanted to prolong your date and watch a movie in the theater room. I already replenished everything needed for the popcorn machine downstairs, and the refrigerator has been fully stocked."

Karter grinned and nodded. "Thanks, Nana. I love the way you think."

"As for your feelings for Dreamy, I believe in love at first sight because sometimes love can't be explained. You just have to go with your gut feeling and hang on for the ride."

"Whoa. I didn't say anything about love," Karter whispered, and glanced toward the stairs. "All I said is that I like her."

"*A lot*," Nana finished on a laugh.

Karter chuckled.

"Don't fight it, my love." Nana patted his cheek like she used to do when he was a kid. "I want you to be happy. Life is too short to try and control every aspect of it the way you often do. Just enjoy the process. Have fun. You deserve it. Besides, I can tell you're really feeling Dreamy."

"How? You just met her."

"Well, for one, you brought her home with you, and it wasn't just because of the dress."

"I've brought women home before."

"*A* woman, and even then, you didn't let Valerie traipse around here on the first date. Actually, you went out with her a few months before you brought her here, and even longer before you introduced her to Morgan."

Karter nodded. "True." That probably was a sign then that he hadn't completely trusted her.

"Have you ever wondered why you're quick to take risks in business, but not in your personal life?" Nana asked.

"It's different. I know business. I know money. Some of those decisions are based on gut instinct, while others come from research. But when it comes to matters of the heart . . . there are no guarantees and few opportunities to make an educated guess. I'm just not willing to take the same risks. Besides, I did that with Valerie and look how it turned out. I got my heart crushed, and it's not something I ever want to experience again."

And then there was Angelica, but Karter never let her get close. Partly because they both knew going in that what they had would never amount to anything serious even if she tried.

That wasn't to say that he didn't want to take a chance on Dreamy. Actually, he already had, since he did ask her out for dinner and invited her into his home. Karter just wasn't sure how much more he'd be able to risk when it came to whatever was developing between them.

"After dealing with Valerie and Angelica, it's hard to open myself back up to another woman." Actually, it wasn't just hard, it was scary as hell. "I need someone I can trust. Someone I can trust not to use me for their own gain, and someone who doesn't stir up drama at every turn."

Nana leaned her hip against the counter and folded her arms across her chest.

"Well, you'll never know if Dreamy is that someone if you don't give her a chance. I'm talking about a chance without putting up your usual barriers. For what it's worth, I like her."

Yeah, me too.

"I like Dreamy because I've already started to see a change in you. Coming home at a decent hour and bringing me flowers"—she nodded toward the red roses on the edge of the island—"you seem happier . . . lighter."

Karter could admit to all of that, but he couldn't say for sure if the change in him had anything to do with Dreamy. At least not all of it. If he were honest, it probably had more to do with his wanting more out of his life. Dreamy just happened to be the cherry on top.

Speaking of cherry on top . . .

His mouth went dry and his pulse amped up at the sight of her wearing his shirt. She stood at the entrance of the kitchen looking adorable but unsure as she wrung her hands together. At her feet was Melvin, who stared up at her, probably wearing the same expression as Karter. Clearly, the dog was just as enamored of her.

As Karter's gaze took her in, a rush of heat plowed through his body. Her hair was pulled into a messy ponytail on top of her head, and she no longer had on the killer high-heel shoes. In their place was a pair of fluffy purple socks.

But it was his shirt on her that had his body tightening and his blood rushing south. With the garment stopping at her knees, it gave Karter an unobstructed view of her long, shapely legs. He didn't realize it before tonight, but he was definitely a leg man, and boy did she have a beautiful pair of legs.

He stood from the bar and approached her.

"I hope you don't mind," she said in a rush and pointed at her outfit. "If you do, I can—"

"I don't mind at all. As a matter of fact, that shirt looks a hell of a lot better on you than it does on me."

She glanced down at herself. "Think so?"

"Positive." She looked so good that Karter was struggling to keep his hands to himself. What he really wanted to do was reach under the shirt and let his hands explore every inch of her lush body.

Maybe later.

Recognizing her anxiousness as she fidgeted with the sleeve of the shirt and moved from one foot to the other, Karter figured it was a good time to whisk her away to the walk-out basement.

"You know what, Nana?" he said. "If it's okay with Dreamy, we're going to hang out downstairs in the theater room, watch a movie, and eat cake."

Dreamy graced him with a huge smile, and Karter couldn't wait to get her alone again. He grabbed the small tray of food and reached for Dreamy's hand.

They were almost to the basement stairs when Karter remembered something. "Nana, if Morgan looks for us, let her know where we . . . Actually, tell her to call my cell phone. We don't want to be interrupted unless it's an emergency."

"Got it."

Every step Dreamy took, Melvin was right beside her.

"You've made quite an impression on my dog."

Dreamy bent down and petted the puppy. "He's such a good boy. Yes, he is," she cooed. The dog ate up the attention, barking and jumping on her in an effort to lick her face.

"Melvin," Nana called. "Come here. You need to stay up here."

The dog whined, and at first it seemed he wasn't going to obey, but then he let out a little bark and trotted to Nana.

"And he's smart too," Dreamy said.

"Yeah, so smart he eats shoes."

Dreamy laughed. "I heard about that. I also heard that this is your favorite shirt. Are you sure you don't mind me wearing it? What if—"

"That's not my favorite shirt," Karter said, laughing. "That's a shirt that Morgan bought me for my birthday when she was a kid. She thinks it's my favorite because I still have it. She was so proud of the gift. I didn't have the heart to tell her that I'll probably never wear it because it's a little too loud for me."

"Ahhh." Dreamy laughed. "Okay, I won't tell her."

Still holding her hand, Karter guided her down the stairs. The walk-out basement was his sanctuary. Besides a theater room, there was a mini kitchen, game room, and another guest bedroom with an en suite bathroom.

The home might've been large enough for a big family, but Karter loved how he, Nana, and Morgan could all be there without getting in each other's way.

"It's like an apartment down here," Dreamy said as she roamed from one room to another. "It's so big, but still warm and inviting."

"I'm glad you think so. Now let me take you to the theater room so we can continue our date."

Dreamy grinned and slipped her hand back into his. "Lead the way, Mr. Redford."

THIS IS TOO COZY, DREAMY THOUGHT.

She and Karter were snuggled together on an ultra-comfortable reclining love seat in his theater room. Add that to the dimmed lights, and one of her favorite movies—*Love Jones*—playing on the large screen, and you had the perfect romantic setting.

Exactly what she *didn't* need.

With her overactive imagination revved up, she was bound to

do something crazy. Like climb on top of Karter and kiss him senseless, or insist that they act out one of her many fantasies.

She couldn't.

She wouldn't.

This was their first date.

What would he think of her?

Karter was turning out to be everything she wanted in a man. Resourceful. Kind. And the perfect gentleman. This evening would definitely fall under best first date ever. It didn't matter that everything that could've gone wrong pretty much had, but being with him felt natural. It felt perfect.

Too perfect.

She curled her feet beneath her and rested her head on his shoulder. He placed a kiss on her forehead and put his hand on her bare thigh. If he knew that the way he was running his hand up and down her thigh was turning her on, he would stop. Maybe.

Dreamy tuned back in to the movie, but a second later, her mind drifted again. She wanted Karter in every way a woman could want a man, and that scared her to death. They didn't know each other. Not really. Yet she felt so comfortable with him. It was as if they'd been hanging out for years. It didn't seem possible that she could be falling for him so soon, but that's exactly what was happening.

And was it crazy that she wanted to jump his bones?

Of course, she would never act on that. She couldn't. No way would she put herself out there . . . in case they weren't on the same page. Then again, if she was reading him right, they wanted the same things. Each other.

No. No. I'm going to keep my mouth shut and my hands to myself.

It was too soon to start fantasizing about a happily ever after. Besides, she had already gotten her heart crushed by a man only months ago. No way was she going through that again anytime soon.

"I can hear you thinking, and you're drowning out Larenz Tate's poetic masterpiece," Karter said.

Dreamy laughed. Her mind was all over the place probably because of Larenz Tate. From the moment she had first seen him in *Love Jones*, she had fallen in love with the actor. And it was this scene, when he was doing a spoken-word piece for Nia Long after just meeting her, that Dreamy imagined marrying the guy.

"I was thinking about how much I love Larenz Tate," she said.

"Yeah, I can understand that. He played this role masterfully. I remember the first time I met him. He—"

"Whoa! Hold up." Dreamy placed her feet on the floor and sat up. "You've met him? *Larenz Tate*?"

Karter turned his amused gaze to her. "Yeah, a couple of times. He's a nice guy. Maybe I'll introduce you one day."

"Seriously? If you do, I'll be forever in your debt."

A slow smile spread across Karter's lips. "Is that right?" he said, his deep voice dropping an octave as his gaze volleyed from her eyes to her mouth, and back to her eyes again.

"Yup. You make that happen, and you can ask anything of me."

"Those are strong words. You don't know what I might ask of you."

"I said *anything*. That's how much I love him."

"Hmm . . . I'm not sure how I feel about that."

Dreamy gasped when Karter slid his arm under her and lifted her onto his lap. He was a big guy, and she assumed he was as strong and powerful as he looked, but he had just proven how strong he really was.

Heat rushed through her body while she straddled his thighs and felt his hardness between her legs. His large hands cradled her butt cheeks, only intensifying the precarious position she was in.

"What are we doing?" she asked breathlessly, her heart beating a little faster. Their mouths were mere inches from each other, and it was taking a will of steel to not grind against him.

"I'm going to show you why you should choose me over him. I'm way more interesting than Larenz."

Dreamy gave an unladylike snort. "More interesting than Larenz Tate? I don't think so."

Karter narrowed his eyes and squeezed her butt while decreasing the distance between their mouths. "Why is that so hard to believe? I own several companies. I'm extremely resourceful. I plan exciting first dates, and I'm better looking than he is. Oh, and I'm definitely taller. More than that, though, I can have you screaming my name within minutes of getting you naked."

Heat soared through Dreamy's body, and it was as if someone had turned the heat up to a hundred degrees. She wanted him to prove that last part, but she also wasn't ready to stop their banter.

"I'm not going to concede that any of that is true," she breathed, her pulse amping up at just thinking about him getting her naked and making her scream. "Besides, it's probably not a good idea to stroke your oversize ego and make your head any bigger than it already is."

"Too late," he said, rotating his hips beneath her, and Dreamy moaned at the feel of his erection pressing against her core.

With her willpower snapped, she cupped his face between her hands and covered his mouth with hers as she ground her body against him. Forget bantering. She wanted this man more than she wanted her next pair of high-heel shoes.

But first, she wanted him to make her scream.

Chapter Nineteen

DON'T DO IT! IT'S TOO SOON!

That irritating voice of reason from earlier shouted inside Karter's head again, but he was too far gone to listen. The feel of Dreamy's body on top of him, grinding against his shaft, had his brain going haywire.

He wanted this too much. He wanted *her* too much to stop.

It had been a while since he'd been with a woman, and if Dreamy kept moving the way she was moving, their little interlude was going to be over way before it got good. He was as hard as granite, and with the rocking of her hips, he was growing harder by the second.

"Karter." She moaned against his mouth. That single word held so much passion and desire.

Dreamy moved her hands to the back of his head, and their kiss grew hungrier with each lap of their tongues. Karter didn't want to slow things down, but he needed to make sure they were on the same page. By the way she was grinding against him, it was safe to say they wanted the same thing. No doubt she could feel how turned on he was and knew the effect she was having on him.

"Dreamy."

"Don't stop," she breathed. "Don't stop."

Karter repositioned his hands, moving them from her butt to her hips, determined to gain some type of control. Pulling his mouth from hers, he peppered feathery kisses against her cheek, and worked his way down the length of her scented neck. Sliding his hands beneath his shirt that she was wearing, Karter marveled at how soft her skin was as he explored every dip and valley of her womanly curves.

She didn't want to stop, and he wanted more.

Safe to say we're on the same page.

"I need you out of this shirt," he said.

Dreamy sat back slightly, removed her cell phone from the breast pocket, and dropped it in the seat next to them. Without having to unbutton the shirt, Karter helped lift it over her head, then tossed the garment to the floor.

Damn. What a sight.

He slowly raked his eyes over her dark skin and full breasts. "You're absolutely beautiful," he said.

She gave him a timid smile. "Thank you."

Dreamy had a body that demanded attention even when it was covered in clothes. But knowing what she was working with beneath her colorful attire had his shaft hard enough to punch a hole through his pants.

Her breasts were more than a handful, and Karter planned to pay them the attention they deserved. Lowering his head, he swiped his tongue across one pert nipple, and she hissed then moaned when he squeezed the other between his finger and thumb.

Oh yeah, he was going to have fun with her enticing body. He still planned to make good on her screaming his name before she was completely naked. Right now, all that was left was her thong, but soon, it would join the shirt on the floor.

Her arms hung loose around his neck, and she arched her back, giving him better access to her breasts as she whimpered and continued rocking against him. Karter sucked, squeezed, and teased her nipples. Her erotic sounds of pleasure grew louder and more animated with each lap of his tongue, urging him on, making him want to give her as much pleasure as possible.

Wanting to feel more of her, he slid his hand down the front of her body. The little strip of material she was using as panties wasn't much of a barrier to get to what he wanted. He pushed the material to the side and slid his thumb over her clit, adding just enough pressure to make her moans even more intense.

He slid a finger inside of her and then another. "Damn. You're so hot and wet for me."

Dreamy fisted his shirt and held on tight as she rode his hand. "Oh, yes," she breathed. Her head lolled back, and her labored breathing met his ears. "Ka-Karter." She whimpered, her moves growing jerkier as he increased the pace. "I—I . . ."

"Come for me, baby," he crooned, covering her mouth with his as he glided his fingers in and out of her.

Dreamy moaned against his lips, but then ripped her mouth from his. She screamed his name and tightened around his fingers as her release came fast and hard.

"Ohmigod, ohmigod, ohmigod," she murmured over and over again and slumped against him while gasping for air.

Karter placed a lingering kiss against her cheek, then repositioned his hands, moving them to the bottom of her thighs as he prepared to stand. "Let's take part two to the bedroom."

PLEASANTLY WORN OUT, DREAMY LAID HER HEAD AGAINST KARTER's shoulder as he carried her to the other side of the massive basement. She should be embarrassed by her state of dress, or lack thereof, but at the moment, she didn't care. True to his word, he made her scream his name.

Another first.

In her limited sexual experience, Dreamy had never screamed a man's name. Ever. Until tonight. Until Karter.

"Okay, I choose you," she said, still trying to catch her breath after that powerful orgasm. "I don't need to meet Larenz."

Karter laughed and strolled into the guest bedroom, closing the door with his foot. "Good to know. You've made the right decision."

He laid her in the center of the bed and climbed in beside her. When he lowered his head to kiss her, it was slow, tender, and oh so sweet. If this man was trying to make her fall more in like with him, it was working. Dreamy had never been with a man who made her feel so cherished and desired. Sure, Brandon started out that way, but it quickly changed to comfortable and familiar.

Her arm slid around Karter's neck as he nipped at her lower lip, then her top one. She was under no illusion that he was perfect, but she had a feeling that what she was experiencing with him, would be a norm.

"I'm feeling a little underdressed here," she said against his mouth before pulling back slightly. She was very comfortable in her skin, but it was starting to feel a little strange that she was mostly naked while he still had on his clothes. "And you're a little overdressed."

"You think so?" Karter stood and turned on the bedside lamp, giving the room a romantic vibe. "I can remedy that." After locking the bedroom door, he started unbuckling his pants. "You sure about this?" he asked, digging through his pocket and setting his wallet and cell phone on the bedside table. "Because if you're not, I—"

"Take off your clothes," she said. "And do it slowly."

The fantasy Dreamy had during the meeting the other day immediately came to mind. Never in a million years did she think she'd be here with him . . . watching him strip.

Karter's signature crooked grin made an appearance as he shook out of his dress shirt and let it fall to the floor. Next went his white T-shirt, leaving the top half of his body on full display.

If Dreamy thought he looked hot with clothes on, seeing him shirtless stole her breath. Wide chest. Thick biceps. And a six-pack that she'd seen on men only in magazines. The man was built like a damn truck. She marveled at the way his corded muscles contracted with each move he made.

She didn't take her eyes off him as she started to pull the covers up over her legs.

"Don't even think about covering that amazing body," Karter said. His baritone had lowered to a deep, groveling bass. "I want to see you, all of you, while I'm shedding my clothes. Unless of course you want me to stop."

"Don't you dare. Take it off, baby!" She giggled. "I've always wanted to say that."

Laughing, Karter toed off his shoes and unfastened his pants, letting them puddle on the floor.

Wow. This just keeps getting better.

Bracing a hand against the wall, he removed his black socks and added them to the pile of clothes. All the while, Dreamy barely pulled her gaze away from the black boxer briefs and how thick his shaft looked inside of them. But the moment he slid them down his legs, her heart beat a little faster. The throbbing pulse between her thighs was suddenly unbearable, and she couldn't wait to have him inside of her.

"Is this better?" he asked, and crawled onto the bed, coming toward her like a tiger on the prowl.

"Oh, yeah. Much, *much* better," she said on a breath seconds before his mouth covered hers.

As their kiss deepened, her arms tightened around his neck. Between his intoxicating scent and the way his body felt against hers, she could barely think straight. She savored his taste—a combination of chocolate and liquor—while they devoured each other's mouths.

Man, he was a good kisser.

So far, the man could seem to do no wrong in her book. All he did was make her want him even more. Wanting to feel more of him, she slid her hand between their bodies. When she found what she was looking for, Dreamy worked her hand up and down his shaft, rubbing, squeezing, tugging on him until she had him groaning her name.

"Babe," he said, palming her butt as she stroked him faster and harder.

Karter cursed under his breath and gasped for air as he tightened his hold on her. "Damn, that feels good," he said. "Too good, and if I let you keep doing that, you're going to make me come before I'm buried inside of you."

Before Dreamy could respond, Karter eased out of her grasp and had her flat on her back before she could blink. He lowered his head and placed a kiss on her lips, then slowly traced a sensuous path down her neck, lingering at her shoulder blade before going lower.

Everywhere his lips touched, her body heated, and she squirmed and squeezed her thighs together as the sensational ache between them grew more demanding. She almost came undone when he cupped one of her breasts seconds before his tongue swiped over her sensitive nipple, sending a wave of desire plowing through her body.

"Karter . . . that feels . . ." A moan ripped through her before she could get the words out and he moved on, paying the same homage to the other breast.

Goodness, this man.

Dreamy didn't know how much more she could take as she arched into him. She wanted him inside of her, but the way he licked and sucked and teased her nipples almost made it hard to breathe, let alone think straight.

"God, you smell so good and taste even better," he mumbled against her breast. "I'm torn between taking this slow or—"

"We can go slow next time but right now, I want you."

"I want you, too, baby."

He kissed her, then reached over to the bedside table. Fumbling with his wallet, he pulled out a foil package. No surprise that he was prepared. He came across as a man who was always prepared for anything.

"This is nice and all, but it has to go," he said of her thong, and made quick work of sliding it down her legs, taking the fuzzy socks with it. "Now, where was I?"

Karter hovered above her and reclaimed her lips, kissing her passionately as he nudged her legs apart. When the tip of his penis teased at her entrance, it was all she could do not to come right then. Her heart was beating so fast and hard, she was sure it would beat right out of her chest. The man had her so turned on, there was no way she'd last much longer. And when he eased into her, all thoughts ceased.

*Oh yes. Yes. Ye*s, her mind chanted as they moved together, their bodies in perfect sync as Karter set the pace and slowly picked up speed. He seemed to go deeper and harder as he drove in and out of her, and Dreamy's control slipped more with each thrust.

Pleasure swirled inside of her, increasing in intensity like a tropical storm hitting the coast, and her nails dug into his back as she struggled to hang on.

"Karter," she whimpered, her head thrashing back and forth against the pillow as the pressure inside of her increased. She was close. She was so . . . A spine-tingling orgasm roared through her body, sending her world spinning out of control.

Karter was right behind her, groaning her name as he pounded in and out of her like a man possessed before his release took him over the edge of control.

He collapsed on top of her, and his breath was warm against her neck as he panted loudly. "Man, that was . . . incredible." When he started to lift off her, Dreamy held him close.

"Don't move. Not yet." They lay there bound together, each struggling to catch their breaths.

Yeah, that was definitely incredible . . . and intense, Dreamy thought as her breathing slowly went back to normal.

Karter eventually rolled off her and pulled her to his side, placing a kiss on her sweat-slicked forehead. Lying on his chest with her arm across his stomach, Dreamy couldn't think of any place she'd rather be.

"So," Karter started, his voice piercing the quietness in the room, "you still in love with Larenz Tate?"

"Who?" Dreamy feigned ignorance, and smiled when Karter started laughing.

Later for Larenz. There was a new man filling her fantasies, and his name was Karter Redford.

Chapter Twenty

STUFFY MY ASS.

At the restaurant, Karter had referred to himself as a stuffy old workaholic. Dreamy understood why he might've added the "old" part since he was a few years older than her, and maybe even the workaholic title. However, she wasn't sure why he referred to himself as stuffy. From what she'd just experienced with him, there was nothing stuffy about the man. Better adjectives would include *exciting*, *creative*, *generous*, and *attentive*, and she could come up with a host of others if she weren't exhausted.

Two more rounds of the most incredible sex she'd ever experienced, and she didn't think she'd ever be able to move. The intense connection that she felt for him defied logic, and she was so glad she'd said yes to dinner. Otherwise, she might've missed out on this incredible man.

Too spent to do much else, Dreamy lay there staring up at the wood ceiling while Karter was in the bathroom disposing of the condom. Considering it was almost two in the morning, it was safe to say that she wasn't going home tonight. Though she had texted

Jordyn a few hours ago, telling her not to wait up, she should probably tell her that she'd see her in the morning.

She just had to drag herself out of bed and find her phone.
Maybe later, she thought, and her eyes drifted closed. Seconds later,
they reopened when Karter exited the bathroom.

"Do you mind grabbing my phone before you get back into
bed?" she asked.

"Sure. Do you need anything else?"

"No, that's it."

He went back to the bathroom and emerged wearing a white
terry cloth robe, then left the room. When he returned, not only
did he have her cell, but he also had the shirt she'd been wearing as
well as bottles of water.

He handed her the phone, and Dreamy saw that she had a couple of text messages. One from Jordyn checking to make sure she
was all right, and the other from . . . Brandon?

She hadn't heard from him since the night of his party, except
for when he'd texted her the next morning. He told her to stop by
and pick up a few things she had left at his place. She texted back and
told him to throw whatever it was in a dumpster and jump in after
it. Dreamy hadn't heard from him since.

So why was he reaching out now? She debated deleting the message without reading it first, but went ahead and skimmed it.

Thinking about you. Give me a call.

She cursed under her breath, and started typing, *Go to hell*, but
stopped short of sending the text. Instead, she wouldn't give him
the satisfaction of responding. After deleting the words, she blocked
his number.

Was a text from Brandon the universe's way of reminding her
about the vow she had made to herself? She was supposed to be

staying away from men and focusing on herself. Not only did she break the vow, she obliterated it by falling for someone like Karter.

It had been heartbreaking when Brandon kicked her to the curb, but Dreamy had gotten over him fairly quickly. But with Karter? What she felt for him was so much more intense than anything she ever felt for Brandon. That made a relationship with Karter that much more dangerous.

Were they moving too fast?

Would he turn out to be a jerk like Brandon?

Or worse, would he make her fall in love with him, then dump her?

"Dreamy?"

Dreamy startled, and her head jerked up to meet Karter's concerned eyes. "Huh?"

"Everything okay?" He slipped off the robe and tossed it on the bench at the foot of the bed. All the while his attention stayed on her.

Her heart leaped at the sight of his naked body. The man's physique was truly a work of art.

With her gaze following him back to the bed, she said, "No, everything is perfect." *You're perfect*, she wanted to add, but didn't. She had to figure out how to continue getting to know Karter without totally losing herself in the process.

For now, she would just enjoy the time they had together.

Dreamy shot off a quick text to Jordyn, who was probably still up studying, and then she remembered to check the lottery numbers. The Powerball jackpot was up to $230 million, more than enough to take care of her family for the rest of their lives and start the nonprofit.

Dreamy sighed after a quick Google search revealed that they didn't even get one number. She tried not to let that fact get her down, but hopelessness lodged in her chest. She needed a break.

Her family needed a break. Even with the raise that Gordon gave her, things were still tight.

Don't give up. Your day is coming. She just had to hang on to that thought. *My day is coming.*

Disappointed, Dreamy set the phone on the bedside table closest to her.

She needed a win. Her family needed a win.

"You sure you're okay?" Karter asked again.

She nodded, refusing to let anything get her down. "I'm here with you. What more could a girl want?"

After one of the best dates she'd ever had, and sex that had her toes curling, she had nothing to be down about. Everything always worked itself out. She just had to stay positive. Stay encouraged.

"Since you're still awake, we can head upstairs and sleep in my bedroom if you'd like. The bed is bigger and it would probably be more comfortable."

"Unless that's what you prefer, but I'm fine here. This mattress feels like I'm stretched out on a fluffy cloud, and it's perfectly comfortable." Truth was, she didn't think her bone-weary legs would carry her up all of the stairs.

"Wherever you are works for me."

Karter sat on the edge of the bed and opened one of the bottles of water and passed it to Dreamy.

She didn't realize how thirsty she was until she demolished three-quarters of it before handing the bottle back to Karter. Apparently, he was just as thirsty since he had already drained his.

After turning off the lamp on the bedside table and plunging the room into darkness, he wrapped his strong, hard body around her. Dreamy snuggled closer, laying her head on his chest and her arm across his waist.

It had been a long time since she'd shared a bed with a man, especially all night. She kind of liked it. No, actually, she loved it, and for the first time in a long time, she felt like she was right where she was supposed to be.

"Karter?"

"Yeah, baby," he said, and his sleep-filled voice was deep and sexy.

"Just so you know, I don't usually . . . I'm not easy. Sleeping with a man on the first date is not something I normally do."

"I didn't think you did, and in case you're wondering, this was not a one-night stand or a one and done, or whatever the hell people call it these days."

"Then what was it?" she asked, though she had already decided that it wasn't a one-night stand. What they shared had been spectacular and special. It felt . . . real. It felt . . . permanent.

There was a long hesitation before he spoke again. "This is you and me dating."

Dreamy couldn't stop the grin from spreading across her face. She didn't know what she expected him to say, but that wasn't it. They had moved faster than she was accustomed to, but as long as their connection felt right, she planned to roll with whatever came next.

"That would make me your girlfriend. Are you sure you're ready for that type of commitment?"

"Considering I ruined a couple's meal tonight, almost burned off my arm, and might've destroyed your cousin's dress, I think I should be asking you that instead. Do you think you're ready?"

"Yes," Dreamy said without a second thought. "But if Morgan wasn't able to fix Jordyn's dress, you better get ready to deal with your girlfriend's cousin."

Karter placed a lingering kiss on her forehead. "I'm up for any challenge when it comes to you."

"Yeah, just keep telling yourself that."

DREAMY SLOWLY OPENED HER EYES, SQUINTING AGAINST THE sunlight peeking through the slats of the blinds covering the only window in the bedroom. She wasn't sure what time it was, but whatever the time, it was too early to be awake on a Sunday.

Without turning to see if Karter was still asleep, she patted her hand on the mattress where he should've been. Cold. Meaning he'd probably been up for a while.

Part of her wanted to get up and go in search of him. The other part, though, wanted to lie there and pretend she had the luxury of doing absolutely nothing for the rest of the day.

That would be nice.

Normally an early riser, she just didn't have it in her to move. Her body, and every muscle attached to it, was wonderfully worn out, and she wasn't sure if she could move even if she wanted to.

But her bladder was making the decision for her.

Dreamy climbed out of bed and slipped into the robe that Karter had left on the bench. Rubbing her eyes and yawning, she stumbled to the attached bathroom. Maybe she could get a little more sleep before she had Karter take her home.

Instead of turning on the light, she let the sunlight streaming through the rectangular windows near the ceiling guide her way. She quickly relieved herself and padded to the sink. It wasn't until she washed her hands that she flipped on the overhead lights and gasped.

Her hair, resembling an eagle's nest, was going to be a pain to comb through. Long strands stuck out every which way, while the right side of her hair was matted down.

She quickly ran her fingers through it, trying to make it look halfway decent. Normally, after getting it done at the salon, she'd wrap it or braid it before going to sleep to keep it from tangling.

Last night—actually this morning—she had been too exhausted to even think about her hair.

The one time I need a wig . . . Guess it'll be a ponytail kind of day.

As Dreamy stood in front of the mirror, trying to wrangle her hair, she marveled at the luxury of the space. Like everything else in the house, the bathroom was large and painted in a soft yellow. The highlight was the soaker tub for two. If she had time, she wouldn't mind going for a swim in it, but she feared she'd love it too much.

Even planning to win the lottery, Dreamy struggled to imagine what it would be like to live in luxury. Would money change her? Would she become a snob and start treating people like second-class citizens?

God, she hoped not. Karter and Morgan were born into wealth, and they didn't act as if they were better than everyone else. Hopefully, that would be the same for her.

"I won't change," she mumbled to herself.

Once her hair looked halfway decent, she glanced to her right, near the other sink, surprised to see a colorful cosmetic bag. A handwritten note was attached to it.

Thought you'd probably need some of these items. Morgan.
PS I had some clothes dropped off for you.
If you're reading this note, they should be nearby.

Dreamy glanced around the bathroom but didn't see any clothes.

She read the rest of the note.

PPS The dress is fixed. Yay! It'll be back from the cleaners before you leave. Now your cousin won't kill you.
Oh, that means I saved your life! You're welcome. Xoxo

Dreamy laughed and reread the last part of the note again.

Morgan had the dress cleaned? How? When? What the hell time was it anyway?

Dreamy padded back to the bedroom and glanced at the clock that was on Karter's side of the bed.

Eight fifteen.

How was it possible that she found a cleaners that opened so early in the morning?

She turned to go back into the bathroom, but pulled up short when she spotted a shopping bag. The name of a high-end store was stamped on the front of it.

She walked across the room, assuming those were the clothes that Morgan mentioned. Excitement bubbled inside of her as she started pulling items out. An orange T-shirt with Boss Lady stamped on the front of it immediately caught her attention.

"Aww, this is too cute and perfect."

Next were art deco leggings that were made with her in mind and contained every color under the sun.

As Dreamy kept digging through the bag, she also found underwear. All of the items still had the tags on them, and her eyes bugged out at the prices.

Good Lord. There was no way she could afford this stuff.

At the bottom of the bag was a box. *Converse.* Another wave of excitement charged through her body as she hurried and opened the narrow box.

"Un-frickin'-believable," she murmured, holding up the orange Chucks. And they were the right size too.

"I see you found the clothes," Karter said as he entered the bedroom with a tray of food. He nudged the door closed and strolled over to the bench at the foot of the bed.

Dressed in a blue tank top that fit loose on his body but showed off his large biceps and a pair of running shorts and shoes, he appeared more relaxed than she'd ever seen him.

"Who are you people?" Dreamy asked, holding up the shoes in one hand and the clothes in the other. "How in the world did you guys accomplish this before eight a.m.?"

"I can't take credit. Morgan is a master shopper, and her connections stem all the way to Paris. When she says she knows people? She *really* does."

"So your sister did all of this here, fixed a dress, and is having it dry cleaned all before eight a.m.?"

Karter shrugged. "I guess she's like the Army, does more before eight a.m. than most people do all day."

"Funny, but seriously. This is too much. I just hoped the dress could be fixed. I didn't expect her to do all of this." Dreamy looked at everything again before returning her attention to Karter, who moved the tray from the bench to the bed.

"And you . . ." she started, eyeing all of the food, coffee, and orange juice. "I knew you were special, but since we've met, you've treated me . . ."

She didn't have the words. The last twenty-four hours felt like a dream. A beautiful, magnificent, unbelievable dream.

"I know you guys have money, but I guess I just didn't realize just how much . . . influence you have with money."

"It's not just about having money, Dreamy. It's also about building relationships. You can have all the money in the world, but if you don't have connections and strong relationships, all you have is . . . money. Money alone is not always enough."

She snorted. "Only a rich person would say something like that. Trust me, if I had money, it would be enough."

He pulled her into his arms, and she wrapped her arms around his midsection before they shared a sweet kiss.

"Okay, if I had money and you, that would be enough."

Karter laughed. "Glad I made the cut. Now, let's eat."

He led her to the bed and they climbed on, each sitting on either side of the tray.

Dreamy shook her head. "This looks amazing." She bit into one of the croissants, and her attention drifted back over to the clothes. "I don't know how I'll ever be able to repay Morgan for all she did."

Karter's brows dipped into a severe V. "She would never take your money." When Dreamy started to speak, he lifted his hands to stop her. "Not because you and I are dating, but because she's one of the most generous people you'll ever meet. She loves doing stuff like this, especially for those she likes. Besides, being a stylist is basically in her blood."

"Still . . ." Dreamy said, looking at the items. "Not only did she get the sizes right, she also nailed my color scheme."

"I might've told her you like bright colors, but she figured out everything else herself. I'm telling you, next to my mother, she's a super shopper. Add that to her fashion expertise, and you have a woman who could dress anyone and nail it on the first try."

"And yet, she doesn't know what she wants to do with her life. Interesting."

"It is, isn't it?" Karter said.

As they ate, Dreamy thought about him and his family, and how much she enjoyed meeting them. They were turning out to be nothing like she expected.

"You probably guessed this, and don't take this the wrong way, but I always thought most rich people were snotty, rude, and acted as if they're better than everyone else," she said.

Karter brushed back a strand of her hair and wrapped it around his finger. "Some are, and I know a few of them, but I've learned that you can't generalize people like that. I know it suits many people, but it would be like assuming every secretary only wants to be a secretary, and we both know that's not true. Because soon, you're going to be a badass boss lady running a nonprofit that's going to change the life of many women."

Dreamy nodded. "Good point, and that's true. No more assuming."

"You have nice hair. I always thought women wore wigs because something was wrong with their hair or that they didn't have hair. That's not the case with you."

"Well, you know what they say about assuming," she cracked.

Karter grinned at her. "I do, and though you look sexy as hell in your wigs, I prefer your natural hair. But," he said quickly when she started to speak, "that's not to say you shouldn't wear wigs. I have no problem with them. Hell, I even chase them down when I have to, but I'm just saying I like being able to run my fingers through your hair."

Dreamy's eyes drifted closed as he massaged her scalp. "That feels so good. If you keep that up, I might want you to massage a few other areas on my body."

"Hmm . . . I love it when you talk dirty."

Dreamy sputtered a laugh and looked at him. "How was that talking dirty? I was talking about massages."

Karter moved the tray and inched closer to her. "Well, what I heard is that you wanted to pick up where we left off a few hours ago."

"Well, we need to get your hearing checked, old man."

"Old man? I'll show you who's an old man."

Before Dreamy could think her next thought, Karter had her flat on her back and had covered her body with his. Old man . . . had she said 'old man'? What she should've said was hot, sexy, virile man who already knew her body better than she did.

How the heck was she going to protect her heart when he was turning out to be everything she'd ever wanted in a man?

Don't think. Just go with the flow.

Chapter Twenty-One

"ARE YOU SURE YOU DON'T WANT TO COME IN?" DREAMY ASKED when Karter walked her to the door of her house.

"I would love to, but it's already hard leaving you here when what I really want is for you to spend another night with me."

The night turned into day, and they ended up spending much of the time lounging around in his bed and hanging out on the back deck playing with Melvin. Well, she played with Mel-Mel while Karter just looked at him. Actually, now that Dreamy thought about it, Melvin looked at his human in much the same way. It was as if they were still feeling each other out.

All Dreamy knew was that the time with them had turned out to be one of the most relaxing weekends she'd ever had. One night and a day with Karter, and she was hooked.

Holding the dress and shoes in one hand, Dreamy wrapped her other arm around his waist and reached up on tiptoe to kiss him. "I'll see you Tuesday evening, right?" He had agreed to help her more on her business plan. Dreamy just hoped they'd be able to focus on work. It was becoming clear that it was impossible for them to keep their hands off each other.

"Yeah, but that's, like, two days away. What am I going to do with myself until then?" he asked, frowning as if he really didn't know.

"Oh, I don't know. Maybe close a million-dollar deal. Help a small business turn a profit for the first time since they opened their doors. Or, maybe you can take another couple of days off because rumor has it, you work too much."

"Does that mean if I take some time off, you'll go away with me for a few days?"

Dreamy leaned back to look at him. "I said *you* should take a few days off. I didn't say anything about traveling or me joining you. Besides, I have to work and I have classes."

He placed a kiss on her forehead. "Then I guess there's only one thing for me to do—go to work."

Unlike him, she wasn't in the position to drop everything and traipse around the country. Her responsibilities didn't allow for much free time, at least not for traveling. But there was nothing more she wanted than to spend more time with him.

"Maybe we can plan to get away after midterms," she said.

"I'd like that. Give me the dates, and I'll come up with some ideas. But for now, go on in, and I'll talk to you later." Karter kissed her lips and headed back to his car.

Dreamy unlocked the door and practically floated into the house. She set her bag and Jordyn's dress on the sofa, and the smell of barbecue met her nose, reminding her that she had missed family dinner. It was something their grandmother had started when they were kids. It got a little hard to pull off as they grew up and had busier schedules, but Dreamy and Jordyn tried to keep the tradition going whenever possible.

Dreamy walked farther into the house, and her cousin was right where she thought she'd be—at the kitchen table with books and papers spread out.

"Hey, cuz," she said. "I would say I'm surprised you're still up, but I'm not."

Jordyn smirked and leaned back in her seat with her arms folded across her chest. "Well, well, well, look who decided to come home. You're looking awfully cute in your little outfit, and I'm really feeling those orange Chucks."

"They're cute, aren't they? You're welcome to borrow them sometime." She told her cousin about Morgan and the clothes, but left out the part about the dress debacle. "Thanks again for letting me borrow your dress. It's been cleaned and ready for your big party."

"Thanks, and I trust that you got your groove back and are well lubricated now."

Dreamy scrunched up her face. "Why'd you have to say it like that? You make something so beautiful between Karter and me sound so . . . so . . . *something*. Let's just say I had the most amazing time of my life, and I think I'm in love."

Jordyn bolted forward in her seat. "What?" she yelled. "Are you kidding me right now?"

"Calm down. Don't get your law briefs in a bunch, I'm kidding." Dreamy sat across the table from her. "I'm not in love, but I already know that Karter would be an easy man to fall in love with."

"Dreamy . . ."

"I know, I know. We just met, and it's too soon. And don't worry, I'm going into this relationship with my eyes wide open, and I'll be careful. Right now, we're just . . . dating."

"Dating?" Jordyn wasn't currently giving her the *are you serious?* look, but that one word was spoken with enough skepticism to let Dreamy know exactly what her cousin thought of the idea.

"He asked me to go steady with him."

Jordyn raised her eyebrows. "Go steady? Damn, exactly how old is this dude?"

Dreamy snorted. "He didn't really say that, but we are officially dating."

"Wow, after one night. Impressive. You must've put it on him real good."

Dreamy picked up a pen and slowly twirled it between her fingers. That was the problem about sleeping with a guy on the first date. She couldn't be a hundred percent sure if Karter wanted to be with her because he enjoyed hanging out together, or if it had everything to do with the sex. Which was mind-blowing. There was no doubt that they had chemistry between the sheets, but Dreamy wanted to believe they had more than that going for them.

"I have to say. It hasn't gone unnoticed that you have a gift of attracting men who are wealthy," Jordyn said as she started stacking her books on the table.

"Brandon wasn't wealthy," Dreamy corrected. Her ex had been financially stable, but nowhere near the same level as Karter.

"Well, like your mom used to say. It's just as easy to fall in love with a rich man as it—"

"Let's not bring her into this conversation."

"Actually, Tarrah called here looking for you. She said you weren't answering your phone. Or you were just screening her calls."

True on both accounts.

"What did you tell her?"

"I told her you weren't here, and that I wasn't sure when you'd be home. Of course, she asked where you were, and of course I told her that wasn't her business."

Dreamy smiled. She could always count on her cousin to keep it real and have her back. Dreamy would've responded the same way even though she tried to be respectful. Sometimes that was hard. Tarrah had a way of irritating a person with just a few words.

"I hate to ask, because I think you should do whatever you feel, but what happened to your no-dating vow? And please tell me that you're not dating Karter because he has money."

"Of course not! I can't believe you'd even think I—"

"I don't, but I just wanted to make sure he didn't lure you in by buying you expensive clothes, jewelry, or a car or something."

"I like him, Jordyn. I *really* like him, and yes, falling for him this fast is scary. But he's kind, funny, easy to talk to, and . . . I *really* like him."

"Yeah, you said that, but I seem to remember you saying that about a few men you've dated."

"I didn't use that many *reallys* when I said it with the other guys."

Jordyn nodded. "True." She stood and strolled over to the freezer and pulled out a small carton of salted caramel brownie ice cream and grabbed a spoon. "Want some?"

"No, thanks."

"For the record, I like Karter," Jordyn said when she reclaimed her seat. "He made a good impression on me, and I've only heard good things about KR Ventures."

Dreamy listened as Jordyn told her what she knew about Karter's company. Not only was their law firm partnering with KR Ventures, but one of her co-workers was a friend of Karter's. Or at least claimed to be. They only had great things to say about him, his firm, and the numerous charities he donated to.

"For what it's worth, I hope things work out between you two. You deserve someone who is going to cherish you, and he might be that guy."

"Thanks, Jay. We both do." Her cousin was seriously focused

on becoming a lawyer, and Dreamy couldn't remember the last time Jordyn had gone on a date.

"Welcome home, Dreamboat," Gramps said when he shuffled into the kitchen.

Dreamy had to do a double take to make sure she wasn't seeing things. "Gramps, why are you wearing one of my wigs? One of my good wigs at that."

He stopped and patted around on his head. "Oh, I forgot about this thing. No wonder it was getting hot in here," he said, taking it off and rubbing his hand over his low-cut salt-and-pepper hair.

"That still doesn't explain why you had it on."

"You sure you want to know?" Jordyn mumbled loud enough for only Dreamy to hear.

That was a good point. She probably didn't want to know, but she was definitely curious.

"I wanted to give it to my lady friend the next time she came over."

"Well, that's not going to happen because it's mine." Dreamy stood and grabbed it from him, thinking that she might have to start locking her bedroom door. "That still doesn't explain why you were wearing it."

Gramps frowned and looked at her as if she were the one who wasn't making sense. "I had it on so I wouldn't forget to give it to her. What's wrong with you? Did that young man of yours get you drunk or something?"

Dreamy glanced at Jordyn, wondering if she had somehow missed something in the conversation. Jordyn smirked and shook her head while she continued eating her ice cream.

"That reminds me," their grandfather continued. "I want to talk to your young man. What's his name again—Karter?"

Wow, he could barely remember their names, yet he remembered Karter's after meeting him only once.

"Why do you want to talk to him?" Dreamy asked.

"Oh, this should be good," Jordyn said on a laugh.

"Because I need to lay down the law. I want him to know what'll happen to him if he makes you cry the way that last jive turkey did."

Again, Dreamy and her cousin shared a look. They thought with some of their grandfather's antics that he was losing his mind. While other times, he made perfect sense. Like now. Well, except for the "jive turkey" part. Dreamy wasn't sure what that even meant.

She pulled out her cell phone to google it.

Her grandfather knew that she was no longer dating Brandon, but Dreamy hadn't realized that he knew that she had cried over the loser.

She shouldn't be surprised. Gramps had always been her hero, attuned to how she was feeling. He was the only man in her life growing up, and he'd been good at making her feel valued . . . treasured, especially after her mother took off. The perfect gentleman to her grandmother, he expected Dreamy and Jordyn to be treated the same. Dreamy couldn't have asked for a better example of what it looked like when a man truly loved a woman.

"Did you know *jive turkey* is a real expression?" she asked Jordyn.

"Never really thought about it. I assumed it was something Gramps made up."

"Well, if he did, it made it to the dictionary . . . or at least Google."

"Of course it's a real thing," their grandfather said, shaking his head. "You kids today . . ."

"Okay, I'll ask Karter to come by sometime," Dreamy said. "Maybe I'll cook dinner for you all. Then you can—"

"But you can't cook," Jordyn pointed out.

"I can cook," Dreamy defended, and tried to ignore the look her cousin gave her. "Okay, I do all right. You'll see, it'll be fine. Oh, by the way, Gramps, we didn't win the Powerball last night."

He was in the kitchen, leaning against the counter with a glass of orange juice in his hand. "I figured as much since the delivery people didn't drop off my hot tub yet."

"You didn't!" Dreamy yelled, and was out of her seat. "Gramps, you can't go around buying—"

"I didn't, but the day after we win, I'm buying one."

Gramps didn't spend much money, and she should've known that he was messing with her. But a hot tub? She didn't even know he'd ever thought about one.

"You probably shouldn't get one in this neighborhood," Dreamy said. "Unless you want to step outside one day and see your neighbors partying in it."

"She's got a point, Gramps." Jordyn finished off her ice cream and washed the spoon. Returning to the table, she grabbed her backpack. "A hot tub in this neighborhood probably wouldn't be a good idea."

"Actually, maybe we all should sit down one day and discuss how we want to spend the money when we win," Dreamy suggested.

"Well, that's my cue. I'm going to bed." Jordyn turned to leave, but stopped. "Oh, and while you guys are making a list, add a new dryer to it. Ours died this morning."

"Ah, man. Not again. If one more thing breaks down . . ." Dreamy let the words trail off. At this point, they barely had enough to cover their basic living expenses. Neither of them could afford to buy a new dryer, along with a roof, living room furniture, as well as other items on the list of things that needed replacing.

"We won't worry about a new dryer right now," Jordyn said on her way out of the dining area. "I took the clothes to the laundromat and finished the laundry twice as fast as I would've if I washed and dried everything here. So, no worries."

Dreamy propped her elbows on the table and rubbed her temples. Something had to give soon. Their repair list was building, but their finances were staying the same. Her little raise wouldn't put a dent in anything. And though Jordyn had a job waiting for her after graduation, that was months away.

Come on, Powerball! We need a win!

Chapter Twenty-Two

THE FOLLOWING SATURDAY, KARTER WAS ON HIS WAY TO PICK Dreamy up for another date, and as he drove slowly through her neighborhood, his respect for her grew. Her positive and outgoing nature was a stark contrast to the depressed state of the community she lived in.

A wave of disappointment crawled through him. The sun might've been shining bright, but it was as if a storm cloud hung low over the area. Run-down, dingy, and boarded-up houses lined each side of the street, and dirt instead of grass made up their yards. Cars propped up on cinder blocks with missing tires sat in a few driveways, causing even more of an eyesore.

He understood that most families in the area probably only had money for the bare necessities, but it bothered him that people had to live like this. And when children had to go without, whether it be food or sporting equipment, it broke his heart. Too many times he'd taken for granted how blessed he and his siblings had been to grow up in a decent neighborhood with more than they could've ever needed. That was one of several reasons why he constantly donated to organizations that provided assistance to low-income families and communities. He also volunteered whenever he could. But no matter how much money he contributed, or time he invested, it never seemed to be enough.

Karter pulled in front of Dreamy's house, which looked as distressed as the other homes on the block, except hers had a few blooming flowers lining the front of the house. The pop of color was just enough to make the place stand out from the rest. Still, it was clear the structure needed some repairs.

When Karter climbed out of his vehicle, a kid who looked to be about ten rolled up on his bike.

"Hey, man. Give me ten bucks, and I'll keep an eye on your ride for you," the boy said, checking out the vehicle as if searching for something. "And for twenty, I'll even wash the windshield."

Karter dug his money clip from the front pocket of his jeans as he peeped a squeegee, spray bottle, and a rag hanging from the back of the kid's bike. The young man reminded Karter a little of himself at that age. Despite growing up in a household where money was in abundance, he had always wanted to make his own cash. Be his own man, as his grandfather would often say. Clearly, this boy was of the same mindset.

Karter removed a bill from the platinum money clip and held it up between his index and middle fingers. "I'll give you fifty if you clean the windshield *and* make sure no one but you touches my car."

The kid narrowed his eyes. "Let me see it first," he said skeptically. "I need to make sure it ain't counterfeit. If it is—"

"It's real." Karter handed it over, and the boy held it up to the sunlight and inspected it. "You can trust me," Karter said with amusement and stuffed the rest of the cash back into his pocket.

"Nah, man. I only trust God, but this looks legit. You got a deal." The boy shoved the money into the front pocket of his ripped jeans and climbed off his bike. He rolled it over to the sidewalk, proceeded to unload his window-washing equipment, and glanced at Karter. "You only get an hour. So you betta make it quick. And hopefully you ain't here to see Jordyn, 'cause she's mine."

Karter chuckled. "Got it, and don't worry. I have my eyes on Dreamy."

The kid nodded and looked at Karter with a little more respect. "She's cool people, too, but good luck with that. She ain't really into flashy dudes," he said with all seriousness and jerked his head to the Maserati.

"Is that right," Karter smirked. "I guess I need to tone it down a little, huh?"

"Nah, man. You gotta be who you are. Just be nice to her, and she'll probably give you a chance."

Karter was laughing to himself when he rang Dreamy's doorbell and was surprised to hear a dog barking. But the moment the door opened, all thoughts of kids and dogs flew from his mind. He never thought much about a woman's attire, but he found himself always looking forward to Dreamy's outfits. As usual, she didn't disappoint. Her flowery off-the-shoulder blouse and white shorts that stopped midthigh resembled her personality, and he smiled.

"Hey, beautiful," he said, and reached for her.

Dreamy wrapped her arms around his neck and planted a kiss on his lips. "Hey yourself," she said before releasing him and stepping back.

Karter glanced down and frowned. "Melvin?" The dog stood next to Dreamy's legs as if she were his owner, and not Karter. "What's he doing here?"

Melvin barked a greeting, then looked between him and Dreamy before trotting out onto the front stoop. Karter then noticed the leash, which explained why the dog hadn't taken off the moment the door opened.

Dreamy propped her hand on her hip, still gripping the leash.

"If you're asking me that, that means you have no idea that Morgan asked if I'd like to dog sit Melvin today. How is it that you didn't know that he wasn't at home?"

Surprise charged through Karter as he tried remembering the last time he'd seen his puppy. "In my defense, I slept at the office last night. And I worked late the two days before. I've barely been home."

"So why do you have a dog?"

He sighed and ran his hand over his head. "Remember, I didn't ask for him. He was a gift."

"Yeah, yeah, yeah, but you should be cherishing this gift. He's amazing and well behaved for a puppy. But anyway, we're all going to have fun today."

Dreamy handed Karter Melvin's leash, and the dog looked back at him, frowning. At least it appeared he was frowning.

Once Dreamy grabbed her large, colorful bag from the living room, she locked the front door. Looping her arm through Karter's, she led them down the walkway.

"If I knew Melvin was going to crash our date, I would've brought a different car," Karter said. Even though all of his cars were luxury, he would've at least brought the least flashy one.

"That's okay. Melvin's not particular about what he rides in," she said with a straight face, then nodded toward the kid watching his car.

The boy was standing on the curb with his chest poked out and his arms crossed, looking as if he really were guarding the vehicle.

"I see you've met Cash. How much money did he take you for?" she asked.

"Enough to share with another couple of kids," Karter murmured, and Dreamy burst out laughing.

"Don't feel bad. He's been getting his hustle on in this neighborhood since he was four. His savings account could probably rival yours because, according to his father, he saves most of what he makes. He's a hard worker and doesn't play about his money, hence the nickname, Cash."

"Sounds like someone I'd want working for me. Well, maybe after he's of legal age."

When they reached the car, Dreamy said, "What's up, Cash? I see you're out here working."

"You know how it is. I have to handle my business. You out, man?" the boy said to Karter.

"Yeah, thanks a lot for your help." He shook his hand. "I'll probably be coming around often. So hopefully, you'll be available to look after my ride from time to time."

Cash nodded. "Yeah, I got you. The next time is on the house since you're a friend of Dreamy's. Peace out." He flashed them deuces and rode away.

Karter couldn't hold back a grin. "I like him."

"Me too, and you better believe he'll be out here to watch your car the next time you show up."

"I look forward to it."

Forty-five minutes later, they arrived at a city park. What surprised Karter was the row of food trucks lining the edge of the parking lot, and there was a ton of activity everywhere he looked. People were out enjoying the beautiful weather, picnicking, jogging, and tossing balls and Frisbees. This was what he missed while working most weekends, but that was going to change.

"I figured we'd grab some grub from the food trucks, then find a spot to eat," Dreamy said.

"Now I know why Nana insisted I load a couple of beach chairs in my trunk. I take it she knew your plan?"

"Oh, I might've mentioned my date idea to Morgan, who probably shared parts of it with Nana."

Karter loved that two of the most important women in his life were as taken with Dreamy as he was. Neither had been able to stop talking about her since the day she'd stayed the night. A night that he wouldn't soon forget.

They climbed out of the vehicle and grabbed everything they'd brought, and a calmness settled inside of Karter. This moment with Dreamy and Melvin felt so . . . normal, as if they hung out together all the time. He'd been looking forward to the date. Not just because he was getting a chance to get to know Dreamy better, but also because he was doing something other than working.

"Are you sure it's a good idea to bring him out here with all of these people?" Karter asked as he held Dreamy's hand and they headed toward the food trucks.

The last thing he wanted was for Melvin to chase after some of the kids who were running around screaming and having a good time.

"I'm positive. There are plenty of dogs out here." Dreamy nodded to an area where a couple of families were picnicking and their dogs were in the mix. "I figured after we get our food, we'll walk to the other side of the park, where it's a little less congested."

"Sounds like a plan. By the way, I love holding your hand," he said, sounding like a kid on his first date. He kissed the back of her hand and gazed down at her.

Dreamy's features were animated as she grinned at him. "I feel the same way. Now, what are you craving?"

"You," he said simply. "Only you."

"Food. I'm talking about food here," she said on a laugh. "There's burgers, pizza, barbecue, and my all-time favorite—tacos—to choose from."

"Well, tacos are something else we have in common."

"Excellent. My favorite taco truck is here," she said, steering him to the left.

Karter chuckled when he realized where they were headed.

John and Lorraine's truck, Taco Grub, was at the end of the row. Instead of telling Dreamy that he had just invested in their business, he said, "Good choice. I know the owners of that one."

"Even better. Maybe they'll give us a discount. I'm all about saving a couple of bucks."

Karter shook his head with a small smile. "You do know that I'd be happy to pay, right?"

"No way, I'm buying. This was my idea, so it's my treat." When he started to speak, she cut him off. "This is nonnegotiable. So don't even bother telling me why I should let you pay."

Her tone left no room for discussion, and Karter didn't bother, but this was a first for him. He'd never had a woman pay for a date, and it was a bit humbling and touching at the same time.

"Oh my goodness, Karter," Lorraine said when they stepped up to the window. "John, look who's here. What a pleasant surprise."

Karter chuckled, and he didn't miss the way Lorraine's eyes sparkled and her smile grew larger when she glanced from him to Dreamy. He greeted her husband and quickly made introductions. The line wasn't long, but there were a couple of people behind them, probably as hungry as he was.

"Okay, what can I get you two?" Lorraine asked.

They placed their order of fish tacos along with nachos with queso and salsa on the side. Dreamy, who he was quickly learning enjoyed sweets, also ordered churro bites. When it came time to pay, Lorraine wouldn't accept Dreamy's money, no matter how much she insisted. Dreamy eventually conceded, but left a sizable tip in the tip jar.

"You must know that couple very well," she said when they walked away. "I can't believe they gave us all of this food for free."

"That happens sometimes," was all Karter said as they hiked across the park. Seemed they'd walked a mile before Dreamy settled on a spot. It was the perfect day for a picnic, and they had lucked out and found an empty table in the shade near a couple of trees.

Dreamy had thought of everything, including a plastic red-and-white-checkered tablecloth that she pulled from her bag, along with bottles of water that had chunks of ice in them.

"Looks like you really planned it all out," he said, looping Melvin's leash around the leg of the table.

"I tried to think of everything we'd probably need. We'll see if I forgot anything," she said absently as she laid the food out on the table along with a bottle of hand sanitizer.

After taking care of Melvin's food and water, Karter and Dreamy sat down to eat. They talked a little about their morning, and Karter filled her in on why he'd had to put in long hours over the last few days. Hearing himself give the reasons out loud seemed lame even to him. Had Dreamy been available those days, he was pretty sure he would've found a way to spend time with her. Since she hadn't been, he'd poured himself into work.

As they ate and chatted about anything and everything, Karter realized he wanted more of this. The day was peaceful, and just for a little while, he could forget about all of his responsibilities. In addition to that, it was easy to talk to Dreamy without feeling like he had to fill any awkward silences.

"This was a great idea," he said. "Thanks for planning the day."

She graced him with a smile, then wrapped an arm around his shoulder and pulled him close. "Thanks for taking the day off and spending it with me."

"There's no other place I'd rather be."

Karter slid his arm around her waist and lowered his mouth to hers. He'd been thinking about kissing her ever since the other night, when they met up at the community center again to work more on her proposal. Like then, their kiss was hot and passionate, just like she was.

Her soft lips moved against his as their tongues tangled and a burning desire for more of her soared through his body. He couldn't get enough of this woman and had a feeling that kissing Dreamy was going to become one of his favorite pastimes.

Melvin's excessive barking interrupted them, and Karter reluctantly eased his mouth from Dreamy's and glanced down at the dog.

"Looks like he wants to run around with those squirrels over there," Dreamy said, pointing at the two rodents that were sniffing around a few yards from where they were sitting. "Actually, he's probably getting a little tired of sitting around with us." She stood and untied the dog's leash from the table. "Can you walk him around a minute while I clean up?"

"Sure."

Karter stood and reached for the leash, but before he grabbed it, Melvin jerked away and took off. He flew across the grass with his leash trailing behind him.

"Oh no, Melvin!" Dreamy gasped and took off in a sprint. "Stop! Get back here!"

Karter cursed under his breath and ran after them. It was like déjà vu from when they had chased after Dreamy's wig. One thing was for sure—hanging out with her forced him to get in a workout.

"I'll cut him off over there!" he yelled, and ran to the right in the direction that Melvin went. But the damn dog veered to the left and seemed to pick up speed.

Even though the squirrels had scampered up a tree, that didn't stop the puppy from running around. If Karter didn't know any better, he'd think Melvin was screwing with them. Thankfully, there weren't people around. He didn't know Melvin well enough to know what he'd do if there were.

"Stop!" Dreamy was still yelling, but Melvin seemed to be having the time of his life running them in circles. He clearly thought they were playing a game. Just when Karter was close enough to step on the leash, he stumbled, barely catching himself before face-planting into the grass.

He growled under his breath. Now he was pissed.

"Melvin! Get over here!" he yelled. The dog seemed to slow down, but not enough for either of them to catch him.

After about ten more minutes of running circles around them, Melvin trotted over to the table and stopped at his bowl.

Karter jogged toward the table, expecting the dog to take off again, but he didn't. He was lapping up his water as if he didn't have a care in the world.

When Karter reached him, he quickly grabbed hold of the end of the leash. A few minutes later, Dreamy made it back to them. She was laughing hysterically and collapsed onto the grass near Melvin.

"That was . . ." she said, panting, and couldn't seem to get her words to work, which only made her laugh harder.

Melvin happily barked and jumped all over her, and Dreamy didn't seem to care that she was wearing white as she rolled around with the dog.

Karter shook his head. Her laugh was infectious, and he couldn't help but join in, especially as he thought about how silly they must've looked chasing his puppy.

"From now on, he can't come on dates with us," Karter said, making sure he had a good grip on the leash. "And I've had enough of chasing wigs and dogs."

Dreamy burst out laughing all over again.

AS THEY LUGGED EVERYTHING BACK TO THE CAR, DREAMY MAR-veled at how much fun they'd had. At first, she had worried that a picnic at the park was too simple since Karter was probably used to glamorous trips and Michelin-starred restaurants. Instead, he seemed to be open to anything she came up with. He had laughed, cracked jokes, and even tolerated Melvin. That last thought made her smile. After the big chase, he'd been adamant that the dog wasn't allowed on their dates anytime soon.

Karter squeezed her hand, bringing her back to the present as they walked.

"I want to ask you something," he said.

By the seriousness in his tone, Dreamy had a feeling that whatever he was going to ask, she wasn't going to like it.

"Okay," she said slowly, mentally bracing herself.

"Would you come with me to my parents' wedding anniversary party in a few weeks?"

Dreamy's brows shot up. "Me? You want to take me . . . to your parents' party?"

"Yeah, I'd love for you to be there. Unless you think you'll be busy."

"No, no, it's nothing like that. It's just that . . . Karter, your dad is Marcus Redford. A-list movie star, Hollywood royalty—I could go on and on."

Karter shrugged. "Well, he's just Dad to me, and I'd like for you to attend with me and meet them. What do you say? Wanna hang out and maybe even meet a few famous people?"

Of course she wanted to, but in the back of her mind, all she heard was Brandon's voice.

Not cultured.

Not sophisticated.

Not educated enough.

That little irritating voice of self-doubt was good at making an appearance and speaking very loudly at the worst moments.

You are more than enough, she reminded herself. *You are more than enough.*

"I'd love to go with you, and I promise I won't act like a total dweeb when I meet your parents. Specifically, your dad. Your *superstar* dad." She smiled and Karter returned it. "But to be honest with you, because that's what I want between us at all times, I'm scared to death of meeting people in your world. I'm nothing like the other women you've been with. I don't know how to act around the top ten percent." There, she said it.

Karter slowed and moved in front of her, then brushed a loose strand of hair away from her face. "I get it, sweetheart. I never want to put you in a situation where you'll be uncomfortable, but I selfishly want you with me. I'll be right there by your side. So if at any time during the party you want to leave, just tell me. I'll get you out of there. You have my word."

God, this man.

The only people she'd ever trusted to have her back were Jordyn and Gramps . . . and now Karter. It felt good and scary to know he cared about her enough to say those words with such conviction.

"Thank you. And thanks for the invite. I know you have your choice of women to—"

"Stop." He cupped her cheek. "Don't go there. I'm a one-woman man. I know the idea of you and me is scary, and maybe even feels a little crazy, but I'm in this for the long haul. I want to see where this thing between us goes."

Dreamy nodded. "Yeah, me too."

He kissed her lips and they continued walking.

"Plus, if you're still planning to win the lottery, then it might be a good idea to see how the other half lives." He grinned at her.

She smiled back at him. "Yeah, you're probably right."

Chapter Twenty-Three

CAN THIS DAY GET ANY WORSE?

Dreamy slogged out of her marketing night class disgusted with herself. The professor had given a pop quiz and allowed the students to use their books and notes. Normally, that would've made her day, but the one book and notebook she needed had been the ones she had left at home. Why? Because leaving the house in a rush that morning, she thought it was Wednesday, not Thursday. Instead of grabbing her marketing book, she had grabbed her small business one.

She trudged down the hallway and sighed in frustration. It was as if the universe was punishing her for something, and it started from the moment she opened her eyes that morning. Actually, it had started as she was having an erotic dream about her man when all of a sudden, a drop of water dripped onto her forehead. Then another one. And another one. When Dreamy finally opened her eyes, that little roof leak they'd had for months had turned into something more. Something that was now going to cost them a minimum of twelve thousand dollars to repair.

The day went downhill from there. On the way to work, she stopped by the grocery store to pick up some lunch. Irritated by the roofing issue, she hadn't been paying attention and had bumped into a display rack and knocked down a hundred jars of dill pickles. Shards of glass, along with pickle juice, not only splashed all over her but also covered the floor and earned her a *what the hell* from the store manager. Dreamy didn't think she could get any more embarrassed than she'd been in that moment.

At least she finally had something, actually, someone, to look forward to. *Karter*. They'd been officially dating for a few weeks, and it was as if they'd known each other forever. Everything from long walks on the beach to hanging out in a café and working on her school project, they tried to spend as much time as possible together.

Tonight, she was heading to Karter's office and knew he would be the bright spot of her lousy day. They planned to have a light dinner and then continue working on her business plan. With only a few more days before it was due, they were almost done, but she still hadn't come up with a name for the business.

"Dreamy?"

Dreamy pulled up short, and her heart stopped and plummeted to her feet. She didn't have to glance over her shoulder to know whom the deep baritone belonged to. What she didn't know was why he was at her school.

I guess this day can get worse.

When she turned around, she came face-to-face with the man who had humiliated her and crushed her self-esteem. The man she had hoped to never see again. The man she wished would be swallowed up by a black hole and never resurface.

"Brandon," Dreamy said dryly and readjusted her backpack on her shoulder.

A few inches taller than her, Brandon looked larger than life, and as usual, was dressed to impress in one of his custom-made Brioni suits.

The only good thing about seeing him was the fact that she looked great. Maybe the universe wasn't punishing her completely. After being showered with pickle juice, she had gone home to change. Needing an outfit to lift her spirits, she had opted for one of her favorites—a short, red sweater dress with black suede boots.

"You look amazing as usual," he said, eyeing her in that way that she used to think was sexy, but now it just irritated her.

"What are you doing here?" she asked.

"I was the guest speaker in a prelaw class. I guess if you're here, that means you're still in school." The hint of distaste in his tone didn't go unnoticed.

"No, I just hang out here for the hell of it." She couldn't hold back the snark that laced every word.

"That mouth. I see you still say what's on your mind."

He wouldn't be able to handle it if she said all that was on her mind. Because right now, she wanted to call him every name but his own, and she wanted to tell him to go fu—

"I've missed you," he said, cutting into her thoughts as he stepped closer.

Dreamy didn't respond. She wanted to put some distance between them, but she wouldn't give him the satisfaction of knowing that his presence unnerved her.

"Why haven't you returned my calls?" he asked.

"For what?"

"So we could talk."

"Again, for what? I think you said all you had to say at your party."

He ran a hand over his goatee, and suddenly looked a little uncomfortable. "About that night. I had a lot to drink and I didn't mean half that stuff."

"Sure, you did," she snapped. "I'm a firm believer that whatever's in our hearts eventually comes out of our mouths. I'm glad I know what you think of me."

"Come on, Dreamy. I didn't say anything that didn't have a little truth in it. You and I are at two different places in our lives. You still have some growing up to do and haven't even settled on a career yet. I'm a partner at my law firm. How would it look for me to get serious with someone like you?"

Hurt pierced her in the heart at his words, along with the words he had spoken that night they broke up.

Not cultured.

Not sophisticated.

Not educated enough.

"I wasn't trying to hurt you that night. I was only—"

"You know what?" Dreamy got in his face and pointed at him. "I've moved on, and I don't give a damn what you were trying to do. The next time you see me, don't bother speaking to me. Oh, and for the record, now that I've moved on from the likes of you, I have settled on a career."

"Really? And what—"

"And to answer your question about how it would look if you got serious with someone like me? It would look pretty damn good, but you'll never know because you and I"—she waved her finger back and forth between them—"will never happen again. I've upgraded. So, you can stay your pretentious ass away and stop calling me. Oh, and one more thing. Go to hell."

Dreamy turned on her heel, and anger propelled her toward the exit. She shouldn't have bothered saying anything to him because he didn't matter anymore. Yet she hadn't been able to stay quiet. The one thing she regretted about the night of his party was that she hadn't defended herself. She had allowed him to talk to her any type of way, and she would never let another man, or anyone, do that again.

But why did her heart feel as if it would split in two? Why did she suddenly feel as low as she'd felt that night?

Because his words hurt and they hit too close to home.

Her chest tightened, and she hurried out of the building, afraid that she might break down. No way would she let him see her cry.

I'm a partner at my law firm. How would it look for me to get serious with someone like you?

His words bounced around in her mind. He was right about one thing. They were at two different stages in their lives. Granted, she might not be established in her career yet, and she wasn't making six figures, but one day. . . .

Her thoughts veered to Karter. It was the same situation with him, but at least he didn't make her feel less than. The traitorous voice inside her head wondered if it was only a matter of time.

No. Don't let that asshole get inside your head. Your life is getting better, and you're working toward your goals.

Right now, Dreamy had more important business to attend to, and that included Karter. Not only was she anxious to receive one of his tantalizing kisses and a warm hug, but this would be the first time she got a chance to see where he worked. All she had to do was focus on him, and she'd forget all about her loser ex.

She glanced at her watch, glad that it was just a little after seven. Getting out of class early was a plus, but Karter was probably still in his meeting. He had told her to come by right after class, and he'd make sure dinner was there.

She pushed the door open that led to the parking lot and hurried toward her car, which was on the far end of the lot. Dreamy smiled to herself as she weaved in between vehicles. She would never be able to walk across a parking lot again without remembering the night her wig flew off. The night that kick-started her and Karter's relationship.

Talk about having a great story to tell their kids.

Whoa.

Dreamy stopped abruptly, surprised at the route her thoughts had taken. Where the heck had that come from? She and Karter were still getting to know each other, and it was way too soon to be thinking about having babies with him. She didn't even know if he wanted children.

Slow your roll, girl. Slow your roll.

"Focus on the here and now," she told herself, recalling what her grandmother often said. "Tomorrow will take care of itself."

Dreamy climbed into her vehicle and started the car. At least, she tried to start it. Each time she turned the key, the car would just whine and the engine wouldn't catch.

"Come on, baby. Just take me to Karter and I won't ask anything else of you tonight."

Dreamy tried again, only to get the same results. Needing to stay positive, she sent up a little prayer before trying yet again. Nothing.

She pounded on the steering wheel and laid her forehead on it, trying not to cry. First the dryer, then the roof, and now her car. When would things turn around for her? Everything was getting worse instead of better. Her lousy raise was nothing compared to the expenses that were piling up.

She lifted her head and stared out the windshield. "Now what?"

Karter was in a meeting and wouldn't be able to pick her up. Besides, she didn't want to call or ask for anything like this so early in their relationship. And she didn't want to bug Jordyn, who had a late study session on the other side of town. Dreamy hated taking the city bus, especially after dark, though it was only a little after seven o'clock. And an Uber would break her financially . . . unless she went home instead of to Karter's office.

"God, I don't want to cancel." He was so generous with his time when it came to helping her on her business plan, she hated missing

a session. More than that, she hated that she wouldn't get to
see him.

Let's give it one more try.

Dreamy patted the dashboard. "Come on, baby. Please start,"
she begged, struggling to stay hopeful.

She batted away tears that were threatening to fall and turned
the key. This time the car didn't make a sound, and defeat lodged
in her chest. She couldn't keep going like this. Something in her
life had to give.

Dreamy sat there for a good ten minutes staring out the windshield and on the verge of shedding tears. She needed to keep it
together long enough to call Karter and let him know that she
wasn't coming.

Her first instinct was to call his cell phone, but not wanting to
disturb him during his meeting, she called the office.

*"Thank you for calling KR Ventures. The office is now closed, but your
call is very important to us. Please leave a detailed message after . . ."*

Dreamy bit her bottom lip to hold back a sob. She hated being
such a baby, but disappointment was practically choking her. It
wasn't just about not being able to see Karter, but it was everything.
Just when her life started looking up, reality came back to bite her
in the butt.

After the beep, Dreamy left a message for Karter, her heart
breaking a little with each word she spoke. Once she was done and
disconnected the call, she allowed herself a good cry.

Something's gotta give.

KARTER STRUGGLED TO LISTEN AS ONE OF HIS MANAGERS, ED-
ward, discussed a new start-up that they were thinking about investing in. He tried not to have many evening meetings, but this
one couldn't be avoided. One of their managers had been in a bad

car accident and would be out for five to six weeks. Then there was the one on maternity leave. Karter normally didn't have to deal with much day-to-day work, but to keep operations flowing smoothly, he stepped in to pick up the slack. Tonight, his team was meeting to reassign a couple of projects.

But Karter couldn't focus, even when they started discussing a company that he had high hopes for. He was expecting Dreamy soon, and wouldn't be able to think straight until he had her in his arms.

"The business had some turnover in the last two months, and has recently hired a new marketing manager. In the meantime, Tamara has been playing two roles," Edward said of the owner. "Which is not going so well. She's excellent at delegating, but she's just overwhelmed."

As his team talked among themselves, Karter checked his phone. It was seven twenty-five, ten minutes since the last time he'd checked. Gloria usually stayed a little late whenever the group had a meeting in the evening, and he had instructed her to let him know the moment Dreamy arrived. So far, she hadn't shot him a text, and Dreamy hadn't called him.

Karter didn't want to become one of those men who always worried about his woman, but when it came to her, he couldn't help it. His protectiveness had been on high alert since day one. It wasn't that she needed him. She had proven to be very independent, but still, he worried.

Seeing movement in his peripheral vision, he glanced at the door, where Gloria was waving him over. Unease clawed through Karter. She didn't interrupt meetings unless it was important, and he already knew whatever she had to say had to do with Dreamy. He just hoped she was all right.

He quietly eased out of his seat and left the room. "What happened?" he asked before she could get a word out.

"Car trouble. She got stuck at school."

Karter looked at his phone again. "I didn't get a call from her."

"She left a message on the office phone, saying that she couldn't come because her car wouldn't start. Karter, she didn't sound good."

"Damn it. She should've called me," he said under his breath and started to call her cell.

"Actually, I caught her just before she was getting ready to get on the bus and go home."

"What? This time of night? What was she thinking?"

"She was thinking that she didn't want to bother you. She said it would've taken too long to get here by bus, so she was going home, but I stopped her."

"You should've pulled me out of the meeting or let me know what was going on. I would've gone to get her myself."

"Dreamy said not to bother you, but she agreed to let Najee pick her up. She should be here in about twenty minutes."

Karter huffed out a breath. "All right. That's good. I'll talk to her when she gets here, but from now on, if she calls and I'm in a meeting, please pull me out of it unless I say otherwise."

Gloria smiled. "Will do. I'll go ahead and order dinner. I was originally waiting for her to get here when I found out that she had left a voicemail."

"Okay. Instead of setting dinner up in the small conference room, set it up in my office."

"Will do."

After Gloria walked away, Karter called Dreamy. After two rings, she picked up.

"Hello?"

"You should've called my cell," he said by way of greeting.

There was a hesitation before she said, "I couldn't, Karter. I didn't want to bother you, and I didn't want to interrupt your meeting. Not for something like—"

"Dreamy, you're important to me. Do you know how it makes me feel knowing you were stranded somewhere alone? Especially when I could've helped?"

She didn't say anything, and he sighed. New relationships were exciting and nerve-racking at the same time. It didn't help that he'd been out of practice for so long.

"Sweetheart, where are you now? Did Najee arrive yet?"

"Yes, I'm with him," she said in a small voice that pierced Karter's heart. Gone was her upbeat tone that usually shined through even over the phone.

"Are you okay?" he asked, which should've been his first question.

"Yes, but I don't know if I'll be good company tonight. Maybe I should stick with my original idea and head on home."

"Did something else happen tonight?"

"It's just . . . everything, Karter. It's been a rough day and—"

"I want to see you. Have Najee bring you to the office, all right?" Again, there was silence on the other end of the line. "Please, Dreamy. I *need* to see you." He needed to see with his own eyes that she was all right.

"Okay. Najee said we'll be there in twenty minutes."

"I'll see you then."

Karter disconnected the call and returned to the meeting, though his heart wasn't in it. All he cared about in that moment was Dreamy, and he needed to find out what was going on so he could fix it.

Chapter Twenty-Four

DREAMY LAID HER HEAD AGAINST THE BACK SEAT OF THE RANGE
Rover and closed her eyes. She didn't want to get used to riding
around in luxury, but she could see how easily that could happen.
The soft leather wrapped around her like a warm embrace, and if
she weren't careful, the smooth ride would lull her to sleep.

If only she could clear her mind and stop thinking. Not only
had Najee picked her up, but he arranged for her car to be towed to
a repair shop. Like she could afford a tow and repairs, but he had
waved off her concerns. According to him, his boss instructed him
to do whatever was necessary to make sure she was taken care of.

No one had ever come to her rescue like that, taking charge and
making sure she was all right. But this was not how Dreamy wanted
a relationship with Karter to start. She didn't want to be that needy
woman who landed a rich man only to have him take care of all of
her problems.

She pinched the bridge of her nose as exhaustion settled in. *I
should've gone home.* The only thing that had stopped her from

doing just that was it would've put Najee in a position to have to choose whether or not to go against Karter's instructions.

Now Dreamy understood why, years ago, her grandmother had wanted them to put her in an assisted living facility. Her grandmother hadn't wanted to be a burden on Dreamy or Jordyn, saying that she had lived a full and enjoyable life. She wanted them to be able to live their lives without the weight of having to care for her.

That's how Dreamy felt at the moment when it came to Karter. He was used to taking charge and helping people, but she worked so hard to not have to depend on anyone. Yet here she was, using his driver.

This wasn't the first time she'd had problems with her car, and it wouldn't be the last time, especially if she didn't replace it soon. But tonight, it was more than the car situation that had her down. It was everything. Even working toward accomplishing some goals, it seemed to be taking too long to get there, and running into Brandon only reminded her of that. It was way past time that she got her life on track.

"You doin' okay, Ms. Dreamy?" Najee asked from the front seat.

So caught up in her thoughts, she had forgotten that she wasn't alone.

Dreamy opened her eyes and lifted her head. "I'm fine. Thank you for asking, and thanks so much for picking me up. I'm sure rescuing a damsel in distress wasn't a part of your plans for this evening."

His deep, hearty chuckle filled the car and helped lighten her mood. "Are you kidding? I'm always available to help a damsel in distress." He lifted his hand, and between his fingers was a business card. "If you ever find yourself in a bind, just call me."

Dreamy leaned forward and accepted the card. She used her cell phone flashlight to read it. The only information on it was his first name and a telephone number. "Thank you, and no offense, but I hope I don't have to use it."

He glanced at her through the mirror and smiled. "Well, at least you'll have it."

Still staring at the card, Dreamy couldn't help but wonder. "Do you give your card to all of Karter's . . . friends?"

"No. You're the first."

Dreamy sighed. "Probably because his friends don't have car issues . . . or issues period," she mumbled under her breath.

"That's not it," he said simply without additional explanation.

"It's because of the wig situation, isn't it?" she said, hoping she was able to put some humor in her voice. No sense in being a Debbie Downer and ruining anyone else's night. "You're hoping to get another good laugh at my expense, aren't you?"

That got a laugh out of him. "Yeah, sure, let's go with that."

For the rest of the ride, Dreamy gazed out the tinted window, trying to decide what she was going to do about Karter. Her short-comings wouldn't look good in his circle of people, and she wouldn't want to embarrass him in any way. It would be better to break up now before things got too serious between them . . . before she completely fell for him.

God, who am I kidding?

She had already fallen hard for him.

"Here we are, Ms. Dreamy," Najee said when he pulled into a circular driveway in front of a skyscraper. "Sit tight and I'll get the door for you."

Before she could protest and let herself out, he hurried around the front of the car. Najee opened the door and helped her out of the SUV. "All right, Ms. Dreamy, come with me and I'll walk you in."

"Thank you, but can you just call me *Dreamy*? All of my friends do."

He chuckled and offered her his arm. "I think I can manage that if you'll agree to call me if you have any more car trouble."

Dreamy smiled up at him. "You drive a hard bargain, my friend, but I'll keep that in mind."

"Not the response I was looking for, but I guess it will have to do. It was a pleasure seeing you again, *Dreamy*," he said with emphasis when they reached the elevator, and pushed the button. "This will take you directly to Karter's office. Enjoy the rest of your evening."

Just as he started to walk away, the doors slid open, and a woman greeted her with a smile.

"Welcome. I'm glad you made it. I'm Gloria. You must be Dreamy."

Dreamy couldn't help but smile back at her.

"Hi, Gloria. It's nice to finally meet you. Thanks for your help tonight. I really didn't want to bother you guys."

"Oh, dear, don't worry about that. I was glad to help, and Karter was very worried about you."

Dreamy glanced away as guilt lodged in her throat. So much for being independent. She had the man worried when his focus should've been on work.

Why would he want to be with someone who couldn't even afford to buy a functioning car? Or even someone who couldn't get an Uber for fear of not having enough money to pay for a ride across town?

Gloria touched her arm, and Dreamy met her eyes.

"I'm not sure what's going through your head right now, but I know how frustrating car trouble can be."

"It's not just about the car. It's . . ." Dreamy started. She really wasn't sure how to deal with the various emotions swirling inside of her. She also didn't know why she felt so weepy as tears filled her eyes. She batted them away, refusing to break down in front of this woman she'd just met.

"Sometimes we do the best we can do to get ahead," Gloria said quietly. "And just when life seems to be turning in the right direction, a situation, an incident, or even a person comes along and throws everything off."

Dreamy shook her head, surprised by the words. "It's like you know me."

"Life is a funny thing," Gloria continued, picking some invisible lint from her dark skirt. "Sometimes it's like a tornado ripping through our world and we have to hold on tight until the dust settles. So whatever has you down and second-guessing everything, try not to worry about it."

"What makes you think I'm second-guessing anything?"

"I won't pretend I know you or what's on your mind, but when I talked to you earlier, I just had a feeling. Like you were at that point where if one more thing went wrong, it would push you over the edge."

Dreamy gave a little grunt, thinking that this woman was good. In that brief conversation, she'd gotten the gist of what was going on in Dreamy's head.

"I might be overstepping, but let me tell you about my boss," Gloria said quietly.

Dreamy braced herself. What if Gloria thought Dreamy wasn't good enough for Karter? She couldn't take another hit tonight when there were so many doubts weighing on her already.

"Karter is the kindest, most generous and thoughtful person I know, except for maybe my husband, of course. Karter thrives on helping and making life easier for as many people as possible. He's a great man, but don't get me wrong. He's still a man. So you know he's going to screw up on occasion, but he has a huge heart."

"Why are you telling me all of this?" Dreamy asked, unsure where this conversation was going.

"Because it's been a long time since I've seen him happy. You, being you, makes him happy. I'm telling you all of this because I think you should let him show you the type of man he is."

He already has, Dreamy thought. In the short amount of time they had known each other, Karter had been kinder than any man she'd ever been with.

"Thank you. I needed to hear this tonight."

"You're welcome. I'm glad I got the chance to meet you. Karter says you're the sunshine for so many people in your life. Keep letting that light shine."

Dreamy nodded, feeling a little choked up.

Gloria held up an ID card to an electronic reader next to the elevator, and the doors swished open.

"Go on upstairs. Karter is waiting for you."

Dreamy didn't know what to say to the woman, so she didn't say anything. Instead, she hugged her, and was glad when Gloria hugged her back.

"Thank you," Dreamy whispered.

"You're welcome, dear. Have a good night."

"You too."

As the elevator climbed to the top floor, Dreamy wasn't sure what to expect. They had originally planned to have a light dinner while working on her business plan, but she wasn't up for doing homework. Yet it would be inconsiderate after Karter had carved out time for her. Besides, she didn't have the luxury to wallow in self-pity and not accept his help when it was offered. She only had a few more weeks to get the project done, and there was still a lot to do.

The elevator stopped. Dreamy released a nervous breath and gripped the strap of her backpack tighter as the doors slid open. Then she saw him. Tall, muscular, and sexy, he had shed his suit jacket, leaving him in a light gray dress shirt with the top two buttons undone and no tie. He leaned against the wall in front of the elevator doors, legs crossed at the ankles and holding a single rose in his hand.

"Finally," he said, and pushed off the wall.

As he approached her, his concerned gaze raked the length of her body. Once he was directly in front of her, he cupped her cheek and stared into her eyes.

Dreamy's heart squeezed at the tenderness of his touch, and those damn tears pricked the back of her eyes again. For a person who rarely cried, she'd spent the last hour or so fighting tears.

"Are you all right?"

She nodded. Her heart rate ramped up at his closeness. How had she thought she could walk away from him so easily? Just seeing him and standing near him had her body all revved up.

"Hi," she finally said.

"Hi yourself."

He lowered his head, and the moment their lips touched, it was as if a heavy weight had lifted from her shoulders. Or maybe that was her backpack that had slid down her arm and dropped to the floor with a thud.

When the kiss ended, Karter presented her with the single rose. "For you."

Dreamy accepted the flower and brought it to her nose. The enchanting fragrance helped erase more of the melancholy that had been plaguing her for the last hour.

Just when I thought he couldn't get any sweeter . . .

"Thank you, Karter . . . for everything."

"You're welcome." He lifted her chin with the pad of his finger and then went in for another kiss.

Earlier, Dreamy might've had a moment of doubt about the route her life was taking, but a change was coming. She just had to hang on and stay strong.

Chapter Twenty-Five

KARTER LOOPED DREAMY'S BACKPACK ONTO HIS SHOULDER AND reached for her hand. Before she arrived, he'd had every intention of chewing her out about not calling him when her car wouldn't start. He had also planned to give her all of the reasons why it wasn't safe to ride the bus alone at night. He had even intended to lecture her about the importance of having dependable transportation.

But when the elevator doors whooshed open, and he saw the vulnerability on her face, his words vanished. All he'd wanted to do in that moment was hold her, comfort her, and show her how much he cared.

Now he was glad he had taken that route. Within minutes, some of the tension that had clearly been weighing her down had dissipated. She still didn't seem quite herself, but at least she didn't look as if she would burst into tears.

"Beautiful office," she said as they walked hand in hand through the suite. Everyone had left for the day, leaving him to spend uninterrupted time with her.

"Thank you. It took a few years to get it exactly the way we wanted, but it's a great home away from home."

As he pointed out more rooms and offices, Karter found it interesting that he wanted to share so much with Dreamy. Whereas he'd almost married a woman, and he couldn't remember ever giving her a guided tour of the building.

That spoke volumes about how he felt about Dreamy versus Valerie. Or it could be that he was just at a different place in his life mentally and emotionally. Yes, it was a little scary opening himself up to another woman, but when Karter was with Dreamy, he felt more alive than he'd felt in years. He wanted her in his life, and if it meant taking a risk, he was ready.

"That's Gloria's office," he said, pointing to the first door on the right. "I had hoped to introduce you two tonight."

"I met her downstairs when I first arrived. She seems really cool."

"She's great. I didn't realize she was still in the building."

Knowing his assistant, Karter wouldn't be surprised if Gloria had planned that impromptu meeting. She was the most efficient person he knew. No way would she leave until Dreamy arrived safely and according to any instructions that she'd given.

He brought Dreamy's hand to his mouth and kissed the back of her fingers. "I'm glad you're here."

"Me too," she said, sparing him a small smile before looking away.

"I'm sure you're probably hungry, right?"

"Yeah, actually, I am. I didn't realize it until this moment."

"Okay, well, let's eat. This is my office."

"Oh, Karter." Dreamy stopped just inside the door. "You didn't have to go to all of this trouble."

He'd had Gloria set up the table with a light dinner for them. In the center of the table was a vase with two dozen long-stemmed roses. Well, actually twenty-three roses since Dreamy had number twenty-four in her hand.

She moved to the table. "I didn't know you were such a romantic. This is lovely."

Karter didn't necessarily consider himself a romantic, but he liked doing things for her. In the weeks that they'd been together, he'd made small gestures like having lunch delivered to her job and gourmet chocolates another day. The Saturday before, he had taken Dreamy to Temecula Valley, wine country, for wine tasting and a carriage ride. Sunshine, a nice breeze off the ocean, and walking hand in hand for most of their time together had amounted to Karter having one of the best days he'd had in a long time. And Dreamy's reactions to his little surprises only made him want to do more. He just felt so bad that he had to work so much.

But right now, she still didn't seem like her bubbly, talkative self, and Karter was at a loss. He couldn't help fix whatever was going on if she didn't let him in. Being a person who preferred to hash things out instead of letting a situation stew, he needed to figure out how to get her talking.

"Your office is huge, almost the size of a studio apartment."

"Yeah, I spend a lot of time here. Ready to eat?"

She worried her bottom lip and nodded. "I'm sorry I was late. The food is probably cold because of me."

Karter pulled out a chair for her, then started uncovering the dishes. "Nope, it's still warm. Gloria arranged for it to be delivered a few minutes before you arrived. It's fine."

"This looks delicious," she said of the side salad, along with burgers and fries from the restaurant in the building.

"Since you like to keep your meals simple, I figured I couldn't go wrong with burgers . . . and grape Kool-Aid."

"Aww, Karter. I can't believe you remembered that."

"Of course I remembered. I remember everything you've told me."

Once he was seated, they started eating. Dreamy took a couple of bites of her bacon cheeseburger, and her quietness was a bit unnerving.

"Talk to me," he said with more force than intended. "You didn't sound like yourself when I called during your ride here, and I have a feeling it's not just the car that's got you down. What happened tonight?"

Seconds ticked by without her responding. Instead, she picked at her fries, and appeared to be deep in thought.

"Thank you for all you did tonight," she finally said. "I was touched and surprised when Gloria called, insisting that I let Najee bring me here."

"Are you mad at me?" Karter asked.

Gloria had taken it upon herself to set everything in motion as far as getting to Dreamy, but it's exactly what Karter would have done. No way would he have his woman riding a bus when she didn't have to.

My woman.

He liked the sound of that. More than that, though, he wanted to do things for Dreamy. If she'd let him.

She looked at him, and though her eyes weren't as sad, she still seemed troubled. "I'm not mad."

"Then what is it? Did something else happen while you were at school or at work?" He had talked to her after she left work, and she seemed fine.

"I ran into Brandon."

Karter stiffened. Had that asshole done something to her? She had mentioned her ex a few times, and in each instance, the guy sounded like a world-class jerk. Sure, people sometimes talked bad about those they've dated, but Karter had a feeling Dreamy hadn't been exaggerating.

"Did he do something to you? Did he hurt you?"

"Only with his words . . . as usual. He reminded me that I wasn't his equal and not the marrying type since I wasn't at his level. I—"

"Dreamy, people treat you the way you allow them to treat you. You've made it clear that the guy is a jackass. Why would you allow him or his words to affect you? You're too strong of a woman for that."

Karter was a little taken aback when she glared at him as if he were the one who had ruined her day. He was only stating a fact. He wasn't sure what set her off, but if her eyes were weapons, he'd be dead. At least he was getting a reaction out of her, because up until now, he thought that at any minute, she was going to completely fall apart on him.

"Yes, Brandon is a jackass, and right now, you're being one too," she snapped. "Karter, it's not like I intentionally let his words get the better of me. It's just"—she shrugged—"it's been a rough day. Maybe you can't understand that, but there's been one situation after another since the moment I opened my eyes this morning. Running into Brandon and then dealing with that stupid car has been a little overwhelming, all right?"

He nodded, still sensing there was more to her melancholy mood.

"Haven't you ever had a day that was so horrible that you wished you could erase it and start it over?"

Karter grunted. "More times than I can count. I'm sorry about what I said a minute ago. I was just surprised that you let him or anyone get under your skin."

"I try not to, but I'm human. Most days, I can let things slide and just roll with whatever situation comes my way. But tonight, it was just . . ."

Seconds ticked by without her responding, and Karter gently nudged her arm. "It's just what? I can't help if you don't tell me what else is wrong."

"That's just it, Karter. I didn't ask you to help. It's already intimidating dating someone like you, and you and your people made all the decisions tonight. I felt as if I didn't have a say."

"So, you would've preferred to camp out in the parking lot with your car or ride the bus? Is that what you're saying?" He tried to keep the irritation out of his voice, but some slipped through. He wanted to understand, but right now it was like pulling teeth to get her to talk to him. "Are you saying that you're mad at me for trying to help?"

Dreamy huffed out a breath. "I'm not mad at you, Karter. I love that you cared enough to help me. I'll never be able to thank you for everything, and . . ."

Karter slipped his hand behind her neck and kneaded it. The more she talked, the more agitated she was getting.

"And what, baby?"

"I hate being needy. It just brings home the fact that I'm so out of my league with you. Besides that, I'm not used to depending on anyone. It's been my experience that when you do, people will let you down."

Okay, now Karter was starting to understand. "Dreamy, that won't happen with us. I'm in a position to help. Let me when I can."

Her eyes met his. "I have nothing to offer you, and the situation tonight . . . and seeing Brandon really hit me. Since we've met, you've been the giver. Dinner, dress repair, help with my project, you even helped me chase down a damn wig."

Though she was serious, Karter couldn't help but chuckle.

"I don't want to get used to you doing things for me. What if we don't work out? Then I'm back to being on my own, and it'll be harder to go back to business as usual."

"Sweetheart"—he brushed the back of his hand down her cheek, needing to touch her—"I'm in this for the long haul. Why don't we focus on the here and now? I'm not trying to control you, and I definitely don't want you to feel like I'm taking away your independence. That's not the case, but I hope you understand that everyone, even the most independent person, needs a helping hand from time to time. If we're dating, we should be able to call on each other when we need to, right?"

"I guess . . . but when will you ever need my help with anything? This feels so unbalanced."

"The only thing I want is you."

She sighed loudly and dropped back in her seat. Clearly, that wasn't what she wanted to hear, but how could he explain how much joy she brought into his life? It was more than anyone had ever given him, and he recently realized it was what he needed the most.

"Do you know why Morgan gave me Melvin?" he said.

Dreamy frowned before lifting her gaze to him. "I'm . . . not sure."

"She said I was dealing with high-functioning depression."

Concern showed in her eyes. "Are you? What exactly does that mean? You're depressed . . . but still functioning?"

"That's what she thinks, and though I didn't admit to it, she might've been right. A friend of mine died a few weeks ago, and I took it hard."

She covered his hand with hers. "Oh, Karter. I am so sorry for your loss. That had to be devastating."

"I'm not going to lie, it was tough. Delton was like a brother to me, and he died of a heart attack. He was forty."

Dreamy nodded, still holding his hand. "And you probably started thinking that could be you."

"Exactly, but even before then, I was just . . . I guess I was just roaming through life, mainly working myself to death. I had no real direction, and my only goal was to make more money."

"Is Melvin like some type of service dog? I thought the two of you didn't get along."

"We're getting there, and no he's not a service dog. Morgan basically thought that Melvin would help with the stress, pull me out of my funk."

"God, I must be the most unobservant person there is. I didn't realize you were in a funk."

"See, that's just it. Dreamy, since meeting you, I feel more alive than I've felt in years. So when you say you have nothing to offer, you give me more than you realize." When she started shaking her head, Karter continued. "I don't know if you understand just how special you are. I'll admit that it's nice having money and having the ability to change a situation for the better.

"But you have a natural gift that has nothing to do with money or material things. Your positive attitude, your love of life, your quirkiness—it's all so refreshing and fun. And the fact that you want to start a business, a nonprofit, to help women achieve success through entrepreneurship makes you even more special. You're just . . . you," he said on a laugh. He couldn't think of a better way to explain what he saw and felt when he was with her.

Dreamy ducked her head and smiled. She went back to eating, this time with more gusto. "Thank you," she said between bites. "I guess with all of the bad things that happened today, I got stuck in my head."

"It happens, but I hope you know how much I adore you. I don't care that we're at different places in life right now. You bring so much joy and light to this relationship and probably all of your relationships. Don't let people like your ex, or anyone for that matter, make you doubt how amazing you are. Okay?"

Dreamy nodded as she wiped her mouth. Then she leaned over

and kissed his lips. "You bring me joy too. I'm sorry if I ruined or almost ruined our plans for the evening."

"No worries. I'm just glad you're here and that you're okay."

"I'm better than okay."

While they ate, Dreamy told him about her day. Now, Karter had a better understanding of why she had wanted to go home. If his day had gone downhill the way hers had, he probably wouldn't have been up to doing much either. He wanted more than anything to offer to fix the issues, but he already knew she wouldn't readily accept his help. He hoped they'd one day get to the point where she wouldn't hesitate to ask for his assistance. Until then, he'd just be here if she needed him.

Chapter Twenty-Six

KARTER DIDN'T ASK MUCH OF DREAMY. ACTUALLY, THE ONLY thing he'd asked since they'd been dating was for her to be his plus-one for his parents' anniversary party. That was the least she could do.

But she would be lying if she said that she wasn't nervous. She'd had time to prepare, but still her nerves were on edge. She had no idea what to expect. Karter and his siblings didn't say much about their dad, but they made their mother sound like a cross between Miranda Priestly and Cruella de Vil.

How was Dreamy supposed to prepare to meet someone like that? She might've finally been confident in her relationship with Karter, but still she understood the importance of having his mother's approval.

Najee pulled onto the property and followed the long circular drive.

"It looks as if everyone has already arrived," Karter said from beside Dreamy.

They were sitting in the back of his SUV, where he'd been holding her hand for most of the forty-five-minute drive.

Dreamy stared out the window and took it all in. His parents' estate seemed to take up half the block. The landscape was meticulously done with blooming trees and flowerbeds perfectly placed. They even had a huge water fountain in the center of the yard, giving the area a park-like feel.

As they continued up the double-wide driveway, lined with one luxury vehicle after another and personal drivers standing near them, Dreamy was reminded of the type of people she'd be around for the next couple of hours. God, she hoped she wouldn't embarrass Karter or herself.

"Are you sure I look all right?" she asked Karter as Najee crept along behind a line of cars.

"Yes, you're gorgeous. I still can't believe my sister designed that outfit. She's definitely wasting her talents bumbling around my house."

Dreamy smiled and glanced down at the unique off-the-shoulder two-piece outfit that was totally her style. She had been looking through Morgan's portfolio and mentioned that she loved the design. A week later, a package arrived at the house and it was the outfit.

Morgan indeed had mad skills that she wasn't using nearly enough. When questioned about why she dropped out of fashion design school, Morgan had said she didn't have a passion for it. But as far as Dreamy was concerned, Morgan's designs and skills said otherwise.

Najee pulled up to the stately Bel Air home. The elegant, Tuscan-like structure looked like something straight out of *Architectural Digest*. According to Karter, it was an entertainer's paradise, and his mother had done a ton of renovations over the years to take advantage of every feature in the home, including the canyon and city views. From the little that Dreamy had seen so far, the estate made Karter's home in the Hollywood Hills look like a tree house.

"You really grew up here?" she asked.

"Yes, but it doesn't look the same. It's been renovated so many times, I barely recognize the place."

"And it's just your parents who live here?"

Karter nodded as he gazed out of the window. "Well, them along with their housekeepers and drivers. There's a guesthouse out back where their personal security details live."

On-site personal security. So this is how the other half lives.

Karter helped her out of the SUV, and she couldn't stop her body from trembling. The one thing that gave her a little peace was knowing that Morgan, Nana, and Randy would be in attendance. Dreamy had met Randy the night her car broke down. When Karter had found out his brother was in his studio, located several floors down from Karter's office, he had taken Dreamy there to meet him. He was as kind to her as Morgan had been.

Karter escorted her up the walk that led to the extremely tall double doors. Other guests, whom he greeted but Dreamy didn't recognize, were also heading to the front door.

"Welcome, welcome," a woman's voice carried outside.

Karter tightened his hold on Dreamy's hand. "It sounds as if you'll meet my mother first thing. She's greeting people at the door."

"Oh great," she mumbled as her nerves started getting the best of her.

"Babe, don't worry. Just be yourself and try to have fun tonight."

Seconds later, a petite woman with salt-and-pepper hair and reddish-brown skin wearing a light blue evening gown with diamonds dripping from her ears and neck came into view. Beside her was a man Dreamy recognized immediately—Marcus Redford, Karter's father. He looked a little older than he appeared on the big screen, but handsome nonetheless. Karter had his mother's skin tone and light brown eyes, but all his other features came from his father.

"Oh, there's my baby," Karter's mother gushed when she spotted him. She pulled him down for a hug and kissed his cheek. "I'm glad you're here. Angelica arrived and is—"

"Mom, Dad, I'd like for you to meet Dreamy," he said pointedly, his gaze boring into his mother. "Dreamy, these are my parents, Marcus and Kalena Redford."

His father flashed a huge smile, and Dreamy's heart melted.

"Dreamy. Beautiful name for a beautiful lady," he said in that deep voice that he was known for. "It's nice to finally meet you. I've heard wonderful things. Welcome to our home."

When *the* Marcus Redford pulled her into a warm hug, Dreamy's knees went weak. Meeting the movie-star legend was like a dream come true and a moment she wouldn't soon forget.

"Thank you, it's a pleasure to meet you both," she said, her gaze bouncing between him and Kalena.

"Hello, dear," Mrs. Redford finally said, her eyes trailing from the top of Dreamy's head to the hot-pink pumps on her feet. "What a darling outfit. Who are you wearing this evening?"

Dreamy beamed at the question, making her wonder if this was how it felt to walk the red carpet. "It's an original Morgan Redford," she said proudly and almost burst out laughing when Kalena's eyes practically popped out of her head.

"That's one of my daughter's designs?" she said incredulously.

"It is."

"Come on." Karter tugged on her hand. "We're holding up the line."

After telling his parents that they'd see them later, Karter pulled Dreamy farther into the house. The long entryway lined with white walls and breathtaking artwork was as grand as the outside of the home.

Dreamy wanted to act like she was accustomed to nice, beautiful things, but she struggled to keep her mouth from hanging open. She didn't even bother to hide her awe when they entered the foyer. Double staircases led up to the second floor and a ginormous, spiral crystal chandelier hung between them.

"This is . . ." she breathed as she glanced around, unable to describe the magnificence of the home.

"Yeah, it is a bit much," Karter said almost apologetically at the sheer opulence of it all. He pulled Dreamy farther into the home, which got more impressive with each step she took.

Strolling into the main living space was like walking into a grand ballroom. The hum of conversation and jazz playing in the background met her ears, and there were people everywhere. Some huddled in small groups talking and laughing together, while others weaved in and out of the crowd, grabbing hors d'oeuvres and drinks from passing servers.

Dreamy couldn't imagine what it must've been like to grow up in such luxury, and to be surrounded by famous people. She spotted a few familiar faces, actors and actresses she never imagined seeing in person. It was all so . . . overwhelming.

"Dreamy! You made it!" Morgan screamed and barreled toward them. She didn't stop until she had Dreamy in a bear hug. "Girrl, you look *hot*! I knew this outfit would be amazing on you, and the deep pink is perfect for your skin tone."

"I can't thank you enough for dressing me tonight," Dreamy said on a giggle, totally feeling like royalty or at least like one of the actresses in attendance. "Oh, and your mom said the outfit was 'darling,'" she whispered.

Morgan's jaw came unhinged and her eyes bugged out. "Get out! That's high praise coming from Kalena Redford. I can't believe she complimented you. I thought she would've given you the stink eye when she saw you with her precious Karter."

"Oh, she gave me that, too, but she got distracted by your amazing design."

Dreamy hadn't missed the disdain in their mother's eyes or her tone, especially after Karter had shut down whatever she was going to say about Angelica. Karter had already given Dreamy a heads-up about both women, and she was ready for whatever they dished out.

"Thank you so much for coming," Morgan said as if it were her party. "Now I can have some fun."

"Oh, boy," Karter murmured next to them.

Dreamy laughed. "So, what? You couldn't have fun before I got here?"

Morgan pursed her lips. "Seriously? Look around. Does it look like a place to have fun?"

Dreamy had to admit, the party did feel a bit stuffy. From what she understood, this was the cocktail hour and there would be a sit-down dinner, and then dancing. That was the part she was looking forward to. She hadn't been out dancing in forever.

As for the sit-down dinner, there had to be a ballroom somewhere in the place because there were at least a hundred guests in attendance already, and people were still arriving.

"Would you like something to drink?" Karter asked near Dreamy's ear, his warm breath on her skin sending a wave of heat pulsing through her body. She didn't think she'd ever get used to having him so close, and when he was, all she wanted to do was burrow closer.

She placed a kiss on his cheek. "How about a glass of white wine?"

Apparently not satisfied with just a kiss to the cheek, he kissed her lips. "Coming right up."

"You guys are so cute together," Morgan said when he walked away. "I'm glad you two found each other. You're good for him, and I've never seen him so happy."

Dreamy's gaze followed the path he took toward one of the bars in the room, and she smiled. "He makes me happy too. Sometimes I have to pinch myself to prove that this is all actually real."

"It's real, girl. Now come on. Let me show you around this museum."

"Wait, but what about Karter?"

"Trust me. When it comes to you, he's like a heat-seeking missile zooming in on his target. He'll find you. Let's go."

KARTER SIPPED HIS GLASS OF SCOTCH AND SAW THE MOMENT Morgan whisked Dreamy off to God knows where. He had a feeling that would happen at some point in the evening and was glad the two had bonded. They got along like sisters and were a good balance for one another.

He hoped Dreamy's independence and strong work ethic would rub off on his sister. And Karter hoped Morgan would help Dreamy feel less anxious around all of this. His and his family's wealth was a lot to take in, and no matter what he said, it would still be difficult for her to adjust to.

"Well, I was wondering when you'd arrive."

Karter almost groaned at hearing Angelica's sugary sweet and irritating voice behind him. No doubt his mother had sent her to find him. When she had mentioned Angelica the moment she saw him, despite Dreamy standing next to him, he had wanted to shake his mother. He was relieved when she complimented Dreamy's outfit, but he knew the woman well enough to know that her snarkiness would make an appearance before the evening was over.

"Angelica," Karter said when she came into view. "How's it going?"

"It would be going great if you hadn't dumped me for that little hussy you walked in with."

Irritation stirred inside his chest, but Karter tamped it down, refusing to let her bait him.

"It's comments like that that let me know I made the right decision in cutting you loose."

She waved him off. "Oh, please. Our split was mutual, even though I did think that we would still be each other's plus-one for events. I can't believe you left all of this"—she ran her hand up and down her body—"for her. Who is she anyway? I haven't seen her around before."

Karter stiffened and carefully thought about his next words. The last thing he wanted was for his ex to cause any trouble for Dreamy. Angelica didn't want him, but she was petty enough to mess with another woman's life out of spite.

"It doesn't matter who she is. All you need to know is that she's with me."

"So are you saying you two are an item? Or is she just your date for tonight?"

"We're an item."

"I see." She studied him as she sipped her mixed drink. "Is it serious?"

"Yes," Karter said without hesitation.

He had already fallen in love with Dreamy, though he hadn't spoken those words to her yet. And he knew the exact moment it happened—the night Najee brought her to him after her car issues.

The moment the elevator doors had swished open and he saw her standing there, looking all vulnerable, something inside of him shifted. Something he had never felt in his life.

His heart had started racing. His pulse pounded in his ears, and his breathing increased. It had been a scary and exhilarating feeling rolled into one. Though the emotions had been foreign to him, it was in that instant that Karter knew that he had fallen in love with her. That he knew there was nothing in the world he wouldn't do for Dreamy.

If someone were to ask him to explain the feeling that had completely overwhelmed him that night, he wouldn't be able to string the right words together. At that moment, he'd had to be strong for her and hadn't had a chance to really explore what he'd been feeling. In those minutes, when she'd stepped off the elevator, his number one concern had been to make sure she was okay emotionally and physically.

Karter signaled the bartender.

"Yes, sir?"

"Can I get a white wine?"

"Coming right up."

"Well, I'm sure whatever you have going on with this woman won't last," Angelica said with a Cheshire cat grin. "I'll give it a couple of months until you get bored with her. Then you'll be coming back to me."

Karter chuckled and accepted the white wine. "Yeah, you keep thinking that. Enjoy the party, Angelica. I know I will."

Karter strolled away and went in search of Dreamy. He already knew he would never find another woman quite like her.

AFTER DINNER, DREAMY HAD A MOMENT TO HERSELF, AND SHE wandered out to the balcony of the ballroom. Most of the guests had moved to other parts of the house, and there were only a few people outside.

Karter had been right. The place was massive and perfect for holding events, and the view from where she was standing was absolutely breathtaking. Yet Dreamy couldn't imagine living in a house so big even if she could afford it.

"Lovely night, isn't it?" Mrs. Redford said when she stepped up next to Dreamy. She took a prim sip from the glass of red wine that she was holding.

"Yes, it's wonderful out here. You have a beautiful home."

"Thank you. We purchased the place when Karter was around three or four. It didn't look like it does today, but I knew the moment we stepped inside that this was the place for us. We've had some incredible years here."

Dreamy nodded, thinking how interesting it must've been growing up there. Plenty of space to play hide-and-seek, and the perfect stairwell to drop water balloon bombs on people. She smiled at that last thought as she recalled the epic balloon fights she and Jordyn had growing up. They might not have had the biggest or grandest house, but the fond memories were priceless.

Mrs. Redford took another sip of her wine and stared out into the night. Dreamy couldn't help but admire how pretty and poised the woman was standing there in the low-cut evening gown that wrapped around her petite frame to perfection. Had she been born into wealth? Dreamy wasn't sure, but she'd seen her mingling with her guests with grace and confidence. Everything she did and said seemed so natural, as if she'd been a part of the high-society scene all of her life.

When Karter's mother glanced at her, Dreamy offered a smile, then hurriedly looked away, uncomfortable that she'd been caught staring.

"Are you having a good time tonight?" Mrs. Redford asked.

"Yeah, I've had a great time. You sure know how to throw a party. It's been cool seeing so many people that I've seen on TV and in movies. I never imagined that I'd ever meet some of them face-to-face."

"Well, I'm glad you've had a good time, but don't get too comfortable with my son. Whatever is going on between the two of you won't last. I know your type."

And there it is. Dreamy had wondered how long it would take for Karter's mother to show her true colors. For a moment there, she thought the older woman had warmed up to her. Apparently not.

"You say you know my type," Dreamy said, trying to keep her composure and not show any emotion. "So what is it?"

"A gold-digging minx who uses her feminine wiles to seduce a wealthy man like my son."

Dreamy almost laughed at the absurdity, but she was too pissed. "Is that how you snagged Mr. Redford?" The words were out of her mouth before she could pull them back. The snappy response sounded like something Jordyn would've said.

She'd be so proud of me.

Kalena gasped, and her hand went to the teardrop diamond hanging around her neck. "I don't know who you think you are. I will not allow you to talk to me just any kind of way in my own home. Don't think for a minute I approve of you for my son."

Dreamy huffed out a breath and leaned an arm on the wrought-iron railing. "You're right. I should be more respectful, and I apologize for what I said just now. But let me make something clear. First of all, you don't know me. Yet, here you are, treating me like some hoodlum who crashed your party, when we both know that's not the case. Secondly, I don't deserve to be spoken to the way you just spoke to me. So I'd appreciate it if you didn't act as if you're above me. Lastly, if I leave, I'm one hundred percent sure Karter will too. Now is that what you want? Don't you want all of your family here to celebrate your anniversary?" Dreamy asked sweetly, hoping it masked the fury bubbling inside of her.

"My son will not leave if I ask him to stay."

Dreamy tilted her head. "Are you sure about that?"

Kalena waved her off. "Oh, so you think because you spread your legs for my boy that you have some type of control over him? Let me tell you something. You're a nobody. You're not the first woman he's been with, and I guarantee you won't be the last. Like I said, this is only temporary, so don't get too comfortable," she retorted, her bitchiness on full display.

"Don't get too comfortable with what?" Karter's deep voice came out of nowhere, and Dreamy and Kalena whipped around to see him standing at the balcony doorway.

Dreamy wasn't sure how much he heard, but his stormy expression showed he'd heard enough. His eyes softened when he looked at her.

"You okay?"

She started to lie and tell him that she was fine, but decided to go with the truth. She sighed and glanced at his mother. "I've been better. Your mother was officially introducing herself, letting me know who she is."

Karter clenched his jaw. "Of course she was." He slid his arm around Dreamy's waist and placed a kiss against her temple. "Mom, I don't know what you said, but I suggest you get used to having Dreamy around, because you'll be seeing her from time to time."

"Well, that's unacceptable," Kalena snapped. "She's rude, uncouth, and clearly, she doesn't belong around—"

"Enough!" Karter growled. "If that's how you feel, we can leave and I—"

"No, not you," she hurried to say, and gripped Karter's arm when he started to walk away. "I mean . . . I don't want you to leave."

Karter tightened his hold around Dreamy, and she glanced up at him. His jaw clenched as he struggled to stay calm. "This is my woman. If she's not welcome here, then neither am I."

Morgan bounded out onto the balcony but slowed as she took

in the scene. "I'm sure I don't want to know what's going on here, but I need to steal my friend."

Dreamy's left eyebrow shot up as she looked at the woman who had quickly become her friend. She didn't know what Morgan was up to, but she had a feeling it was something scandalous, and she was all for it.

"Ready to have some fun?" Morgan asked with a wicked gleam in her eyes.

The tension from a moment ago fell away, and Dreamy's grin matched hers. She glanced at Karter, who gave an imperceptive nod, and then turned back to Morgan.

"Definitely. Lead the way." Dreamy started to follow her new friend, but stopped. "Mrs. Redford, great party you have here. It was . . . interesting meeting you. Oh, and by the way, I think you might have some spinach crostini stuck in your teeth."

The woman gasped and turned away, probably to dig out the food, while Morgan snickered and pulled Dreamy back into the house.

"Come on, sis," she said. "Let's go and loosen this party up with a little 'Cupid Shuffle.' You lead."

"Sounds like fun."

KARTER GLOWERED AT HIS MOTHER, STRUGGLING TO KEEP HIS anger at bay. "You have gone too far this time. Just when I think you can't stoop any lower, you surprise me."

His mother tsked. "I will not have one of your little friends talk down to me. You didn't hear how she spoke to me."

"I didn't have to hear what she said or how it was said. I know her well enough to know that she didn't say anything that you didn't deserve.

"And she's not one of my *little friends*. She means everything to me, and if you even think about treating her less than respectfully, you'll never see me again."

Karter turned and walked away even though his mother was calling his name. If he stood there talking to her any longer, there was no telling what else he would say. No way in hell was he going to stand around and allow someone to mistreat Dreamy, even if it was his mother.

A few minutes later, he found Dreamy and Morgan in the ballroom. The two of them were indeed leading the choreographed line dance. This had to be a first for one of his mother's parties. Karter couldn't ever remember her having a DJ. She preferred live music, specifically jazz. As a matter of fact, there had been a band upstairs in the living room when he first arrived.

When he zoned in on the DJ, who was set up in the corner wearing headphones and standing over a turntable and laptop, he recognized him. Karter smiled.

Morgan strikes again.

The guy was a friend of hers, and he wondered if their mother knew the music had been taken over by a DJ. If she didn't, she'd know soon enough. The noise level had tripled, and more guests gravitated toward the room. Some stood off to the side watching, like Karter was doing, while others hurried to the dance floor and fell in step.

He chuckled and his gaze went back to Dreamy. It was no surprise that she was a good dancer, adding her own flavor to the moves. Karter's heart swelled as he watched her smiling, laughing, and just enjoying herself. It was as if she and his mother hadn't just exchanged heated words.

She was definitely the woman he wanted in his life.

After a few more upbeat tunes, the DJ slowed the music down, and "When a Man Loves a Woman" by Percy Sledge flowed through the speakers. Karter couldn't have asked for a more perfect song to dance with Dreamy. He weaved around a few people and made his way across the room just as she was about to walk off the dance floor, and she stopped.

Man, she was beautiful, and when she smiled at him as he approached, it felt as if his heart was going to burst with love.

"Dance with me," he said, gently gripping her hand.

"I'd love to."

There were still quite a few people on the dance floor, but Karter found a spot for him and Dreamy. He pulled her close, loving how perfect she felt in his arms.

"You're amazing," he said as they swayed to the music.

She leaned her head back slightly to look at him, and her smile was even brighter. "I think you're pretty special too. Thanks for coming to my rescue with your mother."

Karter shook his head and tried to fight the disappointment that crept in. "I'm sorry for whatever she said to you. Though I knew what she was capable of, I had hoped she'd behave herself tonight. But I don't think you'll have any more problems with her."

Dreamy's left eyebrow lifted skyward. "Seriously? That woman hates me."

"It doesn't matter what she thinks," he said, staring into her eyes. "Because I love you."

A soft gasped escaped her lips, and her eyes rounded. "Wha-what?"

"You heard me. I love you, baby, and if my mother has a problem with that, that has nothing to do with us."

Dreamy stopped moving, and she reached up and cupped his face with her hands. "I love you too," she said, only loud enough for him to hear.

When she lifted up on tiptoe, and her lips met his, Karter knew without a doubt that she was his and always would be.

Chapter Twenty-Seven

"WHY CAN'T YOU JUST DO WHAT I ASK?" GORDON SAID. "THEN we won't have these types of problems."

Dreamy stared at her boss, wondering if he was drunk or on drugs. There was no way he could be in his right mind and say that to her. No frickin' way. She'd had to deal with Karter's mother the other day, and now it looked like she was going to have to put her boss in his place too.

Be nice, her inner voice screamed. Gordon was her boss. At least for now. Until she found another job, she would have to play nice. But starting tomorrow, she was getting serious about looking for new employment.

"Gordon, you asked me to pull the report for the Alexander account, which I did," she said as calmly as she could. "It's in your inbox on your desk. You asked me to send another invoice to the Davis Group. I did that, and noted it on our group calendar. Then you asked me to call Freddie O'Neill and ask if he was free for lunch. I did, and he said he'd meet you at the restaurant at one thirty. Not only did I make reservations for you, I taped a message to your desk with that information, *and* I sent you a text. So what exactly have you asked me to do that I haven't done?"

Gordon pulled his cell phone from the front pocket of his jeans and looked at the screen. "Oh, I didn't realize you texted me. Got it. Whew," he said and headed to his office.

No Thank you, Dreamy.

No Great job, Dreamy.

No I don't know what I'd do without you, Dreamy.

Nothing.

Dreamy sat there for a solid five minutes debating whether or not to quit. If she had to work for him much longer, one of them wasn't going to survive, and she'd end up in jail.

The only thing that kept her from throwing her stapler at him today was the fact that it was in her desk drawer and not easily accessible. And he should probably thank Karter for her good mood. Because of him, she felt like the most cherished woman in the world.

She never knew she could be as happy as she was with Karter. Never in her wildest dreams did she think that she would fall madly and passionately in love with a man like him. Someone who made her feel special . . . like she was the most important person in his world.

After he had explained that even the most independent people needed a helping hand from time to time, Dreamy had agreed to let him get her car fixed. Of course, he wanted to buy her a new one, but she wasn't ready for that type of gift from him. It had been hard enough admitting that she needed help with car repairs. Karter came through for her, though. Now her vehicle looked and ran better than it had before she purchased it from Discount Johnny's Auto Lot.

"Hey, chica! Thank you for my flowers," Mariana said as she entered the office.

"You're welcome, and happy birthday."

"Aww, thanks, girl." She gave Dreamy a warm hug. "I was shocked to see them on my desk. For a minute there, I thought my husband had sent them. If he had, he was definitely going to get lucky tonight."

Dreamy laughed. "Well, let's pretend Luis sent them so that he can have a little fun tonight."

"I'll think about it." Mariana glanced down the hallway that led to Gordon's office. "Before I sit down, is Mr. Man here?"

"Girl, he's here, but don't let that stop you from hanging out for a minute. I need to talk to someone I actually like right about now."

Mariana laughed. "I'm not even going to ask what he did or said this time."

"Good, because if I think about it any longer, I'll probably end up quitting."

"Whoa, that bad, huh?"

"Yes," Dreamy said seriously.

She often joked about going to lunch and never coming back, but lately she was more tempted than ever. If he didn't follow through on his threats of firing her, she'd probably have to quit sooner than later. Mentally and emotionally, she couldn't take his craziness much longer.

"I heard the Powerball is over four hundred million dollars. You got your ticket?"

"Of course, and I have a feeling we're going to win tonight."

Mariana laughed. "You do realize you say that every time there's a drawing, right?"

"Yup, and I mean it every single time, but for real this time." Dreamy rubbed her hands together. "I feel it. It's going to happen. Besides, my left palm was itching this morning, and that means money is coming my way." At least that's what her grandmother used to say.

"Or it could mean that you need some lotion."

They both laughed, and Dreamy was glad her friend had stopped by. For the rest of the afternoon, she planned to forget about Gordon and focus on winning the Powerball lottery.

HOURS LATER, DREAMY DROPPED DOWN ON THE SOFA AND picked up the television remote. It was time for the lottery numbers to be drawn. She wanted to stay hopeful, but if she was going to win, she needed it tonight. The home repairs were starting to pile up, and her job situation was getting worse by the day. It was time for a major change in her life, and a lottery win would be a great start.

"Come on, Powerball," she whispered.

I need a win.

The Powerball lottery announcer came onto the screen. *"Good evening, America. Tonight's Powerball jackpot has climbed up to four hundred twenty million dollars. Get those tickets out, and let's see if you've won."*

Dreamy watched from the edge of her seat, silently praying for a win, knowing everyone else watching was probably doing the same.

"First number tonight is sixty-four. The next number is fifty-four . . ."

Oh my, God. Two numbers.

"And right after that, twenty-three, followed by forty-eight . . ."

"Ohmigod, ohmigod, ohmigod." Dreamy shot up from her seat with a death grip on one of the sofa pillows. Four numbers. They had four numbers! Even if they didn't win the jackpot, they would at least win a hundred bucks, which was better than nothing.

"We're ending the night with the number fourteen."

"Gramps!" Dreamy screamed and started jumping up and down. "Get in here! We have five numbers!"

And for your Powerball number . . . we have the number eleven."

Dreamy froze. Surely, she hadn't heard the lady right. Did she really say fourteen, twenty-three, forty-eight, fifty-four, sixty-four and Powerball eleven? Dreamy had been playing the same numbers for years. Had she really heard right?

"Once again, here are the winning numbers . . ."

The numbers were displayed across the flat-screen television, and Dreamy's knees went weak before she collapsed to the floor and her world went black.

"Dreamy. Dreamy. Wake up!"

"Slap her if you need to. It works. I see it on TV all the time."

Dreamy heard her cousin and grandfather talking, but they seemed so far away.

"Dreamy!" Someone patted her cheek and not too softly. "Come on, girl. Wake up!"

What the . . .

"She's coming around," Jordyn said.

Dreamy's eyes flew open and she bolted upright but cried out when her head connected with something hard.

"Ow!" she screamed, and grabbed her forehead.

"Damn it, girl! Ugh," Jordyn growled, and shoved her before scooting away. "Your hard-ass head is going to give me a damn concussion!"

"I could say the same to you." Dreamy squinted against the sudden pounding in her head. Then she made eye contact with her grandfather, who was looking at her with concern. And then she remembered. The lottery numbers. The *winning* lottery numbers.

"We won!" she screamed as Jordyn was walking away. "Gramps, we won. We're millionaires."

Her grandfather narrowed his eyes. "I think we need to call 911. The girl is talking crazy. How many fingers do I have up, Dreamboat?" He lifted three fingers . . . at least she thought there were three.

"Gramps, I'm serious. We won. We got all five numbers and Powerball. We won four hundred twenty million dollars."

Jordyn stopped and turned. "Say what now?"

Dreamy hurried to her feet, but swayed when the room started spinning. "Whoa." She gripped the arm of the sofa, struggling to get her bearings.

"Sit down before you kill yourself," Jordyn said, pushing her down to the sofa before sitting next to her. "Now what are you talking about? You guys won? Like . . . for real, for real won?"

"They just announced the numbers. Not *you guys*. *We all* won! We won the lottery," she repeated, struggling to believe it herself. "We're like . . . *millionaires*."

She didn't know how else to say it, but hearing the words come out of her mouth made her head spin again. Or maybe it was the jackhammer going crazy inside her skull.

Leaning forward, with her elbows on her thighs, Dreamy gripped the sides of her head with both hands as if that would keep it from exploding.

"Call 911. Girlie has lost her mind, and I'm worried about her. She's possessed about that lottery," her grandfather mumbled and sat in the upholstered chair next to the sofa.

"You mean *obsessed*," Jordyn corrected him.

"Possessed, obsessed, same difference," Gramps said.

"I'm telling y'all the truth. We won." Dreamy sat back slowly on the sofa and closed her eyes. "I can prove it. Give me your phone," she said to her cousin. "Better yet, look up the winning numbers for tonight's drawing."

"Okay, here they are," Jordyn said, but Dreamy rattled off the numbers, without looking, before her cousin could recite them.

"Oh my . . . That's impossible," Jordyn whispered.

Gramps whoop-whooped so loud, Dreamy's eyes flew open. Their grandfather was out of his seat, dancing around to some music that only he could hear. His moves could rival an old . . . old hip-hop dancer's steps, making him look thirty years younger.

"We're rich! We're rich, girls. We gotta go out and celebrate! Let me go get my hat. Oh, and, Dreamboat, give me one of your wigs for my lady friend. I'm taking her out on the town." He started from the room until Jordyn stopped him.

"You're not going anywhere, old man." She stood and started pacing in front of the television. "First of all, you don't have the money in your hands. Secondly, it's too late for you to be going out. Lastly, you're going to need more than a hat if you're planning to leave this house. Those . . ." She waved her hands up and down at him. "Short shorts and too-tight-to-be-considered-decent tank top you're wearing are bound to get you arrested for indecent exposure."

"Are you sure we won?" her grandfather asked as if Jordyn hadn't just said anything. "Because I don't want to start spending money in my head and it turns out I don't have none."

"I'm positive," Dreamy said, and slowly leaned forward to test her equilibrium. "I know those numbers like the back of my hand, but I'll show you the ticket."

Heart hammering with excitement, she ignored the pounding in her head and leaped off the sofa and hurried out of the living room, but her foot caught the edge of the leopard-print rug. Tumbling forward, she cried out when her chin hit the laminate wood flooring. Red-hot pain shot through her face and legs, but she couldn't stop. She jumped up.

Get the ticket, her mind screamed as she tore down the hallway, slipping and sliding in her fluffy socks. She stormed into her bedroom, dived onto the twin bed, and slid across the silky comforter until she reached the other side of the room. She fell again but popped up, ignoring more pain to her knees.

"Would you stop acting crazy?" Jordyn yelled from the doorway.

"I can't help it! We just won an *obscene* amount of money, *millions* of dollars. I don't know how I'm supposed to act. Hell, I can barely breathe." Excitement warred within her as she frantically jerked open her backpack and pulled everything out. "It's in here. I left it in here," she mumbled as unease started creeping in.

When Dreamy didn't find it in her backpack, where it was supposed to be, she rushed to her nightstand. It should've been in her bag, but maybe she took it out for some reason.

Pulse pounding loudly in her ear, she felt panic seeping into her bones. "Come on. Come on. Where are you?" She anxiously shook out a magazine, hoping the ticket would fall out of it. When only perfume advertisements tumbled to the floor, uncontrollable fear shot down her spine. "Omigod, omigod, please, please, please help me."

The lamp crashed to the floor, followed by her alarm clock as she jerked open the drawers and started pulling papers and envelopes out.

"God, *help me*. I have to find it." She heard her cell phone ringing, which only made her crazier.

"Jordyn!" Dreamy screamed at the top of her lungs, trying to keep the tears at bay, but failing miserably.

"I'm right here. Please don't tell me you can't find it?"

Dreamy swallowed, tears blurring her eyes. "We—we won," she choked out, her breaths coming in short spurts. "I know we won, but . . . the ticket is not here."

"Shoot. I guess we didn't win." Gramps plopped down on the bed.

"Okay, Dreamy, sit down and let's figure this out."

All three of them sat side by side on the bed while Dreamy tried to think of every possible place the ticket could be.

"Maybe it's in your car?" her cousin said.

"No. I don't keep anything in that car, and it's nowhere else in the house. I always keep it in the backpack. Oh, God. Karter's always telling me to sign the back of it, and I didn't."

Gramps snapped his fingers and leaped up. "That reminds me. I'll be right back."

Dreamy's tears fell faster than she could wipe them away. "I am going to kill our grandfather if he has that ticket . . . or worse, if he—"

"Here it is, Dreamboat." He proudly held a slip of paper up between his thumb and forefinger. "I forgot to put it back after I used it to floss my teeth."

Dreamy stood, but almost collapsed with relief. "Give me that!"

She snatched it from him and quickly grabbed a pen from her backpack and scribbled her signature. Once done, she stared down at the numbers, then looked up at Jordyn and Gramps.

"We won!"

They all started jumping up and down, as if on a trampoline, screaming at the top of their lungs. After playing for so many years and not hitting the jackpot, they'd finally done it. They were millionaires.

Dreamy heard her phone ringing again and stopped jumping while trying to catch her breath. With her heart still racing, she frantically glanced around the room until she spotted the device on the floor between the bed and the nightstand. Snatching it up, she grinned when she saw that it was Karter.

"We won!" she screamed into the phone.

After a long silence, he finally spoke. "Um . . . you won what?" he asked slowly, and Dreamy laughed because she was sure he knew what she was referring to but found it hard to believe.

"The lottery," she said just as slowly, matching his tone, but then she screeched. "We won the lottery!"

Chapter Twenty-Eight

"WHAT DO YOU MEAN YOU QUIT?" GORDON ASKED, LOOKING AT Dreamy as if he didn't recognize her.

The man's cluelessness never ceased to amaze her. How could he be surprised that she was leaving when he consistently belittled her and made her feel less than? What type of idiot was that oblivious? Surely he had to know how many times she had saved his ass.

But it didn't matter. She'd had enough.

After winning the lottery a few days ago, she had a plan. Well, a rough plan. Dreamy still needed to sit down with Jordyn and their grandfather to work out the details. But quitting her job wasn't supposed to happen for another few weeks. Not until the winnings were deposited into her bank account—but it was too late now. She had verbalized the words that she'd wanted to say months ago: *I quit.* There was no taking them back.

"You heard me, Gordon. I'm done." Dreamy dropped down in her office chair and started going through the desk drawers, pulling out her personal belongings. "I've had enough of you treating me like crap. I hate that after all this time, you *never* show me any respect. And it's not like I haven't earned it, but more than anything, I'm just tired of having to think for you. It's hard enough thinking for myself, and I'm done."

The only issue with quitting her job now was that her finances were going to be even tighter than usual until the lottery winnings were actually deposited into her account, which would take approximately eight weeks. She'd have to figure out something, but it wouldn't include taking money from Karter. He wanted to give her a loan until she received her winnings. Dreamy turned him down. He was the most generous man she'd ever met. Still, she was sticking to her principles and not borrowing money from him or anyone else.

The day after she won the lottery, they'd had a heated discussion because he was concerned for her safety, and he wanted her and her family to move as soon as possible. In California, names of lottery winners were made public. Though Dreamy hadn't given it much thought, Karter feared that the media, so-called friends and family, and a host of other people would start coming out of the woodwork for a handout. He insisted that she, Jordyn, and Gramps would need to find a place with security to live, even temporarily.

So far, only the people closest to her, and Karter's assistant and driver knew about her winning. Dreamy hadn't even told Gordon, her co-workers, or her friend Mariana. But Mariana would know soon when Dreamy presented her with a fat check, as well as a job offer.

Excitement bubbled inside of her. Mariana was going to freak. Her friend was always so supportive and right there to give an encouraging word whenever Dreamy needed one. She just hoped Mariana would take her up on the job offer. Director of the nonprofit once it was up and running. Dreamy was prepared to offer her more money than she currently earned, and a few other perks.

But in the meantime, she was keeping her news quiet.

"I'm not accepting your resignation," Gordon said as if he had a choice.

"Fine. Don't accept it, but I won't be here tomorrow, or the next day, or the day after that. As a matter of fact, I'm *never* coming back."

"But . . . but . . ." He stood there looking like someone had kicked his puppy, and Dreamy almost felt sorry for him, but she had to be strong. Quitting her job was way overdue.

"You're not even giving me a two-week notice. Who's going to train a new person?"

Dreamy dug the large binder from the bottom drawer and set it on the desk. "Whoever you hire won't have a problem. I've written every single detail about the job, about the equipment, passwords, and I even included how you like your coffee. They'll be fine."

"I paid you well and this is how you repay me?" he snapped.

Dreamy reined in the anger that was teetering on the edge of her control. "You might've paid me for what I did around here, but you didn't pay me nearly enough for the mental and emotional stress caused by dealing with you. And, Gordon, you would be amazed at how far a *thank you*, or *good job*, or *thanks for your help* would've gone. You never said any of that. You walk around here entitled like we're all supposed to kiss your ass and thank you for allowing us to, but I'm done."

Dreamy glanced at her watch, noting that she had fifteen minutes before she needed to meet Karter outside. He was picking her up for a quick lunch since he had a meeting nearby. Their lunch conversation should be interesting. What would he think when she told him she had quit? Actually, from day one, he'd been saying that she could do better than working for Gordon.

She looped the strap of her handbag onto her shoulder and

huffed out a breath. "Gordon, thank you for giving me this opportunity. I wish you and the company the best."

Dreamy left him standing at her desk as she walked away. When
she stepped onto the elevator and pushed the lobby button, a wave
of emotions hit her at once. Guilt for the way she was leaving her
job. Anxiousness for leaving a job without having her lottery winnings in hand, and fear. Not only did she not have a job, but what
if for some reason she didn't receive her lottery winnings?

Her heart beat a little faster and her breaths came in short
spurts as her anxiety mounted and the what-ifs played on loop
inside her head. Her arms tightened around her oversize handbag
as the elevator headed down, stopping at almost every other floor.
What if something happened . . . a fluke of sorts and she hadn't
actually won the lottery? She'd be totally screwed, and instead of
looking for a bigger house, she and her family would be stuck in the
shack that they currently called home. The walls would start crumbling around them, and the roof . . . hell, there wouldn't be a roof
because it would literally cave in if they didn't get it fixed.

By the time the elevator doors slid open, her pulse pounded in
her ears, drowning out the usual noise of the lobby. Dreamy
stepped off to the side, near a small seating area, and leaned on the
back of a leather sofa.

Stop. Stop. Stop! she told herself. She was being ridiculous. Getting herself worked up for no reason wasn't going to help her current situation.

Just calm down and pull yourself together.

After a few minutes of deep breathing, a calmness that she
hadn't felt all day settled over her. It was amazing how quickly
negative thoughts could take over her mind, but she wasn't suc-
cumbing to them. She started replaying her daily mantra in her
head, and within seconds, everything around her seemed brighter.

A smile slid across her lips as she embraced her renewed energy.

I got this. Nothing was going to get her down. She no longer had to work for a man she didn't respect and, more importantly, she was a lottery winner.

Dreamy headed to the entrance with extra pep in her step and nodded a greeting at a few familiar faces. But she pulled up short when she spotted the last person she ever expected to see.

Brandon.

"Hey, baby," he said, flashing one of those huge smiles that probably got him a lot of women. "You ready?"

"Brandon, what are you doing here?"

He frowned. "You didn't get my text?"

"No, I didn't."

He pulled his phone from the front pocket of his suit pants. "I texted you a few hours ago to tell you I was picking you up for lunch. I haven't been able to stop thinking about you since running into you at the college."

"First of all, I wouldn't go to lunch with you if you were the last person on the planet. Secondly, why do you all of a sudden want to have lunch with me? Lastly, I blocked your number a few weeks ago when I should've done it sooner. Like after you embarrassed the hell out of me in front of your co-workers and effectively ended our relationship."

Brandon sighed dramatically, and Dreamy wanted to throat punch him. How had she not recognized sooner what an arrogant asshole he was?

"I'm sorry," he said, shocking the hell out of her. He hadn't apologized then, and Dreamy wondered why now. Surely it couldn't be because he thought she'd give him another chance.

"Why are you sorry? You admitted to meaning everything you said to me that night. So why the sudden change of heart?"

"I wish I'd handled that situation better." He moved closer, looking at her with so much compassion she almost believed he was sincere. *Almost.* "Dreamy, I want a second chance."

"Why?" she asked again, feeling a little uncomfortable with his closeness. She started to step back, but he stopped her with a hand on her arm.

"What do you mean, why? We were perfect together."

"Yet you broke up with me."

He threw up his hands. "Damn, how long are you going to hold that against me? I said I was sorry, and I meant it," he snapped. "I'm trying to make things right, but you're not making it easy."

Anger stirred inside of her. "Why the hell should I?" she ground out, aware that people were around. Still. Some things needed to be said. "You suddenly decide that you're sorry, and I'm supposed to just forgive you? I don't think so." She started to walk away, but stopped. "Then again, maybe I should, that way we can both move on."

Hope flared in his eyes. "Exactly. I messed up. I messed up big-time, and I'm trying my best to make things right."

"Oh, no, you misunderstood me. I forgive you, but I also want nothing to do with you. I've moved on to bigger and better things."

He chuckled. "Come on, baby. You're trying to tell me that you've done better than me?"

"Yeah, can you believe it?" she asked sarcastically.

"Look, why don't we go to lunch and talk?"

"We have nothing to talk about."

Dreamy started to walk away, but he grabbed her by the elbow. His hold wasn't hard or uncomfortable, but now she was wondering why he was trying so hard to get back into her good graces.

She eased out of his hold. "Why are you really here, Brandon?"

"I told you. I wanted to take you—"

"I want the truth. What do you want? Because there is no way you just decided to show up and play nice."

He sighed and glanced down at the floor as if realizing the jig was up. When he returned his attention to her, his eyes had softened. For a moment, he looked like the man she had originally fallen for. No one could ever say he wasn't a good-looking man with soulful brown eyes and chiseled features. Which was what first caught her attention when he'd approached her at a bar.

"I really am sorry for my behavior and the way I treated you, but I also figured you'd need a lawyer."

Dreamy's eyebrows bunched together. "What are you talking about? I didn't do anything. Why would I need a lawyer?" He was a brilliant corporate lawyer, and also one of the youngest attorneys at his firm.

"I heard," he said.

"You heard what?"

"That you finally won the lottery."

Realization hit Dreamy upside the head. She should've known he'd heard about it. Why else would he be there? *Silly me.* Just when she was starting to believe that maybe he really was sorry about how things ended between them.

"Congratulations! I know you've always said you would win, and I always doubted you, but wow, you really did it."

"How did you find out?"

Brandon shrugged nonchalantly. "Public knowledge. That's why I think you need my services."

Dreamy couldn't imagine having a bodyguard, something else that Karter had suggested, but if Brandon was bold enough to come to her job, others might start seeking her out as well.

"I don't need you or your services," she said to her ex. "So you can crawl back under that rock you've been hiding beneath, and leave me alone."

"Listen to me," he said between gritted teeth, his grip firm on her upper arm. "That's too much money for you to be trying to manage on your own. Let me and my team help. I can personally—"

"You can't personally do shit for her." Karter's deep voice came out in a low growl, startling them both.

Brandon released his hold and whirled around. He puffed out his chest like he was going to do something. Sure, he was tall, but Karter had a few inches on him, as well as a larger build.

"Who the hell are you, and why are you in our business?" Brandon asked, and then squinted. "Wait, aren't you—"

"The person who will break your damn hand if you *ever* touch her again."

Whoa. There was a lethalness in Karter's tone that Dreamy hadn't heard before, and the way he glowered at Brandon surprised and thrilled her. There was no doubt in her mind that he could make good on his threat.

"Karter." She hurried to his side, hoping to keep any drama from erupting, or blood from being shed. He slid his arm around her waist without taking his attention off Brandon. "I didn't know you were here. You should've just called me. I would've come out."

"Wait." Brandon's jaw dropped to the floor as his gaze bounced from Dreamy to Karter, and back to her again. "You and . . . *Karter Redford*? Together?"

"Karter, this is Brandon."

"I figured as much," Karter said dryly. "What I don't understand is why he's here manhandling you."

Brandon quickly whipped out a business card and flashed a million-dollar smile. "Actually, I'm an attorney, and I was offering to provide Dreamy my legal services." He held the card out, but Karter didn't even bother looking at it.

"She doesn't need it or anything else from you. So stay the hell away from her."

Karter eased his arm from around Dreamy and linked his fingers with hers. An overwhelming feeling of rightness settled around her as they moved away from Brandon. Dreamy didn't bother saying goodbye or looking back. As a matter of fact, from now on, she planned to look only forward. Her life was about to get interesting, and she planned to enjoy the ride.

Chapter Twenty-Nine

AN HOUR AND A HALF LATER, DREAMY WAS DRIVING HOME. Lunch had been fabulous, and as she'd expected, Karter was glad she had quit her job. He thought it was time she focused solely on getting the nonprofit started. He still didn't think it was a good idea to use only the lottery winnings to fund the venture, and Dreamy agreed. She'd use a big chunk of it, but fundraising would definitely be in her future.

She turned left onto her street, but slowed.

What the . . .

A handful of people stood in front of her house. Fear crept through her body as various scenarios played through her mind. Had something happened to her grandfather? Had the house been broken into? What were . . .

The moment she parked, reporters surrounded the car, and camera flashes practically blinded her.

"Ms. Daniels, how does it feel to be a lottery winner? What are you planning to do with the money?"

One question after another was thrown at her as she hurried out of her vehicle.

"Is it true that you're dating the venture capitalist Karter Redford?"

That question made Dreamy pause for a second, but she quickly recovered and darted to the house. Her heart was beating hard enough to be heard down the street as she practically burst through the front door.

The moment she cleared the threshold, she slammed the door and fell against it.

"Oh, my goodness," she murmured and dropped her purse on the sofa.

Jordyn strolled into the living room. "I think it's safe to say people know. The media got here a few minutes ago." She peeked out of the blinds. "Actually, it looks like two more showed up."

"I guess Karter was right," Dreamy said on a sigh. "He predicted this would happen, and we don't even have the money yet. And one of those guys asked me about Karter. How do they find out this stuff?"

This was the first time since dating him that there'd been any media presence. He'd told her early on that they rarely sought him out, mainly because he stayed out of the public eye. Clearly, that was about to change.

"So, what should we do first?" Jordyn asked and sat on the arm of the sofa.

"Well, I already got the ball rolling. I quit my job."

Her cousin popped up. "What? Dreamy! I thought you said that you were going to wait. My little money won't carry us that long, especially if we have to find a more secure place to live."

"Calm down. We'll figure it all out. We always do."

Jordyn shook her head. "We've been trying to keep our heads above water for years. Now with one less income, we can't—"

"We can do this. We've always been able to stretch our funds, and we'll keep doing it until the winnings are deposited."

Jordyn twisted her bottom lip between her teeth. "Yeah, but this situation is different. We need to find a place to live that is more secure. I'm worried about Gramps getting caught by the hordes of reporters and photographers."

"I know." Dreamy paused and sighed. She really didn't want to do this. "So, we do have another option that I was against initially. Karter offered us his penthouse temporarily."

Jordyn's mouth fell open. "Seriously?"

"I know we don't usually take handouts, but we might have to take him up on his offer this time. The good news is, the place is conveniently located not far from your office and my school. So it won't be out of your way or mine."

Her cousin nodded slowly and smiled. "I knew cutie-pie Karter with a *K* was a good catch, but damn. That's beyond generous."

Dreamy laughed and totally agreed. She was still a little concerned about accepting help regarding their living arrangements, but she didn't want to flex her independence at the risk of her or her family's safety.

As for Karter, she couldn't imagine going through this change in her life without someone like him by her side.

"Okay, so the thing is," she said, and headed to the kitchen with her bag, "now that people know, we should plan on packing the bare necessities and move out tonight."

"That can be arranged. I have a study group later, but it won't take long for me to pack a couple of bags for me and Gramps."

For the next thirty minutes, they sat at the kitchen table and Dreamy filled her cousin in on what happened at work. She also told her about Brandon, which was a big mistake considering how Jordyn freaked out. She only calmed down when Dreamy told her how Karter swooped in and handled her ex.

"Now, where's Gramps?" she asked, surprised he hadn't made an appearance. "We all need to sit down and talk about next steps."

"You called?" their grandfather said, strutting into the kitchen looking like a pimp. He was dressed to the nines in a suit and a pair of shiny shoes, both of which she'd never seen before, along with a black fedora with a feather on the left side. "So, what do you think?" he asked, doing a slow turn as Dreamy sat dumbfounded. With a wrinkle-free shirt and clean-shaven face, he literally looked like a million bucks.

"Okay, who are you and what have you done with my grandfather? And how did you get all of this?"

"My closet. I've been waiting years to wear this stuff again. I figured since I'm hanging out with your rich boyfriend later, that I—"

"Wait. What?"

Gramps stopped moving. "He didn't tell you? We're going to some fancy-schmancy bar for a drink. I told him I wanted to talk to him, and we agreed that'll be this evening."

"He didn't even say anything," Dreamy said as their grandfather joined them at the table. "Just don't embarrass me, Gramps."

He grunted as if that was the most ridiculous thing he'd ever heard. "Now would I do that?" His expression was so serious it made Dreamy and Jordyn laugh.

Dreamy dug through her bag for her notebook. For years, she imagined what it would be like to win the lottery. But no amount of planning could've prepared her for the mental and emotional roller coaster that came with winning.

The last few days had been exciting and scary as she thought about what to do with her portion of the winnings. Over the years, she had created lists of ideas detailing what to spend the money on. Recently, she'd broken it down into three columns with dollar-amount headings. She'd wanted to be prepared for whatever she won. Their winnings were twice as much as she had expected.

"Anyway, we have to discuss how we're going to spend the money on our current needs," Dreamy said, and opened her notebook.

"I already told you girls that I want you both to split my share of the money. All I ask is that you give me enough to pay for a nice assisted living place. I don't need nothin' else."

"Quit talking crazy, old man. You're staying with one of us forever. Case closed," Jordyn said. "Speaking of splitting the money. I shouldn't get thirty-three percent of it since I didn't buy into the lottery."

Dreamy slammed down her pen. "Jordyn, we're not going to keep arguing about this. The three of us are family. When one wins, we all win. Case closed."

Her cousin threw up her hands. "Fine, but I would've been happy with just a new car and enough money to pay this last semester of law school."

"Well, you'll be able to take care of those expenses and have money left over," Dreamy said.

"All right. Whatever you say."

"I'm glad you girls will finally get to live the life I've always wanted for you. I only wish your grandmother was here to get in on the fun," Gramps said.

Dreamy covered her grandfather's hand. "Yeah, I know, but I'm sure she's here in spirit."

"I'm sure she is." Gramps stood. "I'm going to take a nap. Let me know when Karter gets here, or whenever we're ready to spend the money. Whichever comes first."

Dreamy laughed. "Will do." Once he was gone, she turned to Jordyn. "I'll call Karter and let him know that we're going to take him up on his offer to use the penthouse. Knowing him, he'll probably insist on sending someone over to help move us. In the meantime, let's get packed."

Before they could leave the kitchen, someone rang the doorbell. Dreamy assumed it was one of the reporters and considered not answering until the person started banging on the door.

She tiptoed across the room and looked through the peephole, then jumped back. "Crap."

Jordyn stood a few feet behind her. "Who is it? A reporter? The police?"

"No, worse. My mother."

"COME ON, SWEETHEART. AT SOME POINT YOU'RE GOING TO HAVE to talk to her," Karter said with his arms securely wrapped around Dreamy.

They were standing near the railing on the rooftop deck of the penthouse and gazing out over the city. One thing about Karter and his family, they did a masterful job of finding properties with unbelievable views.

She and her family had arrived twenty minutes ago with Tarrah in tow. Dreamy still couldn't believe her mother had shown up out of the blue. Then again, yes, she could believe it. She should've known that once Tarrah learned about the lottery win, she'd show up with her hand out. Granted, she hadn't asked for money, but only because Dreamy hadn't given her the opportunity. Had it been up to her, she would've insisted that her mother stay at the house while the rest of them stayed at the penthouse.

"I can't deal with my mother right now," she said, snuggling closer to Karter when the wind picked up. It was cooler than it had been lately, but still warmer than most parts of the country.

"Well, you're going to have to deal with her at some point. I have a feeling she's not going away until you guys talk. Besides, you forgave Brandon and closed that chapter of your life. Now you should do the same with your mother. Who knows, maybe you two can make peace and live happily—"

"That's not going to happen, at least the happily-ever-after part. I decided when she left me on my grandparents' doorstep and never came back for me that I didn't want her in my life. That hasn't changed, and I'm comfortable with that decision."

"Then tell her that. You hiding up here is only prolonging the inevitable."

Dreamy released a noisy sigh. "You're right, as usual."

Karter placed a kiss against her temple and held her tighter. "I love being right."

Dreamy chuckled and turned to face him. Her arms slid around his waist. "And I love you," she said. "Thank you again for letting us stay here. It was extremely generous, and I'm sorry I fought you on the idea."

"No worries. I know how independent you are, but your safety is important to me, and I'm glad you came around."

Karter lowered his lips to hers and kissed her sweetly. Dreamy couldn't think of a time when she'd been happier than she was with him. She couldn't wait to see what came next for them. No doubt it would be spectacular.

When the kiss ended, Karter rested his forehead against hers. "You ready to do this?"

"As ready as I'll ever be. Seems this is a day of facing my past. First Brandon, now Tarrah." Dreamy had convinced herself that she had forgiven her mother years ago for abandoning her, but clearly, she hadn't. Otherwise, she wouldn't have had a problem with her showing up. But like Dreamy had told Brandon, in order for her to move on, she was going to have to forgive.

A short while later, she and Karter walked hand in hand down the stairs and entered the living room. Her grandfather was camped out on the sofa that faced the largest television Dreamy had ever seen.

Gramps turned to them. "I'm getting one of these for my bedroom," he said, pointing at the TV. "And I'm getting a toilet that has a seat warmer. When I'm not watching TV, I'll probably just hang out in the bathroom."

Dreamy couldn't help but laugh. Her grandfather was a character, and she couldn't imagine her life without him. She walked over to the back of the sofa and bent down and kissed his cheek.

"Start making a list, Gramps. That way you can get everything you want."

He stood slowly and walked around the sofa before stopping in front of her. "I'm sorry, Dreamboat. I shouldn't have told your mother about the lottery. I didn't know she'd show up."

"No worries, Gramps. It's time she and I had a talk. Where is she anyway?"

"In the study," he said. "And if she's looking for a handout, I'll give her something out of my portion of the money. You hear me?"

Dreamy started to argue, but instead said, "Yes, sir."

"Okay, babe. Gramps and I are going to head out," Karter said.

"Wait," Dreamy said in a panic. "You're leaving me here with her?"

Karter's eyes softened and he cupped her cheek. "Yes, but you know I'm only a phone call away. Your grandfather and I have plans."

"Yeah, we're going out on the town tonight," Gramps said, turning off the television and grabbing his hat. "So don't wait up."

"Fine. Just leave me here while you guys go out and have fun, and, Gramps, please try to stay out of trouble."

"I'll try, Dreamboat, but I can't make any promises."

Karter laughed and kissed her before they left the apartment.

Dreamy sighed and went in search of her mother. When she made it to the study, which was decorated similarly to Karter's office at work, Tarrah was sitting on the sofa typing away on her cell phone.

"Mom," Dreamy said, and strolled into the room.

Tarrah's head shot up, and then she stood. She started toward Dreamy, but stopped and looked more uncomfortable than Dreamy felt.

"This is a beautiful place, and your boyfriend is gorgeous. Clearly, he's loaded. I always said, it's just as easy to fall in love with a rich man as it is a poor one. Dad told me Karter's father is that famous movie star. Have you met him?"

"I have." Dreamy walked farther into the room, but kept her distance. "Is that why you showed up, so you could check out my boyfriend?"

Tarrah huffed out a breath and ran her fingers through her long, wavy hair. The woman didn't seem to age a bit. There'd been a time when people said that the two of them could pass for twins, and now Dreamy had to agree. They looked so much alike, it was almost scary.

Of course, there were differences. Tarrah favored muted colors for her attire. Her wardrobe was basically black, white, and gray. The few times that Dreamy had seen her, she couldn't remember her mother ever wearing any bold colors. Tarrah also never left the house unless she was dressed to impress, like now. According to her, you never knew who you might meet on the street. Might as well make a good impression. Her mother also hated wigs.

"Listen, I'm sorry about just showing up. I didn't mean to upset you."

"Why are you here, Tarrah?" Dreamy knew her mother hated it when she called her by her first name.

Tarrah pursed her lips, then ambled over to the humongous

window behind the desk. She stared out of it for a few minutes before speaking. "I've missed you guys, and I've been thinking about coming back to LA," she said, and turned to face Dreamy. "I'd also like for you and me to try and rebuild our relationship."

Dreamy stared at her mother for a moment, then released a humorless laugh. "You're kidding, right? I start dating a rich man *and* win the lottery. Now you suddenly want to get to know me and play the part of a loving mother? I don't think so. Why are you really here? The obvious guess is money."

"When did you get so disrespectful? That's not how I raised—"

"See, here's the thing, you didn't raise me. Unless you're counting the first twelve years of my life, and even then, you barely gave me the time of day."

"That's not true," she snapped.

"It is true. So don't stand there pretending that you all of sudden care about me."

A heavy silence fell between them. Dreamy would never know if her mother was on the up-and-up, and that was okay. They could be mother and daughter from a distance, but nothing more.

"I forgive you, Mom," she said just above a whisper, and by her shocked expression, Tarrah heard her. "You can't stay here with us, but we'll be happy to put you up in a hotel for a couple of days while you're in town. Oh, and Gramps will have some money for you soon. Be sure to see him before you leave."

"You're kicking me out? But I'm your mother."

"That may be, but I think we should stick with our usual arrangement of living on opposite sides of the country and talking on the phone on occasion."

"But you said you forgave me," her mother said in a small voice, and Dreamy's heart melted a little.

"I do, Mom. I really do, but I'm not ready to have a relationship with you. Not the type that you're claiming to want."

Tarrah nodded and walked back to the sofa where she'd left her purse and suitcase. "I understand. Hopefully in time, you'll change your mind and reach out to me. Until then, I'll respect your wishes."

"Thank you. I appreciate that."

This was the most cordial they'd been in years. Maybe . . . just maybe one day they could at least be friends. Especially since Dreamy already knew that anything was possible.

Chapter Thirty

KARTER GLANCED UP FROM THE DOCUMENTS IN FRONT OF HIM just as Gloria entered his office wearing a familiar scowl. He sighed, and dropped his pen onto the desk, knowing that look on her face well. The look of disappointment.

After Delton died of a heart attack, she had told Karter that he was next if he didn't make changes. He tried. He lasted for a few months, thanks to Dreamy coming into his life. But lately, he had fallen back into old habits.

"Do you want me to order dinner before I leave?" Gloria asked, stopping a few feet from the desk.

A quick peek at the time in the right-hand corner of his laptop revealed that it was seven o'clock. Shit. He hadn't called Dreamy as promised.

Where had the time gone? He arrived at work at five that morning with back-to-back meetings that had started at nine. Karter couldn't believe how fast his days went, but it didn't matter at the moment, because he was pretty sure Dreamy was pissed and wouldn't accept any more excuses.

He huffed out a breath and wiped his hands down his face. "Yeah. Dinner would be good since I can't leave until I finish going through this report."

"You can leave whenever you want. You're the boss, Karter. That report isn't going anywhere, and I don't know why you insist on putting this type of pressure on yourself. You control what goes on around here."

Karter rubbed his tired eyes. The last thing he needed was a lecture. "Gloria, please don't start. I know, but—"

"But nothing! You're doing it again. Acting like you're the only person who can do this work. You have a staff. A very capable staff, I might add. Yet you're operating like you used to when you first started the business.

"You have to know by now that there's more to life than work. You're like a son to me, and I hate what you're doing to yourself. And don't get me started on how you've been treating Dreamy. If you keep this up, you're going to lose the best thing that's ever happened to you."

He already felt guilty about canceling on Dreamy two times this week. The last couple of months, actually. He'd just gotten so busy with work and had fires to put out daily. She told him that she understood, especially since she had work to do too. Still, he knew last night she had been disappointed about having to go to the theater with her friend Mariana instead of him.

"After I close this deal, I'll take a couple of days off."

Gloria rolled her eyes and shook her head. "Sure you will," she said, her voice flat. "What would you like for dinner?"

"Surprise me."

She turned on her heel. "Oh, I'll surprise you all right," he heard her mumble as she walked out the door.

DREAMY WAS HAPPY WHEN GLORIA CALLED TO SEE IF SHE HAD time to bring dinner to Karter. It was just the opportunity she needed. They both had been so busy lately, but Karter was the one who kept canceling their dates.

Now that Dreamy had found a large office suite to house the nonprofit, most of her time was spent there. She and Mariana, who had quit her job to work with Dreamy, were there daily getting the place in order. They made a great team and were getting a lot of prep work done.

It would be a while before they officially opened the doors to the nonprofit, but she had finally submitted the paperwork for her 501(c)(3). It would take months to get approved, but it was a major step in the right direction.

She strolled into Karter's office building and checked in with security. Had she not had help from Gloria and Najee tonight, she wouldn't have been able to pull off this little surprise. The two had been a godsend.

As Dreamy took the elevator to the top floor, she glanced at her appearance in the mirrored wall to her left. She'd come a long way from her shabby-chic style, but hadn't given up on her unique taste altogether. The orange multicolor boho maxi dress that fastened on the left side of her waist had a deep split that showcased her left leg with each step she took. It was bold and daring, and Karter wouldn't be able to resist her. She gave him a pass for canceling a couple of dates, but not tonight. Tonight, he was going to take time to have dinner with her whether he liked it or not.

A wicked smile spread across her lips as the steel doors of the elevator whooshed open. It was time she showed her man what he was missing each time he canceled on her.

Dreamy stepped out into the quiet hallway. Now that she was

no longer working at Mathison's, she stopped by KR Ventures often, except for the last couple of weeks. Karter was putting in extra hours because the company had taken on more clients and one of his managers was still out. That was forcing him, in his opinion, to pick up the slack.

"You made it," Gloria said when Dreamy stepped into the suite.

"Yes, thanks to you and Najee. I appreciate you giving me the heads-up about dinner. I should be able to take it from here."

"Great. Good luck with him. He can be so stubborn at times."

Dreamy laughed. "Yeah, I know. I also know how serious he is about work. Hopefully, he won't be mad at the intrusion."

"He could never be mad at you, dear. He's been working nonstop, and I think you showing up tonight will be the perfect excuse for him to take a break. You're probably the only person he'll listen to."

"I don't know about that. He canceled on me twice this week."

Of course, he promised to make it up to her, but Dreamy was concerned that he was falling back into old habits. He had told her that, before she came along, he easily put in sixteen-hour days. That wasn't healthy for anyone.

"Trust me, he's crazy about you. He's just been distracted lately, but I'm glad he has you to shift that distraction." The older woman grabbed her handbag from the desk. "I'm heading out. I'll lock this door and you can go on in."

"Okay, thank you."

"It's my pleasure, dear. Have a good evening."

"You too."

Dreamy watched her leave, hoping that the woman was right about Karter being okay with her just showing up. She inhaled a deep breath and released it slowly.

Here goes nothing.

When she reached the door to his office, she knocked, and then a muffled voice told her to come in.

"I know it's late, Scott, but I need those numbers run . . ."

His voice trailed off and his eyebrows shot up when he saw Dreamy. His gaze did a slow glide down her body and back up again before lingering on her breasts, which were barely contained inside the colorful dress. A slow smile spread across his tempting mouth.

For the first time since planning this surprise, Dreamy relaxed. He appeared genuinely happy to see her, and relief spread through her body. She strolled in, closing the door behind her. She moved to the opposite side of the room, where the table was located.

"Scott, let me call you back. Actually, I'll give you a call in the morning." He hung up the phone and stood. "Hey, sweetheart. This is a pleasant surprise."

"Hi yourself. I heard that you might be hungry."

As he rounded the desk and strolled toward her, Dreamy eyed him, giving him a once-over similar to the one he had given her, noting that he had shed his suit jacket and tie. That left him in a white shirt with the sleeves rolled up to his forearms, and navy-blue pants. He looked comfortable, but the lines at the corners of his eyes showed he was tired.

"I'm hungry all right, but suddenly it's not for food." He reached for her hand before lifting her arm as if he were going to spin her. "You look absolutely breathtaking."

Dreamy grinned, and when he released her hand, she stepped into his open arms. Without another word, his mouth met hers. She'd missed him, and if the kiss was any indication, he'd missed her too.

It didn't matter how often they kissed, whenever their lips touched it felt like Christmas morning with a ton of gifts under the tree.

The man's masterful lips and tongue never failed, and Dreamy was glad that she got to reap the benefits of his skills.

She didn't want to think about how he'd mastered his abilities. He slowly lifted his head, and a smile spread across his face. "God, I'm glad to see you."

She eased out of his hold and started removing items from the picnic basket. "You could see me every day if work wasn't more important."

He pulled out a chair for her. "Work is definitely not more important than you. It's just that several deals are happening at the same time, and we fell behind."

Dreamy nodded. She didn't bother reminding him that he was the boss and that he should be able to better balance his work and personal life by delegating. That conversation would be a waste of hot air and time. Besides, she didn't want to come across as nagging.

Karter sat in the chair closest to her. "Whatever you brought smells amazing."

"I wasn't sure what you had a taste for, but I figured I couldn't go wrong with carne asada and fish tacos."

"Yum. My favorite, and I'm starving. I missed lunch."

The words were barely out of Karter's mouth before he took a huge bite of one of the fish tacos. He moaned with pleasure, and again, Dreamy was glad she'd agreed to stop by.

"They're good, as usual," he said, wiping his mouth and going in for another bite.

Small talk flowed easily between them as they discussed their day. He told her about a couple of deals he'd made in that week alone; it was no wonder he was busy. Dreamy wasn't sure what drove him. He had already amassed more money than he could spend in a lifetime, and that didn't even include his trust fund. She had no idea why he continued to push himself.

"Next week probably won't be much better," he said after polishing off three tacos. "I have a couple of board meetings to attend, and one of those companies is in the process of rebranding. The other one, I need to work with my team on coming up with a new marketing strategy."

"Why?" Dreamy asked, and sat back in her seat. "Why do *you* have to do it, Karter? You've said yourself that you have some of the best people working for you. So I don't understand why you have to have your hands in everything."

He wiped his mouth with a napkin and sighed loudly. "For the same reason you've worked tirelessly to get the nonprofit up and running. I want these companies to be a success."

"And the only way they can be a success is if you're a part of every aspect of the business? Then why do you need the teams that you've put in place? Aren't you able to trust the people you've employed?"

Except for the sound of a helicopter in the distance, the office was silent. He toyed with the napkin in his hand as he studied her for the longest time. Dreamy had no idea what he would say, and though she hoped she hadn't overstepped, she really did want an answer.

He rubbed the back of his neck before he finally peered in her direction. Worry lines creased his forehead, and he looked more tired than he had when she first arrived.

"You're working yourself to death," she said quietly. "Help me to understand why."

He gave a slight shrug. "Work is what I know. In addition to making money, I love the challenge. I enjoy taking a struggling business under my wing and turning it into a company that turns a profit within a year. You know that about me."

Dreamy listened as he rattled off reasons why he worked so much. She understood them, and could even relate on some levels, but . . .

"What about me?" she said. "What about us? If you're working yourself to death, we'll never have the type of relationship you told me you wanted. The type of relationship I want. I love that you love your job and your company, but will you always work long hours and cancel on me every week? I enjoyed attending the theater with Mariana, and she loved the outing, but I wanted to go to the theater with you that night. Not her."

Dreamy stood and slowly started clearing the table. On her way back from his trash can, he stood and reached out and grabbed her wrist. Pulling her close, he stared down in her eyes.

"I love you," he said with such passion.

"I love you too." Dreamy slid her arms around his waist.

Karter cupped her cheek, and her eyes drifted closed as she leaned into his gentle touch. Though Dreamy talked to him every day except today, she hadn't seen him in four days. She missed him. Missed being in his arms.

"I'm sorry I bailed on you. I promise it won't happen again."

"Okay," she said, but knew they would probably have to revisit this conversation. Letting down the people you claim to love sometimes came with running a business, but at least he'd think twice before canceling.

His office phone rang, and he groaned. Touching his forehead to hers, she could see the battle brewing inside of him. To answer the phone, or not to answer. It was almost comical. Almost.

She pulled back a little and smiled. "Go. I'll be right here when you're done."

He gave her a quick peck on the lips. "Okay, I'll make it quick."

As Dreamy listened to Karter talk numbers, an idea brewed inside her head. She was glad he had taken time to have dinner with her, but her body craved more.

She headed to the door, and turned when Karter called out her name in a low voice.

"Don't leave," he whispered, his hand over the receiver. "Don't leave yet."

She smiled, gave him a thumbs-up, and locked the door. His eyebrows lifted as if he could read her mind.

Dreamy had never had office sex, and since she'd shared so many firsts with Karter, she might as well add to the list.

He was still standing behind his desk, the telephone plastered to his ear as he watched her every move. How he was able to listen to whatever the caller was saying, and yet focus on her, was a mystery. But Dreamy took full advantage, thinking she might as well give him something to look at.

She undid the two buttons that held the dress closed and let the garment slowly slide down her arms.

"Damn," Karter hissed, then breathed a thin apology to the caller.

Dreamy grinned, loving the effect that she was having on her man. With the dress puddled at her feet, she was left in a skimpy red lace lingerie set. Her favorite red high heels covered her feet. Next came a seductive pose that would make the strongest man weak for what she was offering.

"Jim, I have to go. I'll call you tomorrow," Karter said as Dreamy slowly strutted toward him.

She couldn't hold back the laugh at how fast he disconnected the call. In hindsight, this was how she should've started their evening together.

"Damn, baby. You play dirty."

She moved to stand between him and his desk. "Desperate times, my love. Desperate times."

He grinned and fingered the front closure of her bra. "Easy access. Just the way I like." He masterfully flicked the bra open with two fingers and slid the straps down her arms before setting it on the desk. "I should've checked for the goodies you had under your dress the moment you strolled through the door."

"Yeah, but you were too busy with business as usual."

"Well, right now I'm ready to do a little business *not* as usual. I'm thinking"—he peppered kisses along her jawline and worked his way down—"that maybe we can create another first for us."

"Funny, I thought the same thing."

Dreamy moaned when he nibbled on her neck, which was sure to leave a mark. As his mouth kept going lower, so did his hands. Before long, her panties had been discarded.

"Damn, woman, you're killing me here," he said, eying her as he fished a condom out of his wallet. He dropped the leather billfold to the floor and quickly sheathed himself.

Dreamy squeaked then laughed when he caught her off guard and turned her to face the desk.

"You're pretty strong, old man."

Moving up behind her, he wrapped his arm around her waist and nudged her legs apart. "Let me show you what this old man can do," Karter said near her ear, and placed kisses along the side of her neck.

Feeling his hardness against her ignited the sexual hunger that had been brewing since the moment she walked in. She leaned against him as his lips continued exploring her neck, and his hands kneaded her breasts. He squeezed and tweaked her nipples, and everywhere he touched and kissed, her body burned with need.

Still cupping one of her breasts, Karter moved his other hand lower over her belly and didn't stop until his finger teased her clit.

"Oh, yes," she breathed, trying to hold herself upright though her knees had weakened at the way he was pleasing her. She moaned with pleasure, marveling at how well this man had learned her body, better than she knew her own.

"God, you feel so good. I love when you're so wet for me," he crooned near her ear. "But I want more of you."

Karter gripped her hips, and Dreamy braced her palms on top of his desk as he nudged her legs even farther apart. His penis bumped against her moist opening seconds before he slid into her.

They fit so perfectly together, and she moved with him as he drove in and out of her, steadily picking up speed with each thrust. Her heart hammered, and already she was barely holding on as she neared her release. He felt so good buried deep inside of her, stirring her passion to the brink of losing control.

"Karter," she breathed, and her words stuck in her throat as he pumped harder and faster. His fingers dug into her hips as he gripped her tighter and continued pounding into her.

"Dreamy," he moaned, and she could feel him pulsing inside of her as he pushed her to a point of no return.

"Ohh, yes. Yes!" she screamed over and over again and gripped the edge of the desk as her body trembled with her release.

She would've melted to the floor had Karter not been holding her up as he pumped in and out of her, his movements growing more jerky moments before he growled his release.

They both slumped forward, and Karter had one arm around her waist and his other hand braced on the desk.

"I will never be able to get enough of you," he panted near her ear, and tightened his hold. "I love you so much, baby. I promise I'm going to do better. You're going to notice the changes."

"I know." She leaned her head back and placed a lingering kiss on his cheek. "And I love you too. More than I can ever express."

Dreamy knew from day one how important Karter's work was to him. If it meant meeting him at the office occasionally for a little rendezvous, so be it. She'd do it. She was fully invested in their relationship, and she was sure they'd find a good balance. She just hoped it was sooner than later.

Chapter Thirty-One

"I LOVE YOU," KARTER SAID AGAIN AS HE STOOD BEHIND DREAMY, unable to stop touching her. They were in his office bathroom, trying to pull themselves back together. But each time she attempted to snap her dress closed, he undid it.

Dreamy giggled and swatted his hand away. "I love you, too, but you're making it very hard for me to get dressed when you keep trying to take off my clothes."

"Maybe you can just stay here and sit around in your underwear while I finish this last bit of work."

"Yeah, like that's going to happen. You know you can't handle all of this." She pulled the dress open again, revealing the gorgeous bra and panty set, and Karter chuckled.

"Okay, you're right. Finish getting dressed."

"I will, but I think I'll have more success if I leave you in here and I go back into your office."

When she walked out, her rose scent trailing behind, Karter inhaled deeply. He hadn't been kidding when he said he couldn't get enough of her.

I'm going to marry that woman, he thought as he rolled his shirt-sleeves down and buttoned the cuffs. He never knew he could love someone as much as he loved her. And all he could think about lately was making her his wife. They'd been together for only a few months, but he already knew she was the one for him.

Man, I'm tired.

Still feeling a little winded, Karter braced his hands on the counter and closed his eyes. He didn't feel so good. It probably had everything to do with the long hours, and the lack of sleep lately.

I'm going to do better. Starting tomorrow.

"KARTER, I STILL CAN'T BELIEVE WHAT WE JUST DID IN HERE," Dreamy said as she hooked her small purse across her body. "Again, another first with—"

A large crash in the bathroom stopped her in her tracks. "Karter?" she called out. When he didn't respond, she hurried across the room.

She knocked on the door, which was partially closed, and eased it open.

"Oh, my God! What happened?" She dropped to her knees where he knelt near the sink, beads of perspiration dotted his hairline. It wasn't until she got a good look at the grimace on his face that she knew something was seriously wrong.

"Can you speak? Tell me what's wrong!"

"My . . . chest," he wheezed.

"Oh, dear God. Okay, baby. Let me call for help."

Stay calm. Stay calm, she told herself as she fumbled through her purse for her cell phone, then dialed 911. Her hands were trembling so badly, she could barely hold on to the device. Dreamy was able to keep herself together, but barely, especially when the operator started asking her questions. With the phone on speaker, she sent a quick text to Najee. The former Marine would know what to do until help arrived, and she was sure he was somewhere nearby.

"Ma'am, stay on the line. An EMT is on the way."

Dreamy sent up a silent prayer that they'd get there in time.

She held Karter, keeping him upright. "Hold on, baby. Please, please hang on."

An hour later, Dreamy paced the private waiting room that the hospital staff had directed her to. Who knew they had a special area for celebrity patients? This was another time when she was grateful that Najee and Gloria had come to the rescue. She wouldn't have known about the special wing of the hospital. Whenever she was with Karter, they'd never had any problems with the media, but he did a good job of keeping a low profile.

Dreamy stopped near the window and stood there with her arms folded across her midsection. The last time she'd been at a hospital for an emergency was when her grandfather had had a mild stroke. She had already lost her grandmother and had been terrified she would lose him too.

Now this.

She couldn't lose Karter. Not now. Not ever. He was her everything, the love of her life, and the man she intended to marry and start a family with someday.

Dreamy blinked back sudden tears and sent up another prayer.

Please don't let him die.

Please don't take him away from me.

There was a commotion at the door, and Dreamy turned to see what was going on.

"What's happened? Where is he?" Karter's mother, Kalena Redford, stormed into the waiting room, looking around like a woman possessed.

Dreamy started to speak, but the older woman bypassed her

and went directly to Gloria, who had just returned from the ladies' room. Kalena rattled off questions a mile a minute. No way could Gloria understand all that the woman was asking.

Dreamy tried not to judge or take offense that Kalena didn't say anything to her. She acted as if she weren't even in the room. She wouldn't take it personally, because if it were her son who had been rushed to the emergency room, she'd be a wreck too.

Just as Dreamy turned back to the window, she heard someone call out, "Mrs. Redford?"

She turned around just as Karter's mother ran to the nurse.

"I'm Mrs. Redford. How is my son? I need to see him right now," Kalena insisted.

Dreamy moved across the room, wanting to hear what was going on. The nurse seemed calm, like she wasn't there to deliver bad news, so Dreamy was optimistic that Karter was going to be okay.

"You're his mother?" the nurse questioned Kalena.

"Yes. Take me to him right now." Kalena started out of the room, assuming the nurse was right beside her.

"I'm sorry, ma'am," the nurse said, "but Mr. Redford asked to see his wife." She glanced down at the electronic tablet in her hand. "Dreamy?" she asked as she glanced from one woman to the other.

Dreamy stepped forward. The confidence that she'd felt moments ago that he was all right was starting to dwindle. "I'm Dreamy. Is Karter all right?"

"He's going to be okay, and he's insisting on seeing you."

"Oh . . . okay."

"Wait one damn minute!" Kalena snapped. "This woman isn't his wife. She's just some . . . some . . ."

"She's his wife," Gloria said quickly, and shoved Dreamy closer to the nurse. "Go. Go and see what's going on," she insisted, then turned to Kalena.

Dreamy didn't know what Gloria was saying to Karter's mother, and at the moment, she didn't care. All she wanted was to see her man with her own eyes and make sure he was okay.

"Right in here, Mrs. Redford."

Guilt lodged in Dreamy's chest. She hated that she had to lie about her relationship with Karter in order to ride to the hospital with him.

It actually had been Gloria's idea. When Dreamy called her in a panic, Karter's assistant was as cool and calm as usual. She offered to contact his parents, and told her to go with Karter and pretend to be his wife if necessary.

Dreamy stepped into Karter's hospital room, glad to see he was awake. He was attached to a machine that was steadily beeping, and he looked as if he had just run a marathon.

"Hey, sweetheart," he said, his voice low and raspy. He extended his hand to Dreamy, and she hurried to his bedside, no longer able to hold back the tears that had threatened to fall earlier.

"God, you scared me to death. Was it a heart attack?" she asked, looking him over.

"No. It was angina, but the doctor warned that if I don't make some changes, the next episode might be a heart attack. They want me to stay the night for observation."

"I love you. I don't want to lose you, Karter." She quickly wiped away a tear that flowed down her cheek. "What can I say or do to get you to take your health seriously?"

"Aww, baby. Come here." She climbed onto the bed, careful not to disturb any of the cords and tubes, and let him hold her. "Starting today, I promise no more long hours, and no more canceled dates."

"You promise?"

"I promise."

THE NEXT MORNING, DREAMY OPENED HER EYES TO THE SOUND of beeping. She glanced across the hospital room, surprised to see that Karter was awake and sitting up in bed, sifting through a magazine.

"Good morning, sleepyhead," he said, smiling. He still looked a little tired, but much better than last night.

"Good morning," she said.

"Tonight, you sleep in a real bed. My bed," he amended.

"Okay, but actually, this wasn't too bad." She had slept in a chair that reclined and had been more comfortable than she expected.

Dreamy wiped the sleep from her eyes and slipped on her shoes. Jordyn had stopped by last night and brought her a change of clothes, which Dreamy really appreciated this morning.

She leaned on Karter's bed and kissed his lips. "How do you feel?"

"I feel good. I'm ready to head home, but the nurse said the doctor won't be in for another hour. I was thinking about not waiting around and signing myself out, but—"

"But you knew I'd shoot that idea down, right?"

"Right. So I'm still here."

"Good. I'm going in search of coffee. I'll see if I can find us a snack that doesn't taste like hospital grub. Something that will tide us over until we get home . . . your home," she said before leaving the room.

As she headed to the cafeteria, Dreamy wondered if that little slipup was her brain—and her heart—telling her that she was ready to take their relationship to the next level. She and Karter had discussed marriage and children in general as something in the vague future, but not in specifics. He knew she loved him, and she knew he loved her, but she wondered how long it would be before they talked seriously about marriage. Soon, she thought. If he didn't bring it up, she would.

A short while later, armed with a coffee for her and orange juice for Karter, along with bagels, Dreamy headed back to the room. Once she made it to the door, she pulled up short when she heard talking. The voices were a little muffled, but it wasn't too hard to make out his mother's voice.

"All I'm saying is you can do better. Karter, you have a reputation to protect, and all she's doing is making you look bad. You saw the way she was dressed last night. She looked like some hooker you'd see on Hollywood Boulevard. And . . ."

Dreamy took a giant step back from the door as her hands trembled slightly. Her first instinct was to hurry out of the hospital and not look back, but she didn't want to worry Karter. She didn't doubt his feelings, and she trusted that his mother didn't have any power over him, but she just couldn't deal with Kalena this morning after such a rough night and not enough sleep.

Dreamy pulled her cell phone from her purse, trying to decide what she was going to do. She needed air. She needed to think.

Typing a quick text to Karter, she didn't know when he would see it, but at least she wouldn't worry him.

I'm leaving the hospital. Spend time with your parents and I'll talk to you later.

Chapter Thirty-Two

"DAD, YOU DIDN'T HAVE TO COME. I KNOW YOU NEED TO BE ON set, and I'm all right. The doctor should be here soon to officially release me, then I'll be heading home."

"What's the point if you're not going to take care of yourself?" his mother said from the upholstered chair near the window. She was flipping through a fashion magazine, looking as if she'd walked off the pages of it.

Rarely, if ever, did Kalena Redford walk out of the house looking less than perfect. Every strand of her hair was always in place, designer clothes covered her from head to toe, and her jewelry screamed of their wealth.

"You do not take care of yourself, which is why we're sitting in a hospital," his mother fussed.

"I take care of myself fine. It's just that I've had a lot going on in the last couple of weeks, but things are going to slow down soon."

"Until the next time you decide to work yourself to death."

"Kalena, leave the boy alone," his dad said on a sigh. "He's a grown man. He knows what he can handle and what he can't."

"And what about that little girl that you're dating?" she said, obviously referring to Dreamy.

"Oh, not this again," Karter murmured.

The heart monitor started beeping a little faster. He never expected much of his mother when it came to her opinion of others. Especially the women he dated. But it bothered the hell out of him when she said anything that was disrespectful about Dreamy. She just wouldn't let up.

Karter breathed in and out slowly as he tuned his mother out, and instead thought about the woman he planned to marry one day. He had purchased the ring, but hadn't decided how or when he wanted to propose. Whatever he settled on, though, would be something special that they both would remember.

Maybe he'd rent a yacht and take her out on the water for a few days. That would be romantic and private. Or they could fly to Paris. Morgan talked about all things French, and recently Dreamy had mentioned wanting to visit Paris one day. But right now probably wouldn't be the ideal time since her main focus was getting the nonprofit up and running.

Either way, Karter planned to come up with the perfect proposal . . . soon.

"I've said it before, and I'll say it again. You can do better," Karter heard his mother say when he tuned back in. "You have to protect yourself and the family from women like—"

"Enough!" Karter yelled. "If you don't approve of Dreamy, that's your problem. But it's a shame you still can't see past your prejudices. That woman . . . *my* woman, has more love and compassion in her pinkie finger than I've seen from you, ever. So back off!"

"You know what? Maybe we should leave," his father said, slipping into his lightweight jacket and putting on his baseball cap. It wasn't a great disguise, but it was probably better than nothing. "That machine has been going crazy since your mother walked in here. Let's go, Kalena."

Karter's mother huffed, and slammed her magazine closed. "I'm just trying to spare him a life of heartache. You would think he'd learned from his broken engagement to Valerie."

"If I remember correctly, you actually liked Valerie."

His mother's pursed lips held back anything she had to say about his ex-fiancée.

"That should've been my first sign to stay away from her, but no, I had to learn the hard way."

"Son, who you decide to marry is up to you," his father said. "Your mother has your best interests at heart, and just needs some time. I think Dreamy is a lovely young lady and would make a wonderful addition to our family."

"And I think he can do better," his mother cut in. "Karter has a certain status to maintain, and that girl is—"

"This shouldn't even matter, but have you forgotten that Dreamy is a multimillionaire?"

Kalena waved him off. "Oh, please. All she did was win some money. Angelica, on the other hand, knows how to carry herself. She knows what it takes to live in our world, and she knows how to—"

"Be a pain in the ass," Karter finished. "No thank you. I'll take intelligent, kindhearted, and compassionate any day. And Dreamy is all of that and then some."

"Then you're a fool," his mother said just as the door swung open.

Karter was disappointed when it wasn't Dreamy who walked in.

"Hey, Nana sent you some clothes," Morgan said, and dropped the bag on the bed. "Where was Dreamy going? I saw her leaving.

When I called out to her, she must have not heard me because she kept walking."

Unease clawed through Karter. She wouldn't leave without telling him. He grabbed his phone from the bedside table and saw her text message.

Damn it. Had she heard everything his mother said? Karter called her cell phone, but the call went directly to voicemail.

He swung his legs over to the side of the bed. "Okay, everyone out. I need to get changed."

His sister eyed him suspiciously, probably knowing that something was up.

"By the way, Nana said that she put your delivery in the bag too."

Delivery? What delivery?

Karter didn't care at the moment. All he cared about was getting to Dreamy in case she'd heard the conversation with his mother.

"Out! Now!" he said to them.

"You can't leave before the doctor releases you," his mother insisted.

"Well, he'd better get here in the next fifteen minutes. Otherwise, I'm out of here."

DREAMY STARED OUT OVER THE WATER, THE SUN GLISTENING off it and the waves lapping against the shore. Shortly after Karter had shown her his "secret spot," she had claimed it as her own. It really was one of the most relaxing places to be.

On the ride to Santa Monica, she had regretted leaving the hospital the way she had. She should've stuck around and told Kalena what she could do with her opinions.

Dreamy had no doubt that Karter loved her. Yet she still let his mother's words get to her, and why? She thought about that question during the ride to the pier, and the only thing she could come up with was Tarrah.

Dreamy still hadn't gotten over her mother's leaving her all those years ago, and deep down, there was still that fear that others would leave her just the way she had. Namely Karter.

In her head, she knew that wouldn't be the case with him, he wouldn't walk away from the love they had. He knew as well as she did that they fit perfectly together, in more ways than one.

But she couldn't help feeling the insidious fear of being abandoned. It would rip her apart if she gave all of herself to the man she loved and he walked away, just like her mother had all those years ago.

Karter's not like that, her brain screamed. *He would never leave you behind.*

"A beautiful day, isn't it?"

Dreamy spun around, and almost tripped over her feet. "Karter?" She placed her hand on her chest as if that would keep her heart from leaping out. "You scared me. Wait, what are you doing here? You should be at the hospital!"

"How can I get any rest when I'm worried about you?" He slowly sat on a nearby bench, which told Dreamy everything she needed to know. He wasn't a hundred percent well, and it made her feel even worse for leaving him. Of course he would come after her.

Dreamy sat on the bench next to him. "I'm sorry. I shouldn't have left. I needed some air . . . and I needed to think." She slipped her hand into his. "Wait a minute. How'd you know I was here?"

"I called Jordyn and told her I was worried about you because you left the hospital so suddenly."

"I texted you."

He gave a slight shrug. "I still didn't know where you were. Anyway, she tracked your phone."

Dreamy squinted. "How?"

He shrugged. "Find My iPhone. But we need to talk about why you left me."

Guilt clawed through Dreamy. "Don't say it like that. I just needed some air."

He slowly nodded as he studied her. "I assume you overheard the conversation with my mother, but you have to know that she doesn't dictate who I spend my life with . . . who I love."

Dreamy nibbled on her lower lip. "I know. I really do know, but I couldn't deal with Kalena today, and I definitely didn't mean to worry you. That's why I sent the text telling you I'd talk to you later."

"I'm sorry about my mother, and that you felt like you had to leave. I was expecting you to go home with me." He leaned forward with his elbows on his knees as he looked out at the water. "And I didn't miss the way you responded before you went to the cafeteria. You tensed when I mentioned us going 'home.'"

"Technically, it's your home, and I—I . . . What are we doing, Karter?"

"Right now we're talking."

She bumped his shoulder and smiled. "You know what I mean. What's next for us? Your mother is not going to quit trying to come between us. And I don't want to come between you and your mom. I'd never be able to forgive myself if that happened."

Karter sat up, wrapped his arm around Dreamy's shoulders, and pulled her closer. He kissed the side of her head and sighed. Dreamy wasn't sure if that was a sigh from physical exhaustion, or if he was emotionally tired. He had to be sick of going around and around with his mother about her. If he wasn't sick of it, she sure was.

"I love you," he said. "I never knew I could love someone as much as I love you. Don't get me wrong. I adore my family, but what I feel for you . . ." He shook his head as if unable to find the right words to express himself.

Dreamy knew exactly how he felt, because she struggled to explain what he meant to her too. It was such a deep-seated love, it was almost scary. Scary because she couldn't imagine living the rest of her life without him in it.

"I love you more than I have ever loved anyone or anything in my life," he continued. "I'd give up all of my millions if it meant keeping you in my life."

Dreamy leaned back and narrowed her eyes. "Is that because you know I'd share my millions with you?"

Karter laughed, and it helped ease some of the tension in their conversation.

"I'm glad to know that, but, Dreamy, I need you to understand that I'm not going anywhere. There is *nothing* my mother can say or do to change that. I just wish you could believe that."

"I do," she insisted.

Karter raised an eyebrow and gave her a knowing look.

"Okay," she said with resignation. "It wasn't because I doubted your feelings for me. It was because it was upsetting to hear what your mother was saying. I try to have thick skin. God knows I try. I try not to let people's words get to me, but they do. I internalize everything, and it's something that I've been working to improve on for years. I'm not there yet. So when people like your mother—and even my mother—come along with their negativity, it bothers me."

"Then we'll deal with our mothers together. Just know that I'll be by your side no matter what either of them says."

"Thank you, but, Karter, I need you to know something. I love you. I love you so damn much, and I want to spend the rest of my life with you."

Now he was the one narrowing his eyes. "So . . . is this you proposing?" he asked, his lips twitching.

Dreamy laughed. "I would, but I don't have a ring, and I'm sure someone like you wouldn't like being proposed to unless I presented you with a ring."

"You know me well," he said, laughing.

He removed his arm from around her and dug through his front pocket. "Good thing I came prepared, because I want to spend the rest of my life with you, too, and would be honored if you would be my wife." He pulled out a blue velvet box.

Dreamy's hands went to her mouth as he got down on one knee in front of her.

Ohmigod. Ohmigod. Ohmigod.

"This is not how I had planned to propose, but Nana . . ." He shook his head and chuckled. "I just love that woman. This morning she had slipped this box into the duffel bag of clothes that she'd sent with Morgan. I figured today is as good a day as any to ask you to be my wife."

"Oh, Karter." Dreamy's heart was beating loud enough to be heard down the street.

"What better time to ask than out here at our special place?" he continued. "Dreamy Daniels, you are my sunshine and you brighten my darkest days. Will you do me the honor of marrying me and spending the rest of your life with me as my wife?"

He opened the box and she gasped. "Holy crap. That's gorgeous." It had an unusual oval stone in the center surrounded by diamonds that also went around the band. "I've never seen anything like that."

"I had it custom made for you. The stone in the center is called morganite. Randy helped sketch out the design, and Morgan assisted with what stones to include. As for Nana's input, she threatened to stop cooking for me if I didn't go ahead and make an honest woman out of you."

Dreamy laughed.

"So, what do you say? You interested in spending the rest of your life with me?"

"Yes. Yes, I'll marry you!"

She lunged into his arms, and he stood with her as people nearby clapped. Just when Dreamy thought she couldn't get any happier with Karter, he did something like this.

"I can't wait to be your wife."

She cupped his face and kissed him with everything in her, hoping he could feel just how much she adored him. They were going to have an amazing life together, and she couldn't wait to get it started.

Epilogue

DREAMY GLANCED OUT AT THE CROWD OF INFLUENTIAL AND FA-
mous people, most she didn't know. This was one time she didn't
like being the center of attention but, thankfully, Karter was at her
side holding her hand.

They were seated at a beautifully decorated table for two on a
stage at the front of his parents' ballroom. Morgan had insisted on
throwing them an engagement party, and for the last few minutes,
some of their family and closest friends took turns toasting them.
Morgan was the last person. Not only had she become one of
Dreamy's best friends, but in her heart, they were already sisters.

She smiled and marveled at how gorgeous Morgan looked as
she climbed the steps to the stage carrying a glass of champagne.
She looked like African royalty with her microbraids piled high on
top of her head, and her makeup flawless. Morgan might claim that
she wasn't passionate about designing clothes, but the multicolor,
sleeveless and backless dress that hugged her petite body and
stopped just above her knees said otherwise. The garment could
rival anything by a famous designer, and Dreamy knew that several

of them were determined to get Morgan on their team. But her future sister-in-law wasn't interested. She had other ideas for her life, and Dreamy couldn't wait to see those plans unfold.

Morgan stood at the microphone that was a few feet away and glanced at Dreamy and Karter. "I honestly didn't think Karter would ever find someone who could put up with him," she said, a wicked gleam shimmering in her eyes. She paused as a few chuckles flowed around the room. "But then this amazing woman came along and knocked him on his butt."

Dreamy laughed, grateful that Morgan was keeping her speech light. After enduring Jordyn and her grandfather's emotional words moments ago, she didn't think she'd be able to keep her tears at bay for much longer.

"Dreamy, there are days when I don't know who is luckier, me or Karter," Morgan continued. "I have learned so much from you over the last few months. You are truly a role model. I know that women around the country, who are looking to start their own businesses, are about to learn what I already know—you're amazing."

As Dreamy listened, there were moments when even she couldn't believe how her life was turning out. She and Mariana were preparing to open the doors of the nonprofit in a few days. They were officially a 501(c)(3) organization, and she was its proud founder. More than that, she was ready to help other women realize their dreams of entrepreneurship.

Her life was perfect. She had officially moved in with Karter, Nana, Morgan, and Melvin a month ago. The living arrangement was wonderful, except Morgan informed them that she was moving out at the end of the month.

It seemed everyone was getting settled, even Jordyn and Gramps, who had fallen in love with Karter's penthouse, which he sold to them. Dreamy missed them all living together, but they all got together often.

Dreamy was still trying to find that balance between work and her personal life, but everything was coming together. Even Karter was getting used to working only ten-hour days and taking weekends off to spend more time with her and Melvin. He and his dog were finally the best of buddies, which was a shock to everyone.

"Karter, you already know you're my favorite brother," Morgan was saying.

"Hey! What about me?" Randy yelled from somewhere in the crowd, and everyone laughed.

"Oops, I mean, Karter, you already know you're *one* of my favorite brothers," Morgan amended, glancing sheepishly at the crowd. When she returned her attention to Karter, her expression turned serious. "You're so special to me, and you're *so* deserving of the excitement and love that Dreamy has brought into your life." She lifted her glass, and so did everyone else. "I love you two more than I could ever express, and I wish you both a lifetime of love and laughter."

Dreamy tapped her glass to Karter's before sipping her champagne. Then he leaned over and kissed her sweetly.

"It's my turn," he murmured against her lips, and stood before she realized what he was doing.

Karter went over to the microphone, removed it from the stand, and then strolled back to their table. He reached for Dreamy's hand and pulled her out of the seat. She wanted to ask what he was doing, but all eyes were on them, and the last thing she wanted to do tonight was embarrass either of them. They'd had enough embarrassing moments to last a lifetime.

With her free hand, she nervously smoothed out the flowing skirt of her orange strapless evening gown. She had protested when Morgan first mentioned throwing them an engagement party, especially when she learned that it would be formal. But it was when Kalena had insisted on hosting the event that Dreamy had given in.

It was an olive branch of sorts. Their relationship was still a bit shaky, but at least the two of them could talk without snarling at each other.

Despite being a millionaire now, Dreamy still liked simplicity. Only on occasion, like tonight, did she give in and do things the way that was befitting of the world that Karter grew up in. Had it been up to her, they would've had a barbecue in the backyard with a ton of finger food and dance music. Instead, she had compromised and agreed to a sit-down dinner that included chicken and ribs, and a jazz ensemble that played during the meal. Later there would be lots of dancing.

"Dreamy, I'll never in my life forget the first day we met," Karter started. There was a twinkle in his gorgeous eyes, and his lips twitched.

She shook her head and groaned, then covered her eyes, already mortified by those memories, while their guests laughed as if they already knew the story. She prayed Karter wouldn't share all the details of that fateful day at Mathison Technology.

"Your colorful attire was what first caught my attention. Then your lighthearted personality, which seems to shine without you even having to say a word, reeled me in. But it's your infectious laughter and your deep-seated joy that has me excited about spending the rest of my life with you."

A rogue tear slid down Dreamy's face, followed by several others. Karter, being Karter, pulled a handkerchief from the inside pocket of his tuxedo jacket and dabbed at her cheeks. That only caused more tears to fall.

Damn tears.

"Baby, I am so in love with you," he said, seeming unbothered by her quiet sobs. "I can't even remember what my world was like before you came along. All I know is that my life is finally complete . . . because of you."

With her heart full enough to burst, Dreamy grabbed hold of the lapels of Karter's jacket and pulled him close. She kissed him with everything in her, wanting him to feel how much she loved and adored him.

The last few months had been a whirlwind, but one thing remained the same—Karter treated her like she was the most important person in the world. She never knew she could love someone as much as she loved him. Like their courtship, she had no doubt their lives together would be full of love, fun, and excitement. Dreamy could hardly wait to experience all that life had in store for them, because she already knew—they were going to be unstoppable together.

Photo by Albert Cooper

Award-winning and *USA Today* bestselling author **Sharon C. Cooper** loves anything that involves romance with a happily-ever-after, whether in books, movies, or real life. Sharon writes contemporary romance as well as romantic suspense and enjoys rainy days, carpet picnics, and peanut butter and jelly sandwiches.

She's been nominated for numerous awards and is the recipient of Romance Slam Jam Emma Awards for Author of the Year 2019, Favorite Hero 2019 (*Indebted*), Romantic Suspense of the Year 2015 (*Truth or Consequences*), Interracial Romance of the Year 2015 (*All You'll Ever Need*), and BRAB (Building Relationships Around Books) Award-Breakout Author of the Year 2014, to name a few. When Sharon isn't writing, she's hanging out with her amazing husband, volunteering, or reading a good book (romance of course).

CONNECT ONLINE

SharonCooper.net/

 AuthorSharonCCooper21

 AuthorSharonCCooper/

 Sharon_Cooper1

Ready to find
your next great read?

Let us help.

Visit prh.com/nextread

Penguin
Random
House